Muscle memory from all the way back to fighting in the empty swimming pool kicked in. I started to pace and survey the floor, if you could call it that. There was standing water in the corners, enough to drown a man in if I could get on his back and push his face down.

The footing's terrible, so nothing fancy. Short, hard punches. I shook out my arms.

Forehead into nose, temple. Again and again. I rolled my neck.

Elbows into throat, knees into groin. I pulled my left knee up toward my chest, then my right.

Don't let him grab hold, because he won't let go. He's bigger and stronger and a black belt in jiu jitsu.

He was watching me, staring me down.

Don't put your eyes on me. I'll close them for good.

I would make it out.

SUCKERPUNCH

JEREMY BROWN

SUCKERPUNCH

JEREMY
BROWN

MEDALLION
P R E S S

Medallion Press, Inc.

Printed in USA

DEDICATION

For Ellen.

Published 2011 by Medallion Press, Inc.

The MEDALLION PRESS LOGO
is a registered trademark of Medallion Press, Inc.

Copyright © 2011 by Jeremy Brown
Cover design by James Tampa
Edited by Helen A Rosburg and Lorie Popp

Typeset in Adobe Garamond Pro
Printed in the United States of America
Title font set in Impact

ISBN: 9781605422251

10 9 8 7 6 5 4 3 2
First Edition

ACKNOWLEDGMENTS

Thanks to my agent, Margaret O'Connor, for believing and to the fighters for doing what they were born to do.

CHAPTER 1

No head butts, groin strikes, eye gouges, or fishhooks.

The Nevada State Athletic Commission was taking all the fun out of no-holds-barred fighting.

The referee jabbered on, and my opponent, Glenn "The Specimen" Porter, stared at me from less than two inches away, so close I had to go cross-eyed to keep him in focus. I thought, *Why bother?* He was an ugly bastard, and I didn't want to look at him anyway.

But I couldn't drop my gaze. Not because it would show weakness or give him the sense I was worried. No, it was because fans love a good stare down, and I could hear them working themselves into a frenzy, higher and higher like a turbine cycling up for take-off. Besides, if things went well for me, it was going to be the longest part of the fight, and I didn't want the crowd to feel cheated on the ticket price.

Porter huffed out through his mouthpiece, emitting an odor of onions and sour milk that crept up my face and threatened to wilt my eyes. Who ate those two things before a fight? It couldn't be healthy, and to me, it was downright discourteous.

The ref finished his spiel and told us to touch gloves, which we did. It was the lightest hit either of us would get for a while. I backed up into my corner of the cage and watched Porter do the same. *Specimen* was tattooed across the top of his stomach. The thing about getting your nickname printed permanently on your skin: you'd better live up to the name as long as you have the skin.

Porter had gained about fifty pounds since the last time I'd seen him fight overseas, possibly due to a knee injury, but most likely because of the drawer of hypodermic needles and closet of HGH the cops had found when they went to his house on a domestic assault charge. Now that he was off the juice, his genetics were allowed to blossom, and his nickname stretched across his pooch with enough space between the letters to make it look like an acronym.

We were both heavyweights, but with a sixty-pound window for us to squeeze through, the label didn't mean much. I was thirty pounds over the minimum bracket of two hundred six, weighing in at two thirty-six the day before. Porter tipped it at two sixty-two, and he looked like he'd stepped off the scale and up to a Vegas buffet. I carried the weight well with six feet and three inches to spread it over. Porter, at a hair over six, looked like a bobber.

The ref checked with Porter. "You ready?"

Porter nodded.

The ref looked at me. "You ready?"

Double thumbs-up.

"Fight!"

I walked to the center of the eight-sided cage, in no hurry but not wanting Porter to get there first and make me orbit him.

He came out slower, his hands down and head tipped back. I guess he didn't watch my tapes.

I was on my toes with my left side slightly back. When Porter came into range, I flicked my left foot forward in a low kick to get his attention. It did. He looked and flinched. My foot hadn't even touched him when I brought the whole leg back at the hip and pivoted forward and sent a Superman punch on a slightly downward angle straight into his mouth. He stumbled backward, and his legs threatened to give out before they knew they were in a fight. I closed the distance and missed with a hook and an uppercut; then he stepped forward and reached out with both hands to try and clinch, make me hold his fat ass up while he recovered.

I pushed his hands off to my left and sent a right cross into his face, which he didn't like and let me know by grunting and bleeding from the nose. The four-ounce gloves laced and taped to my hands were meant to protect my metacarpals, not his head.

I heard the crowd, voicing their primal roars to see someone from another tribe, village, state, country, planet get his skull caved in.

I could do that.

I followed the right cross with a series of left hooks to the body that got Porter to bend over a little, his hands trying to decide which area was more important to guard. If he went with the body, he was going to need more hands.

I have good left hooks. Knockout power from just about any angle, moving in any direction. I train at my cornerman Gil's gym—The Fight House— and the bags there are all slightly curved to the right from the stuffing getting shifted and compressed. Gil bitches about it, but he's the one who makes me work the punches every day. The power comes from the torque in my hips, something I developed a long time ago from constantly looking over my shoulder.

I heard Gil over the crowd, yelling something about clinch and knees.

When Porter's head came down from the hooks, I shot my hands behind his head, wrapped the left over the right on his crown, and pressed my elbows together over his collarbones, pulling his head toward my chest in a Thai clinch.

Porter started walking backward toward his corner, trying to get his arms inside mine so he could lever them away from his head. I held on like a drowning man with a big fat life preserver and drove knees into his belly with each step, switching from left to right, skipping after him until he hit the cage with his back and couldn't run anymore.

You know what they say about cornered animals: elbow them in the face and knee them in the guts.

I've heard it somewhere.

The knees had Porter hunched over, his forearms crossed in front of his abdomen to intercept the next volley. It was a decent defense against the knees, but we weren't in a knee fight. I brought my right elbow in a downward angle across his temple, snapping his head over and opening a nice cut at the edge of his forehead. Blood welled in the opening, a sight sweeter than water in the desert, and coursed down the side of his face.

If I could get it to run into his eye, the ref might stop the fight. It would be a W for me, but the natives wouldn't like it one bit. To the fans, the only thing worse than a judge's decision is an early stoppage due to a cut, like someone taking your candy bar away when you're halfway done because it's too delicious.

Porter started to turtle on me, curling into a ball with legs to protect himself. As soon as he was "unable to intelligently defend himself," the ref would stop the fight. It was a funny term, assuming we started out intelligent. I tried a few uppercuts to see if they would get through, but Porter's arms were pressed in tight, covering him from eyes to belly button. I snuck a wicked left hook into the side, catching him with a good liver shot that acted like a short-fused time bomb.

The liver's great. It's the largest internal organ and gland in the human body, helps with metabolism, plasma protein synthesis, and detoxification. In a fight, however, it's a giant bull's-eye and a traitorous bastard. You get hit with a good liver shot, your legs turn into noodles and all you want to do is roll around and try not to shit yourself.

Porter went that route, his knees buckling and head slumping. He made a sound like a dying buffalo. But instead of dropping all the way down and calling it a night, he decided to impress someone and shoot for my legs. He probably figured if he laid on top of me for the rest of the round, he could throw a punch every thirty seconds or so, get his wind back, and work on rearranging his innards.

It might have worked if he hadn't stuck his head into my left armpit when he drove forward out of the corner. I snaked my left forearm under his chin, grabbed my right hand in front of my stomach, and squeezed, putting his bull neck into a space about the size of a DVD. He drove me backward, trying to find a gap to pry the guillotine choke off, but I squeezed tighter, doing my best to pop his head off his shoulders.

After three seconds I felt a tap on my right arm, the only way a guy in Porter's position can say uncle. The ref was watching for it and yanked on my arm. I released the choke and Porter sagged to the canvas, then flopped onto his back while his cornermen rushed out with towels and water, the two things you need for births and ass kickings.

Everyone from my corner—so, Gil—came in and hugged me. He checked to make sure none of the blood was mine. I have lumps of scar tissue around my eyes and across my forehead tender enough to bust open from a vigorous frown.

"All clear," he said.

We were both relieved. Surgery was somewhere down the line to get the scars cleaned out, but that would limit my training and keep me out of the cage for months.

The ref held my arm up in victory while the announcer bellowed my record, "Twenty-*four* and three!"

I looked around the place, a few thousand people in the arena attached to the casino, spilling beer on each other and pumping their fists under a dome of smoke, cheering and booing, their night made or ruined because I walked out while Porter limped.

I got paid the same either way.

CHAPTER 2

Back in the locker room Gil got my gloves off and tilted water into my mouth until I could hold the bottle myself, my hands free of all the tape and gauze. I sat on the only training table, a solid thing bolted to the floor with clear packaging tape on the corners to keep the leather from cracking any further.

Gil's built like a keg and usually has stubble over most of his face and head, the salt starting to overwhelm the pepper. He's a black belt in Brazilian jiu jitsu. His body shape and short arms and legs make him horrible to grapple with; there aren't any angles to hook, and once he gets hold of you with his gator-bite grip, it's only a matter of time before he bends something important the wrong way. He usually wears an expression of mild amusement during the whole thing, which doesn't help.

Ten years older than me and eons wiser, he's smart enough to train other MMA fighters instead of getting into the cage himself. He has me on the right track, much better than the downhill straightaway to a cliff I'd been on before he found me.

I've been fighting—in one sense of the word or another—pretty much my whole life. The day I took my first step, some jackass asked me to step outside. Trace the scars and dents on my head, you got yourself a pretty good topographical map of Trouble, USA. I moved from playground tussles to brutal street fights to illegal pit fighting before I graduated high school. The pit fighting exposed me to some people with money, and they needed people without it to make sure they kept it. So I did some bodyguard work at clubs and casinos, walking around giving people the stink eye and making paths when I wasn't even old enough to get through the door. I added some side work here and there, delivering important things to dangerous people and keeping my mouth shut about it.

It didn't take long for someone to try to make money off me. One of the VIPs I handled sponsored me in a sanctioned cage fight at a strip club, and I made him ten grand in thirty-seven seconds after I broke my opponent's orbital bone with an elbow. After that I saw an opportunity to make some money do-ing something I was fairly good at. It wasn't a tough decision; there's no 401(k) plan in undocumented close-quarters bodyguard work, unless you count somebody paying for your funeral.

Gil found me when I was twenty-three, strutting around after my fifth cage fight with a two-and-three record. He said my grappling and jiu jitsu sucked and I ought to train with him. He was right, but I was an asshole. My blood was up from another quick KO, and I had some energy to get rid of. He offered a free lesson right then and there and choked me out inside a minute.

I went to his gym the next day and pretty much haven't left since. Now here we were, still on the undercard at a straight-to-video event. I didn't want the spotlight in my eyes, but it wouldn't hurt to have it drop a little brightness into my pockets.

When they brought Porter back, I hopped off the table so they could sit him down. I gave him a half hug. "Good fight."

"Yeah, right." He held an ice pack to his forehead where I'd cut him. The bleeding had stopped, but he had a goose egg that looked like a third eye. "Did I even hit you once?"

"Sure," I said.

"No," one of his cornermen said.

I looked at him and he shrugged.

Porter groaned as he eased onto his back. "I think

that's it for me."

"Give it a few days," I said. "Don't make any decisions in a locker room."

"I was gonna call it quits for sure if I won, retire happy. But I think this is better proof I'm done."

I didn't know what to say to that, so I patted him on the shoulder and shook hands with his guys and walked away.

"That's rough," Gil said when we were through the open doorway into our prep space, cinder-block walls painted white with a drop ceiling, the yellow water stains on the panels looking like rotten fireworks. There was a droopy green couch along one wall in case you wanted to sit down before a fight or had to lie down after it. If you turned around fast enough, you could smell urine, but the source was elusive. Maybe they mixed it with the paint.

"He shouldn't have taken the fight. Credit to him for not ducking me, but it was a bad matchup for him." I sat down on the couch and felt the fight ease out of me. It was a good feeling, knowing the training was worth it and things had come together.

Gil started putting our warm-up gear in his giant duffel bag, which was starting to smell like a bum's shoe. "I was glad to see you go for the choke at the end. Instead of pounding away until he gave up or you wore yourself out."

I shrugged. "It works in just about every other area of my life."

"Idiot," Gil said.

There was a hubbub outside our room, and I leaned back into the couch to get a better view. Three guys in suits were talking to Porter, who was still on the training table. Porter smiled at something and nodded in my direction. The suit in the middle shook Porter's hand and turned around.

I said, "Holy shit."

Banzai Eddie Takanori walked into the room with the two other guys following close behind. One of them was texting with one hand and keeping his suit from touching the wall with the other. Eddie filled the room at five and a half feet of lean Japanese with his hands in the pockets of a black Armani suit, wraparound shades, a neon blue faux hawk, and a chip on his shoulder that caused an eclipse when he stood on his tippy toes. He was about thirty-five but looked five years younger. He was also the president of Warrior Incorporated, the biggest professional mixed martial arts organization in the Western Hemisphere.

The company had been around for ten years but didn't elbow its way to the top of the food chain until Eddie took over five years ago. Each event got bigger than the previous one, more celebrities were shown in the crowds, and better sponsors showed up on the cage padding and canvas.

And here he was. Eddie in the prep room at this event was like Bill Gates stopping by a RadioShack clearance sale.

Gil stopped packing and stared with a focus mitt held in front of his belly. I considered standing up but didn't want to cause offense by being tall.

Eddie's attitude problem mostly came from getting blackballed by the Japanese fighting organizations because he'd grown up in Southern California and could only order Japanese cuisine if the menu had photographs. I say *mostly*, because I'm willing to bet he was an obnoxious prick long before the boys across the Pacific snubbed him.

Eddie looked around the room and stopped halfway through a sniff.

"That smell was already here," I said.

Eddie pointed at me. "You're Woodshed, right?"

"Right."

"And I am?"

"Eddie Takanori," I said. "Mr. Takanori." I finally stood up and shook his hand.

"It's cool, brah. You can call me Eddie. When I'm not around, you can call me Banzai."

I acted like I'd never heard the word before.

"Great fight out there. Did Porter even hit you?"

It was loud enough for Porter to hear, and I saw him look up. I shrugged. "It all happened pretty fast."

"Goddamn right it did," Eddie said.

Porter smiled and shook his head and gave the finger to Eddie's back.

"Hey, we were talking on the way in here, and we've all heard different stories on how you got that nickname. I heard you train in an actual woodshed, throwing logs around and chopping them with axes."

I was stunned he'd heard anything about me at all. I wanted to tell him he was right, but he wasn't. "I got it after one of my first fights. The guy was a bleeder and super pale, like baby powder pale, and by the end of the first round he looked like he'd been in a plane crash. I knocked him out in the second, and the way he landed the paramedics rushed in thinking the poor guy was dead. He was fine, looked like hell, but no permanent damage."

Eddie and the suits seemed to love it. The one with the smartphone watched me past his eyebrows and kept texting.

"So after the fight, the announcer said I took the other guy out to the woodshed and beat him with it."

"With what?" the texter asked.

"The woodshed. The actual structure."

"That's even better than what I heard." Eddie looked at Gil. "Gil Hobbes, yeah?"

Gil said, "Yeah. It's a pleasure to meet you."

They shook hands. Eddie said, "The honor's mine. Anybody who can go down to Brazil and come back with a trophy gets my respect."

The other two suits nodded.

"That was a while ago," Gil said.

"Back before it was cool to know BJJ. That makes it even better. I hear you got quite a gym going here in town."

I thought Gil was going to throw up, but I'd just never seen him flattered before. "Well, we're coming along."

Eddie cocked his head at me. "If your boy here is any indication, I'd say you're doing something right."

Gil sampled the air and raised an eyebrow at the ceiling stains. "Not right enough."

"Well," Eddie said, "let's see what we can do about that. You guys hungry?"

I showered and got dressed while Gil stowed our stuff in the truck; then we followed Eddie and the suit brothers outside. All I had were my jeans and a warm-up fleece over a T-shirt, but Eddie said it didn't matter. We stepped out of the mini event center and into the limo. Gil and I rode backward, facing the bench seat with Eddie in the middle.

He pointed at the suit on his left, the one with the smartphone fused to his mitt. "Guys, this is Benjamin

Walsh. He's the head of marketing for Warrior."

Benjamin was tall and pale and had a dark receding hairline over a face that needed more sleep. I put him in his late thirties.

Eddie turned to his right. "And this guy you might not recognize, but I'm sure you've heard the name. Meet Nick MacYoung, Warrior's official matchmaker. We call him Cupid because he makes the sexiest matchups in the business."

We shook hands with Nick. I asked him, "Do I have to call you Cupid?"

"Please don't." He was close to fifty and had a graying ponytail and a gold canine tooth. His nose had been broken a few times and refused to behave, but he had a genuine smile. I imagined Nick would be a good guy to have a beer with. Benjamin, maybe a root canal, because you wouldn't have to worry about conversation.

Gil said, "I bet your job is a lot harder than it seems."

Nick shrugged. "I love going to work every day."

"Yeah, but with the weight classes you can't do David vs. Goliath anymore, so you have to keep coming up with contrasting styles, grudge matches, something to keep the interest up."

"The fighters take care of all that. I just put them together, and the fireworks happen."

"Don't listen to him," Eddie said. "Of course the

fighters get the majority of the credit, but we put a lot of work into designing the right events at the right time."

I asked Nick, "Who's your all-time dream matchup?"

"I bet he gets asked that a hundred times a day," Gil said.

"That's because it's a valid and intelligent question. Nick? What do you say? Lee vs. Norris? Ali vs. Tyson?"

Nick smiled. "Hélio Gracie vs. Bruce Lee."

I almost hugged him but settled for a low whistle.

Gil kept his composure and gave a satisfied nod. "I'd pay to see that one." By *pay*, he meant cut off his right leg.

We hadn't asked any specifics about why Banzai Eddie was taking us out to dinner, but curiosity was starting to overcome my limited manners. Having marketing and matchmaking on board was a very encouraging sign, but I'd never heard of any fighter going from the undercard at a one-off event to the Warrior limo. It was like winning the townie festival face painting contest, then getting invited to touch up the Sistine Chapel.

Eddie was sharp. He knew what was happening across the car and said, "We'll get to it. I just don't like talking deals in cars. Seems like we're doing something dirty, illegal."

I nodded. He'd said "deals."

Eddie leaned forward. "Our business should be

conducted in the same establishments where multi-million dollar deals go down. We should be one table over from the NFL and NBC. Coke and McDonald's. Nike and Kobe. They don't think we belong in the same tier as them, but we do."

The car floated to a stop at the curb, and Gil reached for the handle but pulled back when he saw the shape of the driver hustling along outside the windows. The door opened and I followed Gil out.

Without moving his lips, Gil said, "Are you fucking kidding me?"

We were behind Caesars Palace near an overhead door with guys in service uniforms rolling heavy carts around. Some staff members on break were standing around a melting ice sculpture of the Leaning Tower of Pisa, tapping their toes in the puddle it was turning into. They stopped long enough to check us out, weren't impressed, and went back to the puddle.

I was impressed. Casinos like having important people come through the front door. It makes the tourists think they should be there too, either to get a photo or because they're just as important. Telling a casino you want the back door—and getting it— means something.

We trailed Eddie, a fast walker on those legs, until we came to a set of double swinging doors propped open with large cans of olive oil. Steam and noise rolled out from the opening, and we went through into the kitchen of Restaurant Guy Savoy.

Gil and I had heard of the place, but we'd never even been in Caesars Palace, let alone what some considered the best restaurant in the city. We looked at each other's clothes and faces and decided there was nothing we could do.

Eddie said something to a waiter, who left and came back with a guy in chef's whites. That guy greeted Eddie like an old friend and didn't even glance at our clothes while he led us to a table near a window that was surrounded by waiters sliding partitions into place to make it a private dining room.

They finished and disappeared, and the guy in whites sat us down, Gil on my left and the Warrior crew across from us, just like in the limo. A waiter showed up with menus and got waved away immediately. The chef told us not to worry, he'd make us all very happy, and he was gone.

I looked around—nice lighting, good smells, a comfortable murmur of conversation from the other tables but nothing intrusive. The tablecloth was probably the softest material I'd ever felt, possibly made from clouds. I sipped the ice water and tasted pure glacier. "What's good here, the club sandwich?"

Eddie laughed. "The only bad thing about eating here is once you do, every other place tastes like dirt.

Now let's talk before the food comes, because I don't want you to think I'm bribing you with the best meal you've ever eaten. And if you're going to walk out, I want you to do it before you get a taste. Is there anyone I need to get on the phone while we do this?"

I was confused and must have looked it.

Eddie said, "An agent, manager, some kind of rep?"

"I guess that's me," Gil said.

"Good deal. You ready, Woody? How would you like to fight on the next Warrior Pay-Per-View card?"

"Yes, please." I suck at poker too.

Eddie clapped Nick on the shoulder. "You see? That's what I'm talking about. No questions asked. Do you want to fight? Yes. Boom. It's on. Now, Woody, I know it's short notice, but your fight tonight wasn't much more than a hard sparring session."

I frowned. "Short notice?"

"Yeah, our next event is the day after tomorrow. Didn't you know that?"

"Whoa," Gil said. "You want him to fight *this* Saturday?"

"That's right, brah."

"Are you adding a fight to the card?"

Eddie smiled. "Nope."

Then Nick smiled. It wasn't quite as charming as before.

"Morris is out," said Eddie. "He pulled a hammie

running up some goddamn stairs."

I said, "And Morris was going to fight . . ."

"Junior Burbank," Eddie said.

I sipped the water again. Someone had pissed on my glacier.

Eddie's team was prepped and drilled for this. Nick said, "Gil, you were saying how tough it must be to find the right matchups, but this one is a no-brainer."

"On two days' notice?" Gil asked. "No brains sounds about right."

Benjamin leaned in and splayed his hands on the table like he was going to do a magic trick. "Rematches put asses in seats and TV buys in the bank."

"Rematch?"

"Woody is the only guy to beat Junior," said Eddie.

Gil laughed, but he wasn't happy. "That was three years ago. At a barn in Illinois."

"It was a sanctioned fight," Eddie said. "It's on both their records. And I know quite a few top ten fighters who got started in that arena."

"How many of them are still fighting on no-name cards for gas money?"

"Hey," I said. "Which one of you is on my team again?"

Gil put a hand on my arm. "I'm just curious. Because you've fought more than Burbank since then and haven't lost, either. But he's been with Warrior for two years, and this is the first we've heard about a rematch."

"The timing's right," Eddie said.

"For Burbank to avenge his one loss?" Gil asked.

I looked back at Eddie, like watching ego tennis.

"I think he deserves the opportunity," Eddie said, "just as Woody's earned the chance to prove it was legit. It's up to them who comes away with the win."

"But you want him to win," I said. "You meaning Warrior, the whole company."

Eddie shrugged. "We want a good fight. It's no secret we've put a lot of marketing behind Junior, but he's easy to market. Big, blond, aggressive. He's what guys want to be like and what women want their guys to be like."

"Not my woman," Gil said.

Eddie opened his mouth to say something, paused, and started over. "Another reason Junior is so marketable is because of what he *isn't*." He looked at me, and I knew what was coming next. "He *isn't* associated with various criminal elements. Or rumored to have been involved in illegal pit fighting. Or—"

"I got it," I said.

"Do you?" Eddie asked. The table narrowed down to him and me. "Because I've heard some things, and while it's really none of my business, if you're going to fight for me, for Warrior, you represent the brand in everything you do. You take a dump and start to walk out without washing your hands, I want you to think, 'Will this make Warrior look bad?' You get what I'm saying? Football players get busted all the time for knocking their wives around, drunk driving, hell, packing an arsenal for the end of days, but see, the NFL is *estab*lished. They can survive it, because people know it's a good product and they want their players to be a little crazy. Makes for good highlights."

"But not *too* crazy," Benjamin footnoted.

Eddie stayed on me. "MMA is young. We're like a new cola coming in and competing with Coke and Pepsi, and if we get a few bad cans poisoning people before we get the benefit of the doubt, they'll pull us off the shelf like that." He snapped his fingers. "Good-bye, Warrior. Bye-bye, Woodshed. You just fought that piece of crap Porter? I'd never let him in the same building as a Warrior event. With his history? No way. And Gil's right; where you just fought, you know what they had in that arena last weekend?"

"No," I said.

"The Nevada State Pinochle Championship. I'm not fucking kidding you. Wall-to-wall sweaters and hearing aids. You want to keep fighting at that level so you can stay under the radar and screw around with who the fuck knows what, let me know right now. I'll take you back to the glorified bingo hall, and you'll never see me again. Other than in magazines, on billboards, the Internet, and TV."

I poked my silverware around. I didn't know who he'd talked to about me or how much he knew. The people with the worst of the info wouldn't have given him anything. Or couldn't. And if he knew any of that, he wouldn't have brought me to Guy Savoy and sat at the same table with sharp knives. I said, "All that stuff is behind me."

"See, that's the sticky part. With a guy like Porter, he gets busted and put on probation. All the world can see whether or not he's keeping his nose clean. But with you, it's all whispers and sideways looks. So either it's all bullshit and you're a Boy Scout with a massive slander campaign, or you just never got caught."

"Which one would you prefer?" I asked.

"I would prefer that you promise me I'm not going to get a call at 4 a.m. telling me you're holding some chick from Cirque du Soleil hostage on top of the fucking Stratosphere."

"You won't get that call," I said. "I don't like heights."

Nick thought that was funny, and Eddie cracked a little smile but got right back to business. "Promise me."

"You want my word on it?"

"I'll take that over a contract any day. But it *will* be in the contract."

I stood up, said, "You have my word," and leaned over the table.

Eddie rose and we shook on it. We sat back down. I felt Gil staring at me.

"You never gave me your word," he said.

"I got a couple you can have right now."

He ignored that and said to Eddie, "I'm going to have to look at that contract."

Eddie pulled a stack of trifolded pages out of his inside jacket pocket and handed them over.

Gil opened them and sat back.

Benjamin said, "So, is any of that stuff true?"

"What stuff?"

"Come on."

I shrugged. "I'm sure whatever you heard was exaggerated."

"I hope so. Because from what I heard, you—"

Gil pointed at page three of the contract and said, "This is only for one fight."

"We're in a tight spot here," Eddie said. "We don't have time to go over Woody's medical records, see if there's anything preexisting that could keep him from fulfilling an extended commitment. If he even wants one. Then there are the exclusivity clauses, sponsorship deals, appearance schedules and fees . . . It's a huge hassle. After Saturday, we can all sit down again and talk about the future."

Gil flipped a few pages. "More money would be nice."

"Always," Eddie agreed.

"How long do we have to consider the offer?"

"Until I stand up from this table." Eddie tapped his fork against the bottom of his water glass. It looked a bit like he was pouting because we weren't bowing while signing the contract with tears of gratitude, but maybe it was just the light. He let the fork fall. "And it isn't an offer; it's a goddamn gift."

"You came to us," Gil said.

"Lucky you."

"Settle down. You can't walk away from this without Woody on board, so let's figure out a better deal."

Eddie stood. Nate and Benjamin did the same.

"Okay, Jesus," Gil said. His pride was like a horse pill with barbs on it, but he was smart enough to know when to swallow it. "We'll sign it. But I want *your* word we'll talk long-term right after the fight."

"Win or lose," Eddie said. They all sat down. I appreciated them looking only a little smug.

Eddie said, "Woody, I want to ask you something I ask all my fighters: Why do you fight?" He had his hand up, forefinger and thumb pressed together like he wanted me to touch on the exact point he was trying to make.

I didn't want to get it wrong. There were plenty of reasons why I'd been *in* fights—survival being the most common—but that didn't explain why I stepped into the cage. Practically ran to it. "It's what

I was made to do."

"Yes." Eddie made a fist and pounded the table. "It's what you were made to do. So don't get caught up in stupid shit you weren't made to do, yeah?"

"Yeah."

"Good. Now let's sign that bitch and talk about how we're going to make Woodshed Wallace famous within forty-eight hours."

CHAPTER 3

The only thing worse than training is losing.

It isn't a close race, but Gil does his best to make it seem that way.

Friday morning I was doing renegade man-makers with forty-five-pound dumbbells, dropping to the floor with them in my fists, exploding through a push-up, then rowing the dumbbells up one at a time like I was starting a lawn mower, all while keeping my feet together and my hips square to the padded floor. Then I got my feet under me and stood, throwing the bells into a push press over my head. When I was horizontal I could see my reflection in the puddle of sweat beneath my face. I looked very unhappy. The circuit was one minute each of seventy-pound kettlebell swings, burpees, pull-ups, frog jumps, and now these bastards back to back. This was the sixth and final circuit.

"It'll be a light day," Gil had said. "Just to keep you loose."

I heard him sip coffee from a mug that was as big as his head, and I prayed for him to die. He'd sent me to bed as soon as we got back from the restaurant, then stayed up all night watching tapes of Burbank's fights. The coffee mug was standard every morning, but today he actually needed it.

It had started out as a great day. Word of the Warrior deal spread quickly, and everyone at the gym was stoked over it. When they heard I was fighting Burbank the enthusiasm dipped a bit; then it was all grins again when Gil told them a camera crew was going to be stopping by. Roth, from Perth, Australia, and rumored to speak English but sometimes had everyone guessing, asked if he had time to get his hair cut.

Gil told him to get everything from the shoulders up taken off. Then he pulled out his stopwatch and my day went to shit.

We were in the open area toward the back of the gym. To my right and past Gil was the half-scale cage with its black fencing and raised canvas. Farther along that wall and about halfway to the plate-glass windows at the front was the boxing/kickboxing ring, the canvas a little higher than the cage's. When I had the audacity to lift my head during the circuit, I could see Roth and Terence Overton in there going at it with boxing gloves, shin pads, and headgear. I envied them.

Rows of hooks and pegs lined the wall behind the cage and ring. Walk along the row and you could smell the various levels of human suffering from the headgear, focus mitts, kicking shields, Thai pads, and boxing and MMA gloves. The first day Roth trained with us about four months ago, he thought it was acceptable to hang his jockstrap there to dry. Gil set it on fire.

The front of the gym space had a reception desk to the right of the glass double doors and behind that a display of the trophies the fighters had won. The belts and prizes I'd taken in various small promotions were dwarfed and hopelessly surrounded by Gil's jiu jitsu haul. Coming back toward me along the left wall were the heavy bags, Thai bags, double-end balls, and a wrecking ball that had an ongoing blood feud with me.

The wrecking ball is a sixty-pound black leather bastard shaped like an acorn, about as wide as me in the shoulders. It's hung from a set of chains, the top of it level with my chin and the bottom almost down to my waist. It's for working body shots, uppercuts, knees, and whatever else you want to throw, as long as you understand it will seek vengeance on the backswing.

Gil knows I hate that thing and loves to watch me argue with it. When he saw how much I enjoyed hitting the regular heavy bags in comparison, he did his best to ruin that too by introducing me to his "Keep the Change" drill.

You seize the bag's chains and jump up and lock your legs around the bag like you're pulling guard. Then let go with your hands and hang upside down so you can see the floor, where Gil dropped a handful of pocket change. Grab one coin at a time—one, because he's watching—and curl your way back up to put the coin on top of the heavy bag. You're done when all the change is off the floor, including whatever fell off the bag from you jerking it all over the place.

All I have left is the Muay Thai bag, and I know Gil is cooking something up about that one.

Under the bags and loose against the wall were the grappling dummies, about fifty pounds each and contoured to simulate an opponent's torso and trunk. They were good for tossing around and drilling ground and pound, but when it came to actual grappling, nothing less than pain on pain would cut it. We used the rack spaces in between the bags for pull-ups; during the circuits just follow the trail of your sweat back and forth and you won't get lost.

In the back where we were the building widened out to my left—from above the whole space looked like a backward L—and along the front wall of the short leg was the iron. Kettlebells, dumbbells, medicine balls, barbells with enough plates to keep a champion powerlifter busy for a few weeks, and an assortment of torture devices Gil had cobbled together out of heavy scraps, brackets, and duct tape.

The wall to my left was padded and clear of anything else so we could use it for shadowboxing, elevators, handstand push-ups, and whatever else Gil devised. Behind me was the half-windowed wall between the gym and the hallway that led to the back rooms. Some of them were air-conditioned. I couldn't remember what that felt like, but I knew it was good.

"Ten more seconds," Gil said.

I didn't believe him. It was probably twenty seconds, but I cranked it up a notch to finish strong.

"You been holding out on me, Woody? Where's this energy coming from? You got him down. He's on the canvas. Finish it. Finish it. Finish it . . . Time!"

I dropped the left hand dumbbell to the floor and fell away from it onto my back. Sweat ran into my mouth and I didn't care. I couldn't get my stomach to expand far enough to get the air I needed. My heart offered to exit through my mouth to give the lungs some room.

"In through your nose," Gil said and sipped more coffee.

I spit out my mouthguard and gulped air. "Call 911."

"You keep saying that. Look at Jairo. He's fine."

I let my head fall to the right and opened my eyes. Jairo Arcoverde was next to me on the mats. He looked like he'd been hit by a planet. He'd done the whole circuit in his forest green jiu jitsu gi, and the thing was almost black with sweat. "Are you dead?" I asked him.

"Yes."

I picked my head up and looked down the line. Jairo's younger brother Javier was facedown and spread-eagle, and beyond him the youngest of the clan, Edson, twenty-two, was sitting against the wall sipping water. I vaguely remembered him dropping out and spending some time with his face in the trash can during the frog jumps.

The Arcoverde brothers were from Rio de Janeiro, Brazil. Gil had earned his black belt in Brazilian jiu jitsu from their father, Antonio, and now the sons were getting ready to represent the family in MMA. It was a good deal all around; the boys helped me and the other guys at The Fight House work on our ground games, and they got to work on their stand-up with us. As a bonus, they also got to work on their conditioning.

Jairo stood up and peeled off his gi top and dropped it on the mat. It sounded like a sack of mulch. He was thirty and bigger than me, six four and about two forty-five—almost as big as Burbank—and had been doing his best to take me down and submit me for the past three weeks when I wasn't drilling the strategy for Porter. More often than not, Jairo got his way. We'd done some stand-up to make me feel better about myself, but the brothers were picking that up faster than I was avoiding tapouts.

The brothers had olive complexions, dark eyes, and cauliflower ears. Jairo's stood out more because of his shaved head, which he claimed helped him slide out of chokes, but I suspected his bust-worthy skull was the main factor. The thing gleamed like polished bronze when they all walked around in the Vegas heat and pretended to shiver and thought it was funny every time. Jairo had a heavy-lidded way of looking bored most of the time, even when he was working to sink an armbar or triangle choke. It was unnerving, like a brain surgeon yawning with his hands inside someone's skull.

We were lucky to have Jairo around for the Burbank fight. He could come close to simulating the size and brute strength I'd be dealing with, but Burbank was much more aggressive. Maybe Gil could poke Jairo with a stick while we sparred. Porter had a similar fighting style, but relying on my prep for him before fighting Burbank would be like eating a crouton each day leading up to a pancake eating contest.

There wasn't enough time to bring anyone else

in before Saturday. Gil had a Rolodex of judo guys, Division 1-A champion wrestlers, and a former Olympic Greco-Roman wrestler from Montana who almost threw me into the ceiling the last time he came through, but they were all either overseas or getting ready for their own fights. Gil and I agreed none of those guys could really simulate what it would be like to fight Burbank, either. They were too little, too slow, too stiff, or too nice.

I'd just about returned to subpanic heart and respiratory rates when Gil said, "Get in the cage."

Jairo and I dragged ourselves over and got our mouthguards back in and wrapped our hands in the training gloves, the same size and weight as the official version but with Velcro straps instead of laces. I pretended to have trouble getting the straps just right so I could take a few more deep breaths, but Gil caught on right away and threatened me with his coffee mug. I followed Jairo into the cage.

The canvas was still the original light gray color in a few spots. They looked like bleach stains on the mottled surface. No one wanted to bleed in training, but it happened. The scar tissue around my eyes had caused the most trouble, ending sparring sessions when a glancing elbow or inadvertent head butt opened a gash. It was important to let those heal completely before a fight; the athletic commission wouldn't let you compete with a preexisting cut. Like not having sex because you'd worked too hard on the foreplay.

Gil got in front of me and Jairo and looked us over. "How you feeling?"

"Good," I said.

"You look like shit."

"Thanks."

"Is that food from last night causing any trouble?"

"Nope." Even if it made my legs fall off, I wouldn't risk a ban of that menu.

"Are you focused?"

"Yes."

"What are you thinking about right now?"

I didn't know the answer to that.

Gil said, "Are you thinking about Junior Burbank or about how tired you are?"

I sucked on my mouthguard. "Both?"

"Wrong. If you're thinking about how tired you are—*at all*—nothing else matters."

"That's true," Jairo said.

I appreciated his input.

"Junior Burbank," Gil said. "He's the guy you're fighting tomorrow. Remember him?"

I nodded.

Gil scoffed. "No one wants you to win this fight. Eddie sure as hell doesn't. A one-fight contract? Please. He wants his golden boy to powerbomb and

ground and pound his way all the way to the belt so
he can sell Junior Burbank chewing tobacco and T-
shirts that are way too tight. Eddie brought you in
to be the guy getting fucked up in a highlight reel.
The clip they show before the rest of Burbank's fights.
Look what he did to Woodshed Wallace, the only guy
to beat him."

I bit down on my mouthguard. The rubber protested.

Gil was good at this. "After that, Eddie's got no use
for you. One and done. What do you think about that?"

"I think he's going to get a surprise."

He smiled. "Okay. So tell me the game plan." Switch
me from running through a wall to chess, just like that.
"And take your mouthguard out. Don't spit on me."

I popped it out. "He's going to try to take me
down. I'm not going to let him."

"And if he does?"

"I'll get back up."

Gil nodded. "Show me."

Jairo shot in again, and again I sprawled on top of
him and shoved him back. I wrapped his head in the
Muay Thai plum on the way up and pulled his face
down into my knee, stopping an inch from impact.
I pushed him away before he could go for a Greco
clinch and moved to my left.

"Good," Gil said. "If you feel that Thai clinch is

tight, keep it. But he's a strong bastard, so be careful he doesn't just pick you up with his head."

The fights Gil watched didn't show Burbank having to defend the Thai plum, but his neck was thick enough he might just bull right out of it. If I got a good clinch on him and he didn't know what to do, I'd put some knees into his belly and liver and legs and hopefully open him up for a couple to the face.

But I had to be careful. If my elbows were too far out, he could get a single underhook by wrapping one of his arms under mine, hooking his hand over my shoulder, and pulling it close to his body. From there he could go to double underhooks and wrap his arms around the small of my back in the Greco-Roman clinch and pull my hips in, and once that happened I'd get a good look at the world upside down.

Gil said, "Let him get it. Work your way out."

Jairo did a great impression of a wrestler and pulled me in. I dropped my weight down, but it didn't matter. He lifted me off the mat and torqued his body to the left fast enough to make my legs flap around like charged fire hoses. He dropped to one knee and set me down gently on my back with his shoulder in my sternum. If he'd gone full force, I probably would have been dazed or had the wind knocked out of me. At the very least something would have shot out of my body from somewhere inconvenient.

Jairo dropped into side mount, his torso on top of and perpendicular to mine. He gained about three hundred pounds and put them all on my lungs. He had his right elbow tight against my left hip and his right knee digging into my right hip to keep me from turning. I bent my right leg and crossed that foot over my left knee to keep him from sliding over into a full mount.

He started pushing my left wrist away from my body, but that was to get me to pull it in so he could grab my wrist with his right hand, wrap his left arm under my triceps, reach through and grab his right wrist, and pop up into a kimura. I didn't fall for it, but it was a decoy anyway. He dropped a few elbows into the air above my face to show he could. Point taken.

Gil said, "Now this is the tricky part."

"Really?" It came out much higher than I'd expected.

Jairo paused but kept his weight on me.

Gil said, "You've been training with Jairo to avoid submissions, but I think Burbank will go for pure ground and pound. So while you're working on angles and creating space, he's going to completely smash your head."

"Tricky," I agreed.

"So you should probably get up. Jairo, don't let him, but pretend you're a big dumb blond wrecking machine instead of a big sexy Brazilian wrecking machine."

"I can't help this," Jairo said.

We got back at it. Jairo wrapped his left arm behind my head to get a better grip and brought his left knee back to drive it into my ribs. I put my right hand on his left hip and pushed him away and off balance. The knee came in, but it hit my shoulder and didn't cause any trouble.

He tried again, and I pushed and rolled to my right and shrimped my right knee up into the space created between us and twisted clockwise on my hip so we were face-to-face. I reached down and pulled my right leg all the way out from under his hip and locked him tight in my guard.

"Good," Gil said. "But now he's going to posture up and rain devastation on you."

Jairo leaned back at the waist and brought half-speed hammerfists down toward my face.

I covered up and moved and kept my head off the mat so it would have somewhere to go in case a hammer slipped through. I caught his right hand in my left and clamped down on the wrist and kept it close to my chest. I tried to pull it across my body to get him to fall to my left so I could roll him that way, but he was too strong. His left fist came down, and I snagged that one and got good hand control. He couldn't hit me anymore, but that went both ways.

Gil said, "Now what? You can keep it stagnant until the ref stands you back up, but that could take all day. Meanwhile, the judges are thinking he's in a dominant position and you're just flopping around on your back because they don't know shit."

"I bait the powerbomb," I said. "Make him stand me up. Or take him down when he tries."

"I'm waiting."

We went through it. Over and over. By the time we were done, we had half a dozen options for if and when Burbank took me down and tried to murder me. I kept saying *if*. Gil stuck with *when*. Jairo stayed out of it. He and I were soaked with sweat and sitting in the cage with our backs against the fence when Gil's wife, Angie, came into the gym.

"Woody, the camera crew from Warrior just called. They're on the way over."

"That was fast." I took a breath through my nose for the first time that day.

"Eddie wants his hype," Gil said. "And you know what he wants you to say."

I stood and waited to see if my body accepted it. I didn't quite die. "I'm not going to say it."

"Come on."

"No."

Angie said, "For me?"

I considered it. She was way too good-looking for Gil, taller than him, and ten years younger, blonde with a light spread of freckles across her little nose.

She taught yoga and Pilates a few nights a week in the gym and spent most of the time trying to keep her class from lying on the bloodstains on the mats.

She had her head tilted to the side with a pouty lip. "Just once?"

"Sorry."

"Come on!" Roth shouted from the ring. He and Terence had stopped sparring and were leaning on the ropes. Terence was from Detroit and didn't say much, but he was grinning.

"You two get back to work," Gil said.

"We want to hear it," said Roth. "Say it, Woodrow. Then tell us what it's like to be famous."

"Shut up."

"For me?" Jairo asked.

"Okay. For you." I wiped a handful of sweat off my face. I looked around the gym at the faces. Edson and Javier had recovered from the circuit and were rolling in their gis. They stopped in mid-pretzel to watch. Roth had a gloved hand cupped to his helmeted ear. I took a deep breath. "I am going to impose my will upon Junior Burbank and prove our first fight was *not* a fluke."

They all booed. Roth threw his mouthpiece at me.

"Go take a shower," Gil said. "You can't be filmed looking like that. There are laws." He turned to Roth. "And if you're done in there, grab a mop and clean these mats."

I followed Jairo into the hallway at the back and down to the right, past the bathroom and then a left into the kitchen. He plucked an apple off the counter and offered it to me.

"Not yet," I said.

He nodded and ate half of it in one bite.

Some of us stay at the gym during training camp to limit distractions and keep Gil from calling us every hour to see what we're doing, so the kitchen has a constant stock of protein shakes, energy bars, lean meats, raw vegetables, and enough ice cream to keep a fat kid quiet for a week. Gil passes out the ice cream as a reward, and if he catches you with any unsanctioned, you work until your stomach gives it back.

I'd been sleeping in the back room, what we called the Hole, for the six weeks leading up to the Porter fight. Going back to when I started training with Gil I'd probably spent more time at The Fight House than at my apartment. Every month I paid the rent and wondered why.

Jairo and I went past the fridge and through the door on the other side of the kitchen into the Hole. It was a big open space with high ceilings where they worked on cars when the building was a dealership. We had a card table and foosball and console video games on the big screen that usually ended with somebody getting submitted on the floor while the game waited for someone to push a button.

I had my cot pushed up against the wall on the right, and past that in the far corner was the square of four showers sectioned off from the rest of the room with exposed framing showing and the drywall panels still taped together leaning against it. The inside was tiled and watertight, but Gil loathed drywall and thought if he let it sit long enough someone would get bored and hang it. I'd seen fighters in camp resort to lighting their leg hair on fire to pass the time, and no one had touched the drywall.

Jairo looked over to the far left corner at the big-screen and the person watching it on the black leather sectional couch. All I could see was the top of a head poking up past the back cushions. The head was covered by a sweatshirt hood the same forest green as Jairo's gi. Jairo said something in Portuguese to the head. The tone sounded a lot like, "Are you going to watch that garbage all day?" The reply was short and made Jairo stop walking. He turned to me and said, "Do you believe that?"

I shook my head.

Jairo muttered into the showers. I picked the stall diagonal from his and got clean and into a pair of loose cotton pants and a Fight House T-shirt for the cameras. The shirt also featured Arcoverde Jiu Jitsu and some sponsors I'd try to thank after the Burbank fight if I could still talk.

When I walked out, the couch head was still hooded and aimed at the TV. I heard Jairo turn off the water, and I got the hell out of there before he came out with whatever rant he'd been brewing during his shower.

I grabbed a protein shake out of the fridge and entered the gym.

The Warrior Inc. camera crew was setting up to run the interview with the cage as a backdrop, using Roth as a stand-in for getting the lights right. He was telling the producer, "As for Woodrow's face looking any better, it can't be helped. If you want, you can keep the camera on me, and he can talk from the next room. Can we do a quick something for me to send to me mum?"

The producer saw me and walked over. "Kevin Jacobson. If we start doing or saying anything you don't like, just holler, okay?"

"Okay."

"Great. You ready for tomorrow?"

"I better be," I said.

"Yeah, short notice, huh?" Kevin seemed like a decent guy, young with a good haircut and rectangular glasses and a wedding ring, but his job was to get me to say things that would create drama and conflict for the fight. I thought there was going to be enough of that, what with the punching each other in the face and all.

It's a business—I get that—but I just don't have it in me to hype a fight.

Besides, when it comes down to it, I'm in there fighting myself. My limits.

The other guy's just a mirror.

"I think we're ready over there," Kevin said. "Now, if we could, let's get you saying something along the lines of 'I'm going to impose my will on Burbank and prove to the fans it wasn't a fluke when I beat him before.'"

They sat me and Gil on the cage apron in the lights, and a burly guy held a microphone over our heads. Kevin pulled a step-up platform over from the weight corner and sat down with the camera on his right. Angie and Roth and Terence and the Arcoverde brothers lined up behind him and crossed their arms and tried to keep serious faces.

Kevin said, "When you talk, look at me, not the camera."

Gil and I looked at the camera; then Gil put an elbow in my ribs.

Kevin opened a black binder and scanned the notes. "All right, guys, we just need a few clips for the preshow and prefight sequences. Eddie really wants this stuff to crackle through the building, you know? Get people in the crowd looking at each other and going, 'Oooh, he's gonna pay for saying that.' Cool?"

Gil said, "Can I say something about Eddie wanting Burbank to win?"

It was my turn with the elbow.

Kevin looked up from his binder. "Well. Uh . . ."

"Don't listen to him," I said.

"No, no, it's good. We can use that energy. But how about instead of saying you think Eddie wants Junior Burbank to win, you say you *know* the *world* wants him to."

"Never mind," Gil said. "But don't get me wrong; we'll take Junior any day of the week. We just get the feeling Woody isn't supposed to win this fight."

"I don't really know about that," Kevin said.

Roth whispered something to Angie, who shook her head and frowned at Gil. He shrugged.

I started to panic. I suspected that pissing off a producer would be like swearing at the kid in the drive-through. I didn't want to get pulled into the hype machine, but I also didn't want any loogies in my burger. "Sorry. We're a bit on edge around here. Like you said: short notice."

"It's all good," said Kevin. "If we could just get through these questions, I'll get out of your way."

"Hey," Gil said, "Woody's right. We're just fired

up for the fight. Please, my full apologies. Fire away."

Kevin was good at his job and jumped into the window. "How is Woody's jiu jitsu?"

Gil said, "Well, it's like watching a bear trying to change a diaper. It's very confusing."

"I'm not very confident," I added.

Kevin looked at us. "Do you want me to use that?"

"No, let's do it again," Gil said. "Serious now. Ready? Okay. Woody's jiu jitsu is improving. He's not gonna win any tournaments yet, but his takedown defense is very good, and if he does get taken down, he knows how to avoid submissions and damage and get back on his feet. And when he does, he's usually pretty upset."

"Nice," Kevin said. "For the show, I'll probably have a drop from somebody, maybe Benton, spliced in saying that 'improving' coming from you is the same as saying it's excellent. Because of how good you are."

"Hell, I can say that," Gil said.

"It will probably work better coming from someone else." Kevin turned to me. "What do you think about Burbank saying your fight three years ago was a fluke?"

"I think he's improved a lot since then, and this is going to be a completely different fight. But I've improved too, so he's not getting the same fighter, either. It's going to come down to who makes the first mistake. And the last one." I nodded. That was some good shit right there.

But Banzai Eddie wanted more, and Kevin wanted to get it for him. He said, "You couldn't knock him out in your first fight. Does that worry you?"

I smiled. "I wouldn't say I *couldn't* knock him out; I just didn't get the chance. He gave me the opportunity to submit him, and I took it. The first and only time I won by an ankle lock."

"I'll take credit for that," Gil said.

Kevin smiled. "So you're going to knock him out this time?"

"I'm not picky. I'll take the win however it shows up. I'd like to keep it out of the judges' hands, though."

"You're a finisher," Kevin said. "That's why Eddie loves you."

Gil swore. "Sorry."

"No problem," Kevin said. "Woody, Junior Burbank said he'd never trained to defend ankle locks before that fight, so it doesn't really count that you beat him that way."

"His record has a No Fair category? Can I get one of those?"

"Good point." Kevin laughed. "If he decides to take it to the ground, what are you going to do?"

I smiled too, but it was getting harder. I leaned forward a little and in my peripheral vision saw the cameraman adjust to keep me in focus. "It's not a dictatorship in there. Not until about two seconds before somebody gets knocked out, so it doesn't matter what he decides. He's a big boy and a great wrestler, so he probably will take me down. I'll get back up. Maybe I'll take him down."

Kevin made a note. "Burbank's coach said they've been watching tapes of you since they got the call that you were the replacement, and in your last four or five fights you've been cut pretty badly, and you open up pretty easily in general. Are you worried that might be a strategy for Burbank, to try to cut you and win by referee stoppage?"

"Are you serious?" I looked at Gil.

He sipped his coffee and stared straight ahead.

I said, "That's pathetic if it's what they want to do. If that happens, I'll go to the hospital, get stitched up, and come back for a rematch *that* night." I took a breath. "But it won't happen, anyway. I have a great corner and we use the best cutman in the business, and if I get cut they'll keep me from leaking too much."

Kevin kept his eyes on mine. He was circling me in the water. "Burbank said no matter where the fight goes—on the feet, on the ground, in the clinch—he'll dominate with his strength and break your spirit. He said he'll see it in your eyes when you break. And when he sees it, he'll punish you for as long as he can before the ref stops the fight or you go unconscious."

"Did he really say that?"

"I've got it on my laptop if you want to watch it."

"No. I'm sure I'll see it enough tomorrow." I stared past him and let what Burbank said work its way in to see how it felt. I could see the cameraman twisting in closer on my face.

"Woody," Kevin said, "do you have a reply to that?"

"Yeah. I don't care what he does. I don't care how much he's improved. I'm going to knock him the fuck out. And if anybody in his corner so much as cocks an eyebrow at me, I'll put them down too."

Gil let the front door close behind Kevin and his crew. He spent a moment squinting through the window while they loaded up their van.

I tapped the Thai bag with slow hooks and tried to look sheepish. It was harder than I'd expected.

Without turning around, Gil said, "You're going to knock out his entire corner?"

I put a soft dig into the bag's liver. "I may have gotten carried away."

"What about the ref? Should I tell him to wear a mouthguard?"

"You heard him. They want to cut me on purpose? Come on."

Gil turned around. "What I heard was Eddie's puppet strings yanking you all over the place. Cuts happen. Sometimes on purpose, sometimes not."

"Still," I said, "you don't call your shot like that."

Gil walked over and stopped the bag from swinging. "Leave it right here. Don't carry it with you into the cage; it'll burn you out in the first minute."

"Right."

"I want to see you drop it."

I took a deep breath and ran my hands up my face and over my head. Reached behind my neck and pulled my hands forward over my shoulders and held them cupped in front of my chest, let them come apart. "Happy?"

"Damn near giddy."

"Woodrow! Look here, mate." Roth tugged Edson toward us, Edson shaking his head and looking embarrassed. "You wanna talk about cuts? Show him."

Edson leaned forward, exposing a puckered line behind his right ear about as long and wide as my index finger.

We all hissed and cringed.

"How'd that happen?" Roth asked.

Edson didn't speak much English, but he understood the question. He started talking in Portuguese, his hands demonstrating something that looked like combat knitting. He paused to make sure we were getting it. Our faces made him frown.

"Did it hurt?" Roth asked.

Gil pointed to his own lip. "You got some stupid right here."

"What?"

"Nope, missed it. Still there."

Edson started again and we got more confused. He gave up and called for Jairo but didn't get an answer. He hollered again, and after a few seconds the hooded couch lump shuffled on bare feet from the back hallway.

Edson said something crisp, and the feet might have moved a fraction faster. Edson rolled his eyes at us.

The feet came to a stop on Edson's left, and the hooded head turned to him and waited.

Edson tugged the hood down and let a spill of black hair fall out. His cousin Marcela was in there somewhere. She was a few years older than him and, from what I'd heard from anyone who'd talked to her, terminally bored. The sleeves of her Arcoverde Jiu Jitsu sweatshirt swallowed her hands with a few inches to spare. She smacked one of the flaps into Edson's face and kicked him in the shin.

Roth loved it. "Sweetheart, will you marry me?"

Marcela pulled her sleeves up and ran her hands through her hair. She produced an elastic band and made a loose ponytail with her dark bangs still wisping down to frame her face. She blew most of them out of her eyes and looked Roth up and down. She said something to Edson that made him cover his mouth.

Roth panicked. "What'd she say?"

"What are you asking him for?" Gil said. "He brought her out to translate."

Roth was on the verge of tears. "Oh, for fuck's sake."

Marcela gave me the once-over too in case I had any ideas. We'd nodded at each other in passing since the clan arrived last week, but I'd been wrapped up in training for Porter. She was small, maybe five three and a sandwich over a hundred pounds. When her hair was loose, it fell halfway down her back. She had very thin, arched eyebrows over eyes the color of wet beach sand, a shade lighter than her skin. I liked the little bump in her nose on the way down to her lips, which were shiny with light gloss and looked comfortable wearing a skeptical twist.

Her neck was thin, and everything below that was a mystery inside the sweatshirt that went almost to her knees. Her toes were unpainted and stubby. The tops of her feet looked calloused; she'd spent some time on the mat.

I wasn't sure why Jairo brought Marcela to the States. Maybe she wanted to see Vegas, but the brothers wouldn't let her out into the city by herself, and they'd pretty much just given her a tour of the streets from their hotel to the gym and back, the boys either training or caught up in other pursuits. Javier wouldn't shut up about some redheaded stripper named Pandora.

Marcela held her arms out and asked Edson something.

He replied and pointed at the scar, then at us.

Marcela snorted. "Oh, you're kidding, right? That stupid thing?"

Edson pointed at Roth, who pointed at me.

Marcela was disgusted with all of us. "You want to know about that scar?"

"No," I lied.

"He was fighting Vale Tudo in Brazil, you know, this means 'anything goes'? It was his first fight. His last too, I think." She frowned at Edson. "He was fighting some skinny guy, all bones, and an elbow cut him in the head there, behind his ear. Edson had him in the guard, and the guy stuck his fingers into the cut and tried to pull it open to let more blood out."

"Awful," Roth said.

"The guy, he wanted to make the cut so bad the judges would stop the fight. It's not easy in those fights. He pulled on Edson's ear with one hand and pushed at his hair with the other. The crowd did not like it, but he didn't care. You could see Edson's bone in there, his skull."

Roth whistled. "Christ."

"Did the ref stop it?" Gil asked.

"No," Marcela said, "the blood wasn't in his eyes, so he could still fight. But the blood was everywhere else. Edson wouldn't tap because he's stupid, and Jairo had to throw the towel in from the corner. It was a big towel, and they pushed it against Edson's head, and it was full of blood before they announced the winner."

Edson saw she was done and smiled and nodded at us. He gestured like he was pulling curtains open and peeking inside; then he pointed to his scar. Gave everyone a thumbs-up.

Marcela shook her head.

Jairo walked up with another apple. "What are you talking about?"

"The scar," Marcela said.

Jairo smiled. "That." He looked at Edson's head and became very concerned. "We did not see sign of brains."

Gil checked his watch. "You ready for the goat rodeo?"

The weigh-ins. Everyone fighting tomorrow had to make weight today. Most guys fighting light, welter, middle, and light-heavyweight walked around ten to twenty pounds over their fighting weight and got down to four or five over by the day of the weigh-in. They cut those last few pounds of water in the sauna, stepped on the scale looking ripped from the dehydration, and couldn't wait to get something down their necks.

The heavyweights had a much larger bracket to

work in, from two hundred six to two sixty-five, so we didn't spend a lot of time consulting the scale. I didn't trust the weigh-in numbers anyway. A heavyweight skipping around at two fifty today could easily be stomping at two seventy tomorrow.

I asked, "Eddie said four o'clock?"

Gil nodded. "It's just past three now."

Marcela perked up. "You're going to the arena?"

"One of the convention rooms attached to the casino," Gil said. "We can check out the arena, though."

"Let me shower," she said and ran out of the gym faster than I'd seen her do anything else.

Roth leaned around Jairo to watch her go.

"Hey, come on," Jairo said.

"Sorry, mate. Why's she so mean to me?"

"Have you seen your face?" Gil asked.

"That'll do from you, thanks."

Jairo folded his arms and spread his feet, ready to discuss. "She don't like the culture in Brazil, you know, the macho kind of guy, and I try to tell her it's a fighter thing. She's around fighters all the time, and we have to be a man in the ring and cage, and outside, we still have to be a man. So, you're like that."

Roth nodded. "What if I sing to her?"

Gil looked appalled.

"Listen," Jairo said, "I think if you do that, she punches you in the face. No joke."

"Well, that's my whole arsenal. Does she like flowers?"

"Yes, she does, but she doesn't like you."

Roth looked at me. "Christ, the whole family's mean."

"You can sing to me if you want."

"Nah, mate, you're fighting tomorrow. I can't have you distracted with confusing feelings for me. And I believe it's my turn to wash the towels, yes, Master Gil?"

"Whatever keeps you from singing."

Roth waltzed toward the back hall, massacring Sinatra the whole way.

Jairo winced. "Punches to the face. I'm sure of it."

"Okay, let's get packed up." Gil took a look at me. "You've done this before. It's the same stage, just a bigger crowd. You won't notice them anyway once you're in the fight."

"I know." I wasn't scared of the fight—that had passed a long time ago—but I hadn't had any time to get used to the Warrior situation. Every time the reality of it popped in, that I was in my first big-time show tomorrow, the fight that could get me facing the right way and not half turned all the time to see what was catching up, my stomach came into my throat to get a look around. I'd be glad when Burbank landed his first punch just so I'd know the waiting was over.

"Hey," Gil said, "this crap is for the fans. The

goddamn hype. This is Eddie's day, so let him worry about it. Enjoy it and don't take any of it too seriously. You already made it through the hardest part right here on these mats. The fight is cake. A surprise cake, but aren't those the best kind?" He grabbed the back of my neck and pushed and pulled me around. "Today is like Christmas Eve, boy. Tomorrow you get to open your presents, right?"

"Right," I said.

He let go. "I don't want to ruin the next surprise, but I think Santa is bringing you Junior Burbank's head."

"Good. I don't have one of those yet."

CHAPTER 4

Walking through the Golden Pantheon Casino, attached to the arena where Warrior holds its events, we had to keep stopping to let Marcela get a closer look at the flashing slot machines and seizure-inducing games that had people either tugging at each other in celebration or giving the thousand-yard stare at what could have been.

Those same people might have called me stupid for willingly stepping into a cage to face assault, but I'd tell them if money and pride are on the line, at least let me fight for them. Football teams don't win or lose on the coin toss.

Marcela cleaned up well. Her hair was still wet, and it reflected the colors in the room and made them much softer on the eyes. She was wearing jeans and a black baby tee with a rounded Arcoverde Jiu Jitsu logo across her chest, and I wanted to thank that old sweat-shirt for hiding her figure back at the gym; it's easier to get knocked out with your mouth hanging open.

There were some fight fans bouncing around the casino. A pair of fratty guys wearing frayed jeans and five shirts between them, drinking something with a lot of straws, took a long look at our group—Marcela, me, Gil, and the brothers. The boys fell in next to Jairo and asked if he was a fighter.

"I do jiu jitsu, but you'll see me soon in MMA," he said, then nodded at me. "This is the guy."

They studied me. One of them said, "You're fighting tomorrow?"

"That's right."

"Against who?"

"Junior Burbank."

The talker smacked his bro in the shoulder. "Oh, shit, this is Woodshed!" Then, in a voice he must have thought was much quieter, "I bet a grand against him."

The friend laughed and shushed him.

"Seriously. Dude, no offense, but I thought you'd be bigger."

"It's because I'm standing next to this house." I indicated Jairo.

"Yeah." Skeptical with a touch of pity maybe. Like I was going to have a short dance in the cage and an extended stay in a hospital. The two of them started to drift away. "Hey, good luck."

Gil said, "Sorry about your thousand dollars."

We showed our passes to a guy in a maroon jacket guarding the backstage door to the conference room, Marcela wearing Roth's pass around her neck. The guy didn't bother to read the names, just waved us in.

The backstage area stretched across the width of the big room and took up a third of the length. It was separated from the public area by a heavy, dark purple curtain on our right that you could probably use as a mainsail on an aircraft carrier, but it would snag too many planes. There was a solid wall on the left, lined all the way to the far wall with folding chairs and tables piled with sponsor junk.

A few fighters stood around, avoiding the bottles of water and sports drinks lined up on some of the tables. If they'd spent the last few hours in a sauna dropping water weight, those bottles would look like the nectar of the gods.

Somebody bumped me from the right. "Keep me away from those tables." It was Terry Crawford, a welterweight fighting on the undercard. A former wrestler, he'd been to The Fight House a few times to train submission defense with Gil. He was getting better, but we all saw him tapping to a choke at some point. I could see his jaw muscles ripping at the gum in his mouth, and he carried a cup for the saliva he managed to work up.

"Hey, Terry, how you feeling?" We clasped hands like arm wrestlers and half hugged, neither of us really leaning into it.

Terry said, "I'll tell you what, man. You get me in the cage right now, just put a brownie sundae on the other side of Nakano. I'll go through him in five seconds and have chocolate sauce on my face in six."

"I feel bad for him already."

"Should be a good one. How about you? Congrats on the fight, but holy shit. The co-main event against Burbank?"

"Yeah, no tune-ups for me, I guess."

"Porter," Gil offered.

Terry stiff-armed me. "That's right. You just fought last night. You're a madman."

"Nah. It was easier than any day at the gym. I feel pretty good. But I didn't have to cut any weight."

He spit into the cup. "Asshole."

"Come on up to heavyweight. You can eat all the sundaes you want. Carbs, even."

Terry snorted. "Yeah, a five-eight heavyweight. They'd roll me into the cage and carry me out in a sack."

It was hard to picture. If he lost any more water weight, museums would be fighting to get him into a sarcophagus. "Why do you do this to yourself? I thought you'd know better by now."

"Bad knee. Can't do much cardio, so I had to stop eating. But what can you do?"

I understood. You said no once, Eddie figured you didn't have the warrior's heart. Or did he capitalize it even then?

Gil piled our stuff onto some chairs and walked over. "You been drilling those defenses?"

"Even in my sleep," Terry said.

"We won't get a chance to see that, though, right?"

Terry glanced around and decided the coast was clear. "Hey, you guys know anybody speaks Japanese?"

Gil and I looked at each other.

I shrugged. "I don't think so. How about Portuguese?"

"Nah. We were talking about getting someone who speaks Japanese in the corner who could understand what Nakano's guys are telling him. So if they're hollering for him to go for a choke, my corner can tell me, 'Hey, watch out for the choke.'"

Gil nodded. "What's the lag time on something like that?"

"Yeah, I know," said Terry. "Plus, those guys don't do a lot of hollering anyway. Just not in the culture. Kinda creepy."

"Here you go," Gil said. "You start to feel his arms or legs coming around your neck? Watch out for the choke."

"You're the best."

"Good luck tomorrow."

Turning away, Terry said, "You guys too. Hey, after party at Stinger."

To me, Gil said, "It's gonna be tough to dance with an ice pack on his throat."

"Anything can happen," I said.

"You seen Burbank yet?"

"I haven't been looking."

Gil, staring past me toward the door, said, "Shit, here comes Eddie."

I turned and saw him coming in with four guys in nice suits with no ties and shirts open a few buttons to show tight T-shirts underneath. Benjamin and his smartphone were in the group, but I didn't see Nick.

Eddie shook hands and half hugged his way through the room, moving fast so no one could hold him up. He looked like a piranha swimming through a pack of sharks with the sharks getting the hell out of the way. He spotted us and vectored in. "Woody, Gil, welcome. You get some sleep last night?"

"I did," I said.

Good enough for Eddie. He said, "You're lucky you already have a nickname, or we'd be calling you the Owl. Everyone I talk to, when I tell them who Junior's fighting, they say, 'Who?'" He'd probably been holding it in all day.

I feigned confusion.

He seemed disappointed for a beat, then got serious. "How we feeling?"

"We're feeling good," Gil said.

Eddie nodded at the Brazilians. "These guys in your corner?"

I said, "They'll all be here tomorrow, but just Gil and Jairo, the big one, are going to corner me."

"We'll get them some passes. Benjamin, get them some passes."

Benjamin went to work on his smartphone.

Eddie said, "Gil, I have some paperwork you and the other guy have to look at and sign, so catch up with me after the weigh-in, yeah?"

"Mm," Gil said.

Eddie gestured at the purple drape. "The buzz out there is crazy. I put a few guys in the crowd with Woodshed Wallace shirts on, and they're telling the Junior fans it might go down right here. That the two of you could flip the switch and start throwing in your skivvies."

"I have shirts?"

"Yeah, they're slick. Benjamin had his people designing them while we were at dinner, and they printed overnight. They smell like shit, but that'll fade. It's got your silhouette kicking in the door of a shed, and the flying boards spell out Woodshed, all splintered and nasty looking. You want one?"

"I don't think so."

"Gil? What size?"

"Four of each," Gil said.

"I shoulda known better. I'll have somebody bring them by. And listen, we're going in the order of the fights for the weigh-ins, so you guys are second to last. I'm not saying be boring, but try not to outshine the main event."

"Hard to do, fighting in skivvies," I said.

"You'll figure it out." Eddie snagged a girl hustling by with a coil of velvet rope in her arms. "Sweetheart, when you're done with that, get four of the brown T-shirts in each size and bring them over here to Woodshed Wallace, okay?"

"Who?"

They banged through the weigh-ins and stare-down photos, some of the guys down to their jocks to get within the limit. We could see most of the stage by standing at the bottom of the stairs that cut through an overlap in the drapes and led to the left side of the platform. Eddie was up there with some of the ring girls and other necessary people, the girls in their bikinis and tennis shoes, blowing kisses and whispering to each other when a fighter had to have a towel held in front of him on the scale.

We couldn't see the crowd, but it sounded big. Davie Benton, the color commentary guy for Warrior, gave the PA system a workout introducing the fighters and asking the crowd if they wanted to see some fireworks between the two guys glaring at each other with no shirts on. Eddie stood back a little bit between them like he was going to have to break something up.

That could work. Like spitting on a forest fire.

"You're next," the guy at the bottom of the steps told me, then clicked a button on a wire running up to a headset and said into it, "Do we have Burbank? . . . Good. Okay."

I couldn't help it. I searched for him. I scanned the tops of the heads backstage for a blond lump sticking up like a mushroom made out of muscles. Nothing. I glanced at Gil and Jairo, standing by our stuff, and Marcela, sitting against the wall looking bored. Javier and Edson were missing. Gil got on his toes to show he was on the lookout too, then shrugged when he had the same luck as me.

I heard Davie holler, "Are you ready? Are you ready? All right, now we have in his first fight for Warrior but bringing a very impressive twenty-four and three record with him—*twenty* of those wins by KO or TKO, folks—a guy who'll take the fight out behind the woodshed and knock the whole place flat, heavyweight fighter Aaron . . . *Wood*shed . . . Wallace!"

"That's you," the guy in the headset told me. "Go, go, go."

I climbed the steps, the lights and noise hitting at the same time like coming up from underwater into the boiling rapids, and I didn't feel the hook or see the net until it was too late.

CHAPTER 5

The crowd was worked up. Credit to Davie, because it couldn't be easy to sell guys standing on a scale. The room held a few hundred people, five tops, but they were all on their feet and taking photos and making vowel sounds for me. Most of them were *ooooo*, preceded by a *B*. I'd been booed before but never with this relish.

It made me smile. They boo you leading up to the fight, then on the way to the cage, during the introductions, and through the stare down. Then you knock someone out and everyone wants to buy you ice cream.

There was a huge Warrior, Inc. backdrop hanging on the purple drapes on my left, the name and logo about the size of a large pizza box and repeated every two feet. If someone took your picture in front of it, they'd get to see the logo at least three times.

Davie waved me over and kept the microphone low and said, "Hey, Woody, big fan." He was much smaller than I'd thought, thin in a tight navy Warrior T-shirt, his forehead up to my shoulder and an inferno of rusty hair almost brushing my chin. Impressive muttonchops clamped his narrow face.

He seemed like a nice guy; serious actor, usually the sidekick to someone bigger, and a fan of the sport who could spread its charms into influential circles. He'd started out as a stuntman, so he had some basis for saying what hurt and what didn't.

Davie raised the microphone. "All right, Woody, you said you're going to knock Junior Burbank out cold."

Fucking Kevin.

"You were the last and *only* person to beat him, but that was three years ago, and you couldn't knock him out then. What makes this time different?" He swung the mic under my mouth and grinned.

Davie was challenging me, and hype be damned, I took it personally. He was close enough to elbow in the temple, see if he still knew how to fall the right way.

I leaned into the mic and said, "This time I'm pissed off. And I'm better at knocking people out than he is at staying awake."

The crowd tried to set a world record for loathing. They chewed on their cameras.

Davie kept a straight face and said, "Wow, bold words. Okay, let's get you on the scale and see what Junior Burbank is dealing with."

The crowd settled down a bit, simmering at a low murmur about how it didn't matter how much I weighed, Burbank was going to toss me into the rafters.

There's really no intimidating way to take your pants off, so I just got them off, movements I've done every day I could remember, but it still felt awkward onstage. I had my fight shorts on underneath, dark green with The Fight House and Arcoverde Jiu Jitsu logos on each hip and sponsors splattered on the thighs and butt. The sides of the legs were sliced halfway up to the waist for sprawling and kicking.

Next came the shirt, followed by one whistle from the crowd that was quickly hushed in case it gave me superpowers. I stepped on the big scale, a doctor's office rig with counterweights and levers and a team standing by should someone nudge it. An official from the Nevada State Athletic Commission got personal with the weights and stroked them around until he was happy.

"Two thirty-five point five," he said.

"Two thirty-five and a half," Davie yelled into the mic.

The crowd jeered, my very weight an insult to Burbank. How dare I?

I flexed—it was in the contract—which shut a

few people up but made most of them louder.

Davie said, "All right, Woody, looking solid, very solid. Now let's get his opponent out here, folks. Maybe you've heard of him. *Ju*nior *Bur*bank!"

I didn't know which the crowd enjoyed more, hating me or loving Burbank. I glanced at the steps, my face blank. If Burbank came bulling over and got right in with a snarl, I'd counter with boredom. If he walked past with no acknowledgment, I'd yawn.

I waited. The crowd was almost ready to overthrow a government. I saw Gil at the bottom of the steps. He shook his head and shrugged. No Burbank.

Davie walked over to me, and I started to come up with a line about Burbank being too scared to step on the scale with me, let alone into the cage. A real gem. But Davie kept the microphone low and said, "Sorry, man."

I didn't know what he was talking about.

Then I looked out into the crowd.

Burbank was making his way from the rear of the room, the fans pulling at him and holding palms out for him to punch, chanting Bur-*bank*, Bur-*bank*.

No one even told me that was an option. I glared at Eddie. He tried to look innocent, but his genes wouldn't let him.

Burbank plowed through with a few stops to swirl an autograph on a shirt or hat or breast; then he high-fived one of the security guys along the front of the stage and jumped onto the stage, which had to be four feet off the floor. I probably could have done the same thing with a three-foot boost.

Burbank turned to the crowd and put his arms out, his mitts spread and big enough to put me and Davie and half the city in shade. He was big and tan and had his blond hair shaved to stubble. It was a serious haircut. He spun around and almost killed one of the ring girls with his chin.

I got ready for the chest to chest, but he stared past me like a salad in a candy shop. So I ignored him right back, but it felt weak and pouty. I put my pants on and pretended the crowd was cheering for that.

"Davie!" Burbank stomped over and gave Davie the half hug, Davie asking him how he felt. "Like an eater of worlds," he said.

"You gonna make weight?"

Burbank scoffed and pulled his shirt off. The crowd swooned. He was bigger than the last time we'd fought. A lot bigger. Back then he'd certainly filled a doorway at six six, two sixty, bulky but a little soft; now he was cut from a sequoia big enough to accommodate a tunnel.

Burbank leaned on Davie to get his warm-up pants off. Davie looked like a spider monkey next to him. Burbank got down to his square-cut boxers, the guys in the crowd a little quieter now, but the women making up for it. Burbank crushed the scale and stood while the official slid things around. He shook his head at a few counterweights, like he'd never had to use them before and wasn't sure they'd work. When he was happy, he said something to Davie.

"Two hundred and sixty-*three* pounds, fight fans! Just under the wire, Junior, great job."

I wanted to shake my head. He'd walk into the cage at two eighty, almost fifty pounds heavier than me. Maybe they'd let me carry a shovel.

"All right, guys, let's get you over here for the photo." Davie walked backward to the right side of the stage near Eddie and the ring girls.

Burbank walked with him and moved to Eddie's left. I stopped on Eddie's right so he was between me and Burbank, his arms already raising to stop Burbank when he spun around with his fists out and in my face.

He ground his teeth together and pulled his neck tight, his eyes wide.

I leaned back to avoid spittle and knuckles.

"Easy, guys, easy," Eddie said. "Don't get a hernia during the weigh-in."

He kept Burbank in check enough for me to lean in a little with my fists up for the photos. My hands looked like Tater Tots about to go into his microwaves. Eddie wanted it to look like we were about to go at each other and couldn't wait for the cage door to close. We couldn't have done better with Spielberg's help.

"Got it," the photographer said and scurried away.

Burbank put his hands down and filled the space between us with the rest of his body. The crowd got louder, but I pushed it away. "So you're gonna knock me out?" he said.

"That's right." I stood my ground but didn't like looking up at him.

He glanced at my brow, then glared at me. "That's gonna be hard to do, all that blood running into your eyes."

"You're going to bleed into my eyes?"

"*Your* blood, ass wipe."

"That's a good plan. Praying the ref will stop it before I put you facedown."

Burbank got closer, which I hadn't thought possible. "No ref here now."

"This isn't boxing. Try to act civilized."

"Guys, enough." Eddie got his arms between us and kept a smile on his face while he tried to push us apart. Moses might have done it but not Eddie.

Burbank tilted his forehead down to press against mine. I got on my tiptoes to push back. I started saying things faster than I could think them up. The room slowed down like it did when the bell rang. I got ready to fight a man in his underwear.

A huge brown arm came over my shoulder and shoved Burbank backward into the swarm of security that was storming up from that side of the stage. More arms wrapped around my chest and pulled me back and off my feet.

Vegas security knows how to stop a fight. I was hustled away, feet off the floor and arms akimbo. I saw Jairo standing in my wake yelling something in Portuguese and gesturing at Burbank with the same brown arm that had wrangled me.

Before I dipped backstage I heard Davie say into the microphone, "Who else can't wait for tomorrow?"

The water bottle in my hand was defective and shaking a little, so I put it down between my feet. I didn't want any shaky water. I sat in a chair with Gil and Jairo in front of me in case the adrenaline wouldn't let me stay put.

We could hear Burbank hollering at the other end of the backstage area, saying we should go *right now*. He kept repeating those last two words. I thought I heard the crowd pick up the chant on the other side of the drapes.

Gil muttered to me about saving it for tomorrow, don't wear myself out, let the other guy get tired—the mantra of a cornerman.

Eddie and some other suits found us. He pushed his way to me and Gil. "Skip the fighter orientation after this. It's the same shit you heard a few days ago, just on a bigger scale. Security doesn't want you and Burbank in the same room again until tomorrow night."

Gil said, "Woody's not the one acting like a cartoon character."

"Yeah, well, your boy didn't exactly diffuse the situation out there. Just take the rest of the day off." He pointed at Gil. "But you still gotta sign that shit."

"Yeah, yeah."

Eddie and his crew rolled away.

Marcela sat down next to me and started reading the label on a can of energy drink. She said, "This has four servings of fruit in it," and looked around for a response. When no one said anything, she said, "Fruit in a can, I don't get. Just eat fruit."

Jairo put the can on the table next to her chair and shook his head.

She said, "Okay, fine," and crossed her arms.

"Maybe it's so you can absorb the nutrients faster," I said. I was breathing too fast and had to make up for it when I was done talking. Deep breaths.

"Through the nose," Gil said.

Marcela glanced at the can. "What, your body wants it faster? Are you sure you can take it?"

"Take it?"

"Your ancestors, they did fine with a banana off the tree."

"I think I'm mostly Scottish. No bananas there."

"So, what? Apples?" Marcela leaned forward and put her elbows on her knees like me.

Burbank had stopped yelling at some point. There was still a hum of energy backstage, but it was pressing against a bubble around us.

I shrugged.

She said, "Who cares. The point is, you don't want these phonies. Your body says no." Marcela tipped the can over and shoved it under a pile of T-shirts with the drink company's logo on them. Satisfied, she slapped her knees. "What are we doing now?"

"I gotta work this out," I said. "Let's go back and hit the bags."

Marcela said something in Portuguese that shocked Jairo.

"No," Gil said. "In this state, you'll bust your hand or stroke out on me. You gotta relax."

"Watch some tapes?"

"I said *relax*, not watch Burbank fights and get even more worked up. Hang out. Get some dinner. Have a conversation about something besides forcing your will on him."

"They made me say that."

"I know." Gil patted my head.

"Take me to dinner," Marcela said. "And to see the fountain."

I raised my eyebrows at Jairo, not sure if he was her official chaperone or what. I didn't want to start any blood feuds.

"Is up to her," he said.

Marcela smacked my arm. "Don't look at him for things about me."

I surrendered. "Okay, where do you want to eat?"

"There is a VIP club here in the building called Chaos. Let's go there."

"Chaos. You've been there?"

"No."

"Is it relaxing?"

"Of course."

Like I'd asked if water was wet. "Okay. You guys coming?"

Gil shook his head. "We go, all you'll talk about is tomorrow. Get away from it for a few hours. No fried food, though."

"Hooray."

"Marcela, will you make sure he eats good stuff?"

She hooked her arm through mine. "I will order for him."

Gil and Jairo headed for the door. "We're gonna find Javier and Edson and sign that shit for Eddie. See you back at the gym?"

"Yeah. Hey, what time?" I asked. I didn't want them to leave. Marcela was intimidating me.

Over his shoulder Gil said, "Not too late."

Jairo nodded.

"So ten? Eleven?"

"Sounds good."

"Which one?"

That only got a wave. Before they walked out the door, I saw Gil nudge Jairo, who looked back with a stupid grin and laughed. Idiots.

I turned to Marcela. She looked right at me with those tan eyes. There were flecks of green in there I hadn't noticed before. She had a small scar at the corner of her left eye that disappeared when her eyebrows lifted and she waited for me to talk. I didn't know what to say. I stuck to things I knew were true. "It's almost six. We could eat now."

"Let's walk around a little first. I'm not too hungry yet."

"Good. Okay." We went through the doors.

"So, what happened back there? Jairo had to run out; then those guys are bringing you to the chair."

I was surprised I had to tell her. "Oh, there was some trouble on the stage. You know, smack talk, posturing, all that."

"You are all so stupid," Marcela said.

I didn't argue.

"Why do you do that?"

"Well . . . ," I said and started searching for the restaurant. If I could get some food in my mouth quick enough, maybe I wouldn't have to answer.

CHAPTER 6

Marcela and I got out of the event center and went through the big opening into the casino, laid out in a huge circle and divided like a pie into different gambling areas. The middle of the pie was all clubs and shops and restaurants; in order to get to them, you had to run the gauntlet of slots, craps, roulette, blackjack, poker, and whatever else they could come up with to get your money. We battled clockwise through the noise and bustle and after fifteen minutes found an entrance into the inner circle.

The long hallway into the core was decked out like a Roman garden, the walls covered in trellis and fake ivy with an electronic sky you could glimpse through the leaves to catch the stars winking at you. They'd done a good job with the constellations. I thought I saw a dollar sign, but it might have been Cassiopeia.

We stepped into the inner sanctum next to a shop that sold realistic Roman fashion. Silver togas and all. I saw the sign for Chaos, then the long line outside the door that looked like tryouts for the douche bag Olympics. Marcela sagged.

"Maybe we can find a vending machine," I said.

She perked up, pointed. "That guy is waving at you."

I saw the Chaos doorman beckoning somebody over. Me?

Well, well.

We showed him our event badges, but he shooed them down. Dressed in a tailored suit that Marcela and I could play hide-and-seek inside, he was close to seven feet tall and had short black hair and no facial hair or visible tattoos.

He smiled and said, "Please, Woody. We know who you are. Shouldn't you be resting up for tomorrow?"

"We won't be out late. Just unwinding a little." I glanced at Marcela to see if she was going to over-rule me. She was busy leaning around the doorman to peek through the door and didn't say anything.

"I heard what happened," he said and tapped a wireless earpiece. "I hope you knock his ass out, man."

"Can I hit him with you?"

"Have fun in there. I'll let them know you're coming, and we'll get a booth ready."

"Much appreciated." I tried to tip him, but he

pushed my hand away.

Marcela and I put on bored faces like the debonair VIPs we were. We went through the door into darkness, and immediately a cool mist drifted over us and our feet swirled through a low-lying fog. We pushed through a thick black curtain that was pulsating to heavy bass and stepped into a room that should have been illegal.

It was dim, illuminated with indirect spots in cool blues, greens, and purples with some red thrown in to draw the eye. Ahead of us was a full bar extending from floor to ceiling with the staff working horizontally, the drinks defying gravity to stay in the glasses as they went to customers who stuck to high-backed stools but should be dropping to the floor in a heap.

Directly over my head a woman walked upside down out of a door that wasn't there and waved to another woman who looked like she was ten feet away on my left, but when she screeched and hugged her inverted friend, I couldn't hear a thing. It wasn't because of the music—I could hear plenty of people talking and laughing and not screaming (which was alarming)—it was because she was really nowhere near me.

The music was some anonymous thump and squawk with an orchestra in the background playing out of sheer terror. I glanced down to make sure I was on the floor and saw that at least the heavy fog was there with me, paying attention to the rules.

Marcela started forward. When she didn't disappear forever, I followed her into the abyss. About five steps in, the mirrors started to make sense, but I still didn't want to reach out to lean on anything in case it wasn't there. The bar became horizontal, and the people at it stopped being magical. I wanted to shake hands with every one of them.

A blonde woman in a nice suit and a purpose walked over. "Woody?" She did a good job of sounding familiar, but there was a slight undercurrent of worry that I wasn't the right guy.

"Yes," I said.

"I'm Bonnie. We're so glad to see you and . . . ?"

"Marcela," I said, presenting her.

"Of course," Bonnie said. "If you'd like to follow me, your table awaits."

We trailed her between more mirrors and floating people, but I didn't wobble or act too amazed. We came out into an open area with a nearly empty dance floor straight ahead and another bar along the left wall. She turned right and led us up a short flight of stairs to a row of booths along the right wall that overlooked the dance floor.

A woman wearing a small white dress and a laurel wreath in her hair waited next to an empty booth.

Bonnie waved us into it.

I took the far seat so I could see the doorway. Old habits.

"This is Stephanie. She'll be taking care of you this evening."

Marcela smiled. "Thank you so much."

"Okay, bye now." And Bonnie was gone.

Stephanie poured us waters and said she'd be back when we'd had a chance to review the menu.

I took a look around. The only mirrors were behind the bar, and I vowed to stay away from them. The room looked like a billowing Roman tent, maybe something the senators would use to host debauchery and assassinations. Six brass poles were spaced evenly down the center of the dance floor, parallel to the booths, with faux torches banded near the tops sending flickering light into the overlapping canvas of the ceiling. The poles were thin enough to be at home on a stripper runway, and there were a few girls out there taking pictures of each other hooking legs around the poles and pulling their bottom lips down with one finger. A few of the bartenders were having a serious discussion about the girls, probably conspiring over which kind of shot would get their tops off the quickest.

"What is this, marble?" Marcela rapped on the table and tried to move it back and forth.

"I think it's concrete, made to look like marble."

"I think it's marble," she said and picked up her menu. She was fun to watch, everything right there on her face. Her eyes drifted over to the dance floor, came back, and squinted at me. "Do you dance?"

It was a trick question. "I have danced before. It's a lot like my jiu jitsu."

She put her hand over her mouth. "Oh, man. No dancing tonight, then."

"Come on. It's that bad?"

Marcela sipped her water and wiped the residue of her lip gloss off the rim with her napkin. "You try too hard. You're always pushing and pulling and squeezing. Sometimes you just have to relax and be patient."

"I tend to lose my patience pretty quickly when someone is elbowing me in the face."

"It's different when you can punch and kick each other. But not that different."

"Do you compete down in Brazil?"

She said, "Yes, of course, and other places. Wherever we go."

"MMA or just jiu jitsu?"

"*Just* jiu jitsu? Please."

Like I'd asked Sinatra, 'You only sing?' I said, "Are you any good?"

"I've won more than lost."

"That could mean anything. Two and one?"

Marcela sighed. "Five-time national champion

and undefeated in three weight classes. I got my black belt when I was thirteen."

"Jesus Christ."

"No, no," she said. "Woody, you can't say that. It's disrespectful."

I liked how she pronounced it. *Woo-dee.* I apologized and said, "Do you have a nickname? For when you compete?"

"Not for that. My family calls me Cela sometimes."

"What does that mean?"

"Mean? It's part of my name. Marcela. Cela." She held her hands together, then separated them. "See?"

"Right, yes."

"The ones with meaning, that's for you boys. You all want to be superheroes with secret identities. You should fight with capes on."

"Easy to choke somebody that way."

"Not for you," she said and hid behind her shoulder. She was a rascal.

Stephanie returned, and we scrambled to figure out what to order. To buy us time she refilled my water and got Marcela a Diet Coke. We both decided on grilled chicken salads, and Stephanie did a good job of making it seem like that was worth all the time it took.

When she was gone, Marcela said, "Why did you pick Woodshed for your name?"

"I didn't. Someone else gave it to me. You can't

pick your own nickname."

She sipped her drink with a frown. She freed the straw long enough to ask, "Why not?" Then was right back at it.

"I don't know. It's tacky. Like a smart person going around telling everyone to call him Einstein. It's not spontaneous. Everyone will end up calling him Whinestein or something."

"So at the gym, the loud guy—"

"Roth," I said.

"His nickname is Cut Snake, he told me. Which means crazy, right?"

"Right. Australians are . . . unique."

"He didn't pick that for himself?"

"He says his mom's called him that since he was a baby."

Marcela said, "It's a good name for him."

"The best one I've heard so far is Adrian's, a guy from Greece who trains with us sometimes. Over there they call him *Akoniti*, which means 'no duster' in Greek, from the old pancration days. They used it to describe a fight that was over so fast it didn't raise any dust from the arena floor."

"I like that one," Marcela said.

I was going to add something about how I hoped he hadn't earned it in the bedroom, but I drank water instead.

She said, "So who gave you Woodshed? And why a building?"

I told her the story, then explained, "There's a phrase when you really give someone a good whipping. People say you took them out to the woodshed. For a beating."

Marcela frowned.

"The guy said I took the other fighter to the woodshed and beat him with it."

She nodded, probably so I would stop talking. She said, "Okay, so you're a building where beatings happen."

"Kind of. Maybe."

Our food arrived, and we spent some time arranging our napkins and sampling the salads with small bites that wouldn't leave anything on our faces. We both wiped after each nibble just in case.

Marcela said, "Did I hear one of the fighters introduced as a goat?"

"*The* Goat," I said around a mouthful that almost ended up in the booth behind Marcela. I kept it in and withered under her disapproval. I got some water down and wiped my face. "The Goat. It's an acronym for Greatest of All Time."

"Of all *time*?" she asked. "Is he?"

"I've never seen him fight. He lost his last two, I think. And he's just a jiu jitsu guy, so he can't be that good."

Her mouth fell open. "I am going to kick your

face." She reached across the table and put a crouton in my water.

I gulped it down and crunched with a smile.

The place was filling up. Every half hour the staff would pick one of the people out of the crowd and put them in a sedan chair and carry them around the dance floor so they could act like an emperor or empress. Some of them did a good job, holding a hand out and gazing above the plebeians. Others clung to the arms and gave out high fives like free bread.

The music and people were making it so we had to lean over the table to hear each other, Marcela talking with her hands and almost smacking me in the face more than once. Each time she stopped what she was saying to put a hand on my cheek and apologize until she finally said, "Here, hold my hands on the table. It's the only way."

I laid my hands palms up on the table, and she dropped hers in, little hand-shaped cookies, and I closed around them lightly and waited.

"I can't do it." She laughed. "I need them free to talk."

"That's why I'm not letting them go," I said.

"Oh, you like your women to be quiet?"

"How would I know?"

She closed one eye and freed a hand to point at me. "You are going to be trouble, boy."

I tried to do a who-me? face, but I don't have one.

Marcela turned my hands over and ran her fingers over my knuckles. She inspected a scar on my left hand near the base of my middle finger that looked like someone had smashed two front teeth into it. "Why did you pick fighting?" I opened my mouth and she said, "And don't give me the nonsense about fighting picking you."

I closed my mouth.

She said, "You seem pretty smart, so that's why I ask."

"Who said fighters can't be smart?"

"You've met my cousins?"

I said, "Jairo has his head on right."

"Psh. That one, maybe he's wise, but I don't know about smart. Someone looks at him cross-eyed and he's got his shirt off, ready to go."

"He's Brazilian."

She didn't have an argument for that.

"You know, it used to be some of the best fighters were also the smartest guys around. Socrates was a soldier in the Athenian army. He treated battles like arguments, no retreating."

"Let me guess: he died in battle."

"No," I said, "he was imprisoned and given a death sentence. He drank poison."

Marcela lifted her glass. "To Socrates."

"You want me to apologize for being a fighter, but I'm not going to. Fighting is fun. It's honest. You can't hide from yourself in a fight. You should know that from your jiu jitsu."

"No, that is grace and strength. And there are rules."

"MMA has rules."

"Ah, but that's not where you started. They talk at the gym, and I listen. You're just like Jairo and the others, fighting since you were little for no good reason."

"I had a good reason," I said.

"What, did they take your cookies? Pull your hair and say you stink?"

I almost let it slide. But she was testing me, pushing me to see if I'd push back. In my experience, the best way to gain the advantage in an argument is to tell the truth; it throws people off. I said, "No. They tossed me in an empty pool when I was eleven. Then they threw another kid in. He was fifteen. Guess who climbed out?"

Marcela eased a cherry tomato into her mouth and chewed it a few times. She pointed her fork at me and said, "You're joking with me."

"Nope."

"Somebody put you in a pool."

"An empty pool," I said. "A full pool would have been more dangerous. I have a tendency to sink."

"Who put you in?"

"There was a gang of Hispanic kids who hung

around the school. They were a chapter of the San Chucos gang, called themselves the Thirteen Bulls. Smoking, trying to look tough, selling drugs. Graffiti. They found an abandoned house a few blocks away and turned it into their hangout, and it had a pool in the backyard. I think they skated in it for a while, but that got boring. One day I was on my way home, and they grabbed me and tossed me in."

"Before they grabbed you, did you know they did that there? The fighting?"

"Sure."

"Stupid, why didn't you go another way?"

"They didn't own the street. I walked that way before they showed up."

Marcela looked at the ceiling and made an appeal in Portuguese.

While she was distracted, I picked a piece of lettuce out from between my teeth.

Marcela said, "You know what I think? I think you wanted them to grab you."

Shit.

"You probably strolled by, stopped to tie your shoe. Hey, I think maybe you rang the doorbell."

"That's ridiculous." The electricity in the house had been shut off.

"No, *you* are. Why didn't you go home and watch TV?"

"Believe it or not, that pool was safer than my house."

"Okay. I believe that," she said. "But still, go to the library. Play fútbol."

"I'm not saying I didn't have choices. I didn't make the smartest ones, but that doesn't mean I deserved to get jumped. I just went about my usual business, and one day they decided to interfere. Three of them grabbed me off the sidewalk and took me around back and dropped me in the pool. There were probably thirty or forty kids standing around the edge, yelling and spitting and flicking butts at me.

"They shoved each other around to see who would fall in. Finally one kid did, the fifteen-year-old, taller than me with some fat on him. He stood as far away from me as he could and started hitting me in the head, big looping things that slapped more than punched, you know?"

Marcela nodded. She had her glass in front of her but wasn't drinking.

"I remember thinking, 'This guy hates getting hit. And he thinks he's whipping me, but I'm standing here taking it. Is this how kids hit?' I barely felt it. It took me a while to realize I could fight back—this wasn't some drunk who'd throw me out the window if I tried. So I did. And, man, I never saw that kid again after that day. I think his family moved to Ohio."

Marcela said, "But you went back."

I shrugged. "I just kept walking home. Some days they grabbed me. Some days they didn't."

"Which days did you like better?"

I looked at her and knew I had lost the argument. I didn't care. "The pool."

Marcela mumbled and attacked her salad for a while. When it didn't fight back enough, she straightened and shook her head. "So, what, you beat up the whole gang? One by one?"

"If I say yes can we change the subject?"

"No."

I said, "I didn't fight anyone from the gang after the first time. Well, there might have been a few. They had more fun watching me against other kids they brought in."

"Just random kids pulled off the street." Marcela was nodding to herself, and I thought she was going to flip the table over. "But not like you. No, those poor boys didn't want to fight. Didn't *like* it."

"Will you calm down? They were from other gangs, smaller ones, trying to get in with the Bulls. If they got past me, they had to fight one of the gang members. Or several. It was kind of random."

Marcela cooled off a notch, but I was still on the endangered list. "How many got past?"

"I don't know. Less than half."

She asked, "Did you kill any of them?"

"Marcela."

"Yes or no?"

"No."

She leaned across the table. "Gangs kill people."

I moved forward almost close enough to touch foreheads and said, "I was never *in* the gang." Marcela stared at me, and I saw the green flecks in her eyes and forgot what we were talking about. She leaned back and I rallied. "They kept me around for fun, but otherwise white boys weren't welcome. When they got tired of watching me beat on kids from other Hispanic gangs, they started looking around for other races. Black kids, Asians, Indians. From India, not here. Oh, and my first Brazilian."

She said, "Listen to you, like we're talking about sex."

"Wait, we're not?"

"Shut up." Marcela resisted for a moment, then asked, "So did you beat him?"

"The Brazilian? Yeah. He was a slick little guy. I didn't know what it was at the time, but he pulled guard on me in the shallow end of the pool. Tried to armbar me. It rained the night before, so I dragged him into the deep end and held his head underwater. Whenever he came up for air, I gave him the good news." I smiled. "I know it sounds bad. But it helped get me ready for MMA."

"That was your plan the whole time?"

"Plan? Nah. My plan was to not get my ass kicked. Then a guy named Shepherd showed up. He was the one with the plan."

CHAPTER 7

Marcela alarmed me by getting another Diet Coke; caffeine and short tempers liked to dare each other. She took a sip and set her glass aside and slid the salt and pepper shakers into the middle of the table. She held up the salt. "So this is you, because you're white." Then the pepper. "And along comes this Shepherd guy."

"He was white too."

"Was?"

I shrugged. "Back then. Who knows what he is now."

She pursed her lips and considered the dilemma. "Well, we have just the one salt, so too bad." She rocked the pepper back and forth toward the salt. "He comes along and says, 'Hello, Woody, I'm Shepherd. Want to fight MMA?'"

"You want me to tell it? Or do you just want to make up whatever sounds good to you?"

Marcela knocked the saltshaker over. "Go ahead."

"Nice man voice by the way. That really sounded like him. Okay, first, I didn't have the Woodshed nickname then—I was just Aaron."

"See, I like that name. You should keep it."

"I still have it," I said.

"Yes, but who knows it? Tell the story." If she was half as tricky on the mat as she was at conversation, she could submit an octopus.

I said, "Since we're on the whole name thing, his real name wasn't Shepherd. He went by The Shepherd, and people just shortened it. He thought of himself sort of like a scout for criminal talent. Liked to find kids with potential and show them how to stay out of the system, work under the radar, and make money for him. He always said the only place to get a better criminal education was in prison."

Marcela asked, "Have you been to prison?"

"No." I waited for her to ask if I'd ever been arrested, but she didn't, so I continued. "Shepherd worked with the Bulls and other gangs—supplying drugs, moving cars they stole, but mostly acting as a go-between for people who needed muscle. He'd tell the Bulls so-and-so needs twelve guys to work security at a party, or this guy needs a car full of guns to escort a truck through north Vegas. Somebody from the gang must have mentioned me, because one day I'm in the pool—I was probably thirteen or fourteen at this point—and I look up and this tall, hefty dude with gray hair is standing on the edge.

"I thought he was some kid's dad at first, but he's joking and talking with the Bulls and they give him a beer and he raises it to me. When I'm done, I climb out and he pulls this ice pack out of nowhere for my eye and says, 'Let's go for a ride.'"

Marcela said, "In Brazil, they never see you again."

"Same here sometimes. But I knew the name Shepherd, and with the way the Bulls treated him, I was honored. I got into his Cadillac, this long, silver boat, and we went for a drive. With the windows up and the air-conditioning on, it was like being in a bubble floating through the city. We stopped at McDonald's and got Quarter Pounders and fries and Cokes."

Marcela said, "This sounds like a good date. Did you hold hands?"

"Okay, no more story."

"Oh, stop it. Keep going, because I still don't see how you're any different than Jairo and the other fools. But not too much more with you riding around with this guy; it sounds goofy."

Pushing and pulling. Reel and slack. I clamped down on the hook and tried to catch up to the boat. "All right, I'll skip the part where we did each other's hair and listened to a mix tape. So we drive around and talk, and he parks outside an apartment complex where I wouldn't normally go without a full police escort. He hands me an envelope, tells me to take it to the fifth floor, and give it to a guy named Tyrone. I step out of the car, and the looks I got would have melted Superman."

"But not you," Marcela said. "Not tough Woody."

I spread my hands. "Well, I'm still here."

"So who was Tyrone?"

"Some dude with another gang. I took that envelope through the gauntlet of hard stares and itchy trigger fingers to the building. The elevator was gone, so I took the stairs. The lights were out and I'm pretty sure there was a dead guy on one of the landings. I kept thinking, 'Just look straight ahead and put one foot in front of the other.' I get to the fifth floor, some guy the size of a bus asks me if I'm crazy. I ask him, 'Are you Tyrone?' To this day I'm amazed my voice didn't crack."

Marcela's eyes were wide, and she had one corner of her bottom lip pulled in.

I drank some water, got an ice cube and worked on it.

She slapped the table. "So he was Tyrone?"

I took another drink. "No. But Tyrone heard me say his name, and he came over and grabbed the envelope. Told me to get the hell out. I did, and it was a lot harder to *not* run down the stairs than it had been to walk up them. Back at the car the air-conditioning hit the sweat pouring out of me and I was trying not to shake. Shepherd laughed, but then he said something, calmed me right down. I'd never heard it before. Made me forget about shaking."

"What did he say?"

"That he was proud of me."

Marcela put her hands over mine and made a sound like she was looking at a puppy. "This guy, Shepherd, he was like a father to you?"

I was uncomfortable. I handle sentimentality like I do sprints: horribly and as short as possible. "Kind of. He got me out of the pool. By the time I was sixteen, he had me delivering packages alone and working the pit fights."

"*Pit* fights?"

"Shepherd and guys he knew would arrange to meet at a spot, and everyone brought some fighters. We all got numbers, and my name went in a hat with everyone else's. When they called my number, I fought."

Marcela hooked some loose hair behind her ear and smoothed it down. It looked like a relaxation exercise, and I gave her all the time she needed. When she was done, she asked, "In a pit? How is that better than the pool?"

"Sometimes it was in a pit, if we met at a construction site or something. Sometimes it was at a parking garage or somebody's backyard. One time it was at an empty hockey rink. Complete disaster."

"So this guy didn't help you at all. Just got you to fight in different places."

"I did the courier work too," I said, "delivering packages."

"What was in them?"

"I never looked."

"Oh, good." She offered me up to the room so everyone could see how much sense I was making. "It could have been drugs, guns, terrorism, whatever."

"It could have been coupons for free French fries."

Her look was flat enough to balance a quarter on edge. "I don't think so."

There was a lot more I could have told her. I'd worked all kinds of action for Shepherd's associates, their associates—whoever needed the things I was good at. But I was having enough trouble convincing her it had been a good thing I'd met Shepherd, so I stuck with him. "When I turned twenty-one, he bumped me up to bouncing in his clubs and escorting VIPs."

Marcela raised her eyebrows a fraction. She was coming back around.

"And their prostitutes," I said and spent the next twelve seconds trying not to get kicked under the table.

No one ever hired me to do the talking.

Marcela said she had to use the ladies' room and left

the table. Ten minutes went by. I'd fought for five times as long and didn't sweat half as much. The server asked if she could take our plates. I was torn between clearing the table of everything sharp and breakable, or making sure Marcela had something besides me to tear into if she came back. I kept the salads.

After fifteen minutes, Marcela returned without any chain saws that I could see. She slid into the booth and said, "I'm ready to go now."

"What? Why?" Feigned confusion is a good way to stall for time.

"You just told me you were a pimp."

"What?" Actual confusion isn't good for much. "No, I was never a pimp. I provided security for people, and some of them happened to be prostitutes. I never . . . no."

"But you gave security to pimps."

"Whoever was paying for it."

"So who was the whore?" she asked. One eyebrow was cocked, but she didn't need to fire any more rounds. It was checkmate.

"Look. What I did then wasn't always nice. It wasn't always legal. But somehow it got me here, and that's good enough for me. I've been in a continuous fight since that first day in the pool to *not* end up facedown in the deep end, and I have no idea when that fight is going to be over or how I'll know it when it is. It feels close, though. It feels like I've climbed out and

I'm just about far enough away from the edge to not get shoved back in."

I was on a roll, but Marcela wasn't really listening. She was looking out onto the dance floor and seemed interested in it, and I got ready to panic. But she didn't want to dance. She said, "I think that guy is staring at you."

I turned and scanned the churning crowd until I saw him. He waved and grew a smile that never reached his eyes. I nodded at him and hoped that was enough to move him along. Instead, he headed to our booth.

The edge of the pool got a lot closer.

CHAPTER 8

The guy disappeared into the crowd like a shark fin slipping underwater.

Marcela said, "Do you know him?"

"I used to. Hopefully he just wants to say hello."

"You're not good friends?"

"We worked together."

"Is *he* a pimp?"

I spotted him a few booths away, edging between people and dodging servers, his eyes on me and the smile still there and still only at his mouth. "No. This guy's a snake."

He got to the booth and said, "*Fuckin'* A-Wall, man, holy shit."

"Lance," I said.

He looked worse up close. I hadn't seen him in over five years. He was thinner than I remembered, his wrist bones poking out enough to open envelopes, arms disappearing into the short sleeves of a purple silk button-up shirt that looked like it had stains on it. I could never tell with those shirts. His neck was straining to hold his head up, and I could see the muscles under his chin working, the tongue doing something in there his lips and teeth were smart enough to hide.

His nose was still smooshed, and his eyes were bright with something. I ruled out admiration and brilliance. He had a crescent-shaped scab on his forehead over his right eye, a strange place to have one without any other damage. It looked like someone, maybe him, had put a fingernail there and pushed.

He tapped his fingers on the edge of the table. "A-Wall, how ya been? Wait, no. Now you're Woodshed, right? Or Woody?"

"Woody," Marcela said.

"Yeah, that's it."

I said, "Lance, this is Marcela. Marcela, Lance."

"Yeah, hi," Lance said.

She kept her hands on the table and twiddled some fingers at him.

"Hey, can I slide in here for a second?"

"We're about to leave," I said.

Lance said, "Okay," and I had to move to my left to make room for him sitting down. He smelled sour. "Salads?" He glanced around the table for evidence of more than that. "What are you guys doing tonight?"

"Just a little dinner. We'll probably head home from here." I yawned to make it seem as boring as possible. Nothing he'd want to tag along for.

"Cool. So what you been up to?"

"Mostly the fighting." I didn't want to ask what he'd been up to; I didn't want to appear on any accessory warrants.

He nodded.

I let the silence stretch into the fidgeting phase.

Marcela had better manners. "What do you do, Lance?"

"Oh, this and that. Sometimes the other, you know, when this and that aren't hiring." He laughed and took a drink of my water. It became his water. "A-Wall—no, shit, *Woody*—he's probably told you about when we ran together."

"This is our first date," Marcela said and winked at me.

"Oh, congratulations," Lance said. "Super. Yeah, we used to bang around town making all kinds of trouble."

Marcela glanced at me, and I shook my head. She asked Lance, "What kind of trouble?"

It took him two stories to get to the favor.

First, Lance told Marcela about the time I held a Saudi prince over the railing of a balcony on the fifteenth floor while Lance hustled the two hookers—"ladies of the night," he called them, using air quotes—out to the car.

Marcela cocked an eyebrow at me, probably thinking pimps and prostitutes were going to be the theme of our relationship. Lance had to hurry and explain that he was the driver, I was the chaperone, and the prince got out of line with a riding crop and leather hoods that were oversized versions of the kind sporting falcons wear. It sounded a little better after that, but I still figured I'd be explaining every detail later.

There was an awkward lull, and I thought that was it.

Then Lance said, "Hey, you still run into Chops?"

"No. Not for, what, maybe six years." Chops had been one of Shepherd's associates. I didn't mention Marcela and I were just talking about Shepherd, and I hoped she would keep quiet about it. Lance never made the cut to work directly for Shepherd and probably still had a gripe about it.

Lance told Marcela, "Chops is a guy we used to work for. I see him now and again. He always asks how our boy here is doing. Now I'd tell him, shit, do a search for Woodshed Wallace, find out for yourself. You know why they call him Chops?"

"How would I know?" Marcela said but made it sound nice, conversational.

Lance hunkered over the table, talking about

important stuff now. "Before I met him, I thought it was because he chopped people up; then I thought that's crazy. Maybe it's because he has wicked mutton-chops, you know big Wolverine shit flying off his face."

Marcela shook her head.

"But no. I meet him, and the guy's face is smooth as a baby's ass. No hair at all. They call him Chops because the fucker's got a fake hand and it's in the shape of a karate chop, and when he gets his panties in a bunch, he starts knocking the edge of it against the table." Lance hacked the concrete or granite a few times, the funniest thing in the world, then must have hit his hand wrong because he hissed and cradled it under the table.

"How did he lose his hand?" Marcela asked.

"I don't know." Lance asked me, "You ever find that out?"

"Nope." I knew, but I wasn't going to say it. Let Marcela think I worked for a nice beardless guy who could take a joke like being called Chops because of a fake hand.

Then Lance told her about the time he was driving stolen air bags to LA with me riding shotgun and some of the bags went off in the back of the panel truck, both of us thinking we were being shot at and trying to fit into the glove compartment. The guy we delivered them to said it happened, something about static electricity tripping the triggers.

Lance said, "Then there was the time we *did* get shot at," and I figured out why he'd sat down.

"We don't need to go over all that again." I turned to Marcela. "It's much more boring than it sounds."

She looked suspicious.

"And we should get going. Lance, great to see you again." I started to slide toward him.

Lance didn't move. He just smiled and said, "Hey, hold on a sec."

I could have moved him, but it wasn't that kind of conversation yet. I glanced at Marcela, and she had a little wrinkle between her eyebrows.

Lance said, "Marcy, hey, it's not as boring as he wants you to think. I don't have to tell the story, but I can show you the scar. You remember that, A-Wall? That surgeon guy they brought in saying I should be dead already?"

"I remember."

"And me saying, 'Well, I *ain't* dead, motherfucker, so get to work.' Marcy, the guy almost pissed himself."

Marcela said, "Who is Marcy?"

Lance ignored her and looked at me. "But the thing I remember most is right before he put me under, you said you owed me one. That made it all worth it."

"Oh, that's sweet," Marcela said.

I was appalled, but the guy deserved an Oscar. I

checked to make sure my fork was still on the table and not in his hand, jabbing into his leg to get some tears flowing.

Lance blinked a few times and said, "Yeah, don't let him fool you. He looks like a lion, but he's just a kitten inside."

Marcela laughed. "No more Woodshed for you; now you're Kitten Wallace."

"Perfect!" Lance said. "No, wait: *purr*fect."

I was surrounded. "Everybody, calm down."

Lance nodded and got rid of his giggles and put his hands flat on the table. "Oh, man." He sighed, then failed at sounding casual. "So, can you help me out with something tonight?"

Behind him on the dance floor, a girl tipped out of the sedan chair and disappeared into the lowly masses. A turquoise high heel geysered into the air and became a trophy that was passed hand to hand until someone threw it over the railing onto the floor near our table.

Lance followed my gaze, then plucked the shoe off the floor and put it on the table. He held the heel in his left hand and the toe in his right and made it tap-dance.

Marcela frowned at it.

Lance spun the shoe, read the label, and checked how far it could bend. "Huh." He kept it in his hands and looked at me. "A-Wall?"

"Woody," Marcela corrected. She stared at the shoe and didn't put much into it.

"Right, sorry. Woody, can you?"

"What is it?" I owed him and it was bad form asking, but if I hurt his feelings, maybe he'd leave.

He didn't. "It's no big deal."

Alarms started going off. I expected the next sentence to either be about storing nuclear waste for him—just for a year—or helping him get his car out of the ocean.

"I owe some money to a guy, and I don't have it yet, and I have to go tell him I'll have it soon. Nothing's going to happen—he's not like that—but it won't hurt to have you standing there with your sleeves rolled up."

I ran through it again in my head. No uranium or scuba gear. "That's it?"

"That's it."

"This guy isn't in Kansas City or anything, right?"

Lance used the shoe to wave that away. "Nah, he's off the Strip. In a bakery."

"A bakery?"

"What do you want, a sign that says Illegal Book-maker?"

I thought about it some more. "How much?"

"Ah, that's not important."

"What I want to know is, do you owe enough to kill *two* people over or just one?"

Lance stuck his bottom lip out at the shoe and shared its loneliness. "It's not that kind of deal."

"When is this supposed to happen?"

He brightened. "I'm already late."

I took a breath. "All right. I have to take Marcela back; then I'll meet you out front. Thirty minutes."

"What?" Marcela cut in. "No, you're not taking me back. It's boring there. I'm coming with you."

"I don't think that's a good idea," I said.

"Who cares?"

"There is that." I asked Lance, "Is this a place where she can wait outside without armored protection?"

"Dude, it's a *bakery*. She can have a muffin while she waits."

"Oh, I like this," Marcela said.

"Good?" Lance asked.

I wasn't ready to call it that yet. "We'll see."

Lance slapped the table and started to slide out but was stopped by a girl in a small black dress who looked like she'd been through an industrial washing machine. Lance recoiled.

"Can I please have my Veronica back, you fucking pervert?"

"Huh?"

"My *shoe*?"

"Jesus, yes. Take it." Lance handed her the shoe.

She leaned on the table and tried to glower at him while she put it on, but it was apparently too hard to do both. She focused on the shoe and spun and clomped away.

We stood and watched her go. Her other foot was bare.

"Damn," Lance said.

Marcela made a noise in her throat. "I hate high heels."

"Yeah?" Lance looked her over. She came up to his chin. "They'd make you taller."

"So why don't you wear them?"

Lance beamed at me. "She's a keeper."

"Like it's up to me." We got to the door and began the expedition of finding the exit in a Las Vegas casino.

CHAPTER 9

We made it onto the Strip and started walking north.
The Golden Pantheon was near the south end, so we
had some ground to cover and distractions to avoid.
A guy handing out flyers and hollering in English
switched to Spanish when he saw Marcela and tried
to give her one of the shiny cards covered in pink and
flesh tones.

She smacked it away and said, "I'm from Brazil,
stupid."

The guy swerved into Portuguese without a pause
and baffled Marcela into taking one of the flyers. She
looked at it and muttered and gave it to me, then
wiped her hand on her jeans. I tossed it into the next
trash can on top of a pile of its kin.

The Strip was full and flowing both ways, people
rushing to the next casino or stopping every ten feet

to take a picture of one another in front of something lit up and sparkling. We found a group of movers and drafted in behind them. The flyer hawkers kept trying, but we walked fast and kept our hands close to our sides.

"How far?" I asked Lance.

"Other side of Sahara, just past St. Louis. You want to get a cab?"

I looked at Marcela.

She said, "I want to walk. I like the smells."

Lance goggled but stayed quiet. Traffic was moving like an old man in a pharmacy, so a cab might not have made a difference.

We were on the east side of the Strip, and I glanced back at the front of Caesars and the people going in the front door. Suckers. We stopped so Marcela could admire the pirate ship across the street in front of Treasure Island. We'd just missed the latest battle, so we continued on and made it to The Venetian before she wanted to stop and stare again.

She pointed at things and gasped and said, "Look. Oh, look."

I nodded and said, "Neat, huh?"

Lance bounced from foot to foot. "It's not much farther. Hey, we can check this stuff out on the way back, really take our time, you know?"

A genius selling seven-dollar disposable cameras

for fifteen bucks out of a backpack noticed we weren't taking pictures—a Class A felony in Vegas—and he handed one to Marcela and turned to me for the money. Marcela already had the foil wrapper open, so I paid.

Lance paced toward traffic and ran his hands through his hair.

"Stand over there," she told me.

I stepped so the tower was behind me and waited. It would look like I was posing in front of a brick wall at this angle, but I'd stood in front of worse.

"Smile."

I moved my mouth but not enough.

She tried to kick me from twenty feet away. "Bigger, Woody. Be happier." She hit me with the flash, and I blinked.

Lance said, "Look, they have postcards for sale right there of the same shot. No, better. They have a full moon in them." He bent closer. "It's fake, but it still looks cool."

"Woody isn't in them," Marcela said.

"Yeah, they're professionally done. Guys, we're running pretty late."

Marcela said, "*You're* running late. *We* don't have to be anywhere."

Lance sagged and looked at me.

"Let's get this over with," I said.

Marcela rolled her eyes. "Okay, fine." She slapped

me with the flash again as I walked toward her. She laughed. "That's going to be a terrible picture."

We scampered across the expanse of Sahara Avenue and managed to get past the Stratosphere without any incidents from Marcela, then cut east through some parking lots and followed a construction site fence until Lance said, "That's it up there."

It was at the end of a strip mall set back from the street between a Thai food place and a pawnshop. Dig through the Dumpster behind the mall, and you'd probably find a couple new elements for the periodic table. The place was called New Harvest Bakery, and the windows were dark. The Thai place was open but dead, and the pawnshop had a curtain of bars locked across its face.

We crossed the empty parking lot. I could see the skeletons of unlit neon signs in the windows. They promised coffee, bagels, sweet rolls, and bread, most of them including some kind of wavy steam lines.

Lance knocked on the glass door and we waited.

A shape walked toward us. A big shape. I figured there must be an overhead door on the other side, because this thing wouldn't fit through the front. The shape peered at us through the glass. Marcela said something in Portuguese, and I agreed.

I heard three locks turn, and the door opened. A face the size of a manhole cover ducked out and said,

"Lance." He smiled at me and Marcela. I felt like a snack. "And friends. You're late, but that's okay. Come on in."

He swung the door out like it was a newspaper, and we filed past him into the cool, dim interior. There were about a dozen round white tables with chairs upside down on them over a dark and light checkered floor; I couldn't tell the colors with the lights off.

Ahead of us a counter stretched the width of the place, and behind that were empty bins waiting for the morning's fresh goods. In the middle of the bins a set of swinging doors with glass portholes led into the rear. It was even darker back there.

Lance said, "These are just some old friends I ran into. Guys, this is Jake." He put his hands in his pockets. "Yeah, we're going to see some sights after this, so I told them to come along. It won't take long."

"Sure," Jake said. He sounded like he had a mouthful of peanut butter, but I figured the words were just tired from traveling so far to get out. He had a brown buzz cut and a goatee that would have made a great toupee for a normal man. He stuck his hand out. "Jake."

"Woody." My hand disappeared, and I planned to never see it again.

He didn't squeeze, though, just shook once and let me go. He did the same with Marcela and said it was nice to meet us. Then raised his hand and asked,

"Who's been frisked in a bakery before?"

Marcela and I looked at each other, our hands down. Lance raised his.

Jake said, "Great. If you could all stand with your hands on the counter and your feet spread, we'll get you in to see the man."

Jake checked me first. He spread one hand between my shoulder blades and kept me pushed forward while he swept up and down one side, then switched hands and sides. He whistled something jaunty. When he got to the bottom of the second leg, he said, "You're pretty solid in there. You work out a lot?"

"Not a lot," I said.

"Genetics, huh?"

I shrugged.

"Lucky bastard." He moved down the counter to Marcela. "Nothing personal, sweetie." He checked her over and wasn't nasty about it, but she still kept her eyes flat and her mouth tight. When he was done, she turned and whipped her hair over her shoulder and spat some Portuguese at him. His eyes got big and he asked me, "She's with you?"

I nodded, hoping she wouldn't turn on me for doing it.

"I take it back. You're a *really* lucky bastard." He stood still and looked at Lance. "Do I have to check you? You wouldn't be that stupid, would you?" Before Lance could answer, Jake said, "Yeah, you would be. Hold still."

Lance's hands slipped on the counter from the rough treatment he got. Maybe he'd caused enough trouble for Jake that he deserved it. Maybe Jake knew Lance would take it and not fight back. Maybe Jake wanted him to fight back.

"Well, you're not that stupid today." Jake clapped Lance on the shoulder and almost put him face-first into the counter. "But you fuckin' stink. You two can follow Lance. He knows the way."

Lance went to the far left end of the counter, past the drink station, and through a hinged gate that let him behind the counter. We followed, me right behind Lance, then Marcela. If I was here to protect Lance, I wanted to be close when he went through the door in case he got jumped.

If he got shot, I wanted a clear path over the counter.

At the gate I turned and saw Jake right behind us. He smiled and shooed me forward. I'd assumed he was going to stay out front with the door, but he just wanted to keep us all ahead of him. I had a quick debate about which was more important—keeping an eye on Lance or getting between Jake and Marcela in case things went bad—and let Marcela step in front of me. Jake knew what I was doing and looked offended.

I shrugged, he smiled again, and we kept moving.

Lance got to the doors. He pushed through the one on the left, and I waited for a ruckus and a mitt to clamp down on my head from behind. None of that happened, and I followed Marcela through into a darker room lined with stainless steel racks on rollers. It smelled like Christmas morning should smell.

Lance inhaled deeply and said, "Man, that's good."

Marcela glanced at me over her shoulder. "We should come here in the morning for breakfast. It smells wonderful."

"Yes, it does," I said.

Jake said, "You get used to it."

Marcela tsked him.

We walked toward the back left corner, past some big industrial ovens and a rack of something still giving off heat.

Marcela stopped and sniffed. "Those are big cinnamon rolls."

"You want one?" Jake asked.

"Woody, will you split it with me?"

I was torn. There are three things it is impossible to look intimidating while doing:

Sucking a thick milk shake through a straw.

Putting on lip balm of any kind.

Eating a messy cinnamon roll and licking your fingers.

Taking a leak with just a T-shirt on used to be on the list until I met a Chechen.

"How about on the way out?" I said.

I could see her disappointment in the low light.

"Go ahead. Take one," Jake said. Was he being nice, or did he want my hands full?

I said, "We'll wait."

"You're gonna need some milk. Them suckers will stick to your neck like molasses in January."

"Yum," I said.

I turned, and a shaft of light cut through the room as Lance opened a door that looked like it led to a closet. Which it did, sort of. We filed into a space about twenty feet long and twelve feet wide, what was probably supposed to be an employee break room. It was so full of electronic equipment and people that if you stuck your elbow out, you'd knock four things over and assault two individuals. Mercifully, Jake stayed in the open doorway and leaned his forehead against the top of the frame.

Tall black metal filing cabinets lined the wall on the left, and I put my back to them; I'd never been ambushed by a filing cabinet. Looking down the length of the room, the left wall was crowded with two eight-foot tables piled with computer monitors showing sports graphs, stats, and updates and phone systems blinking chaotically but making no sound.

The two young guys sitting at the table each had headsets on, and they'd hit a button on the phones and say, "Talk to me . . ." They'd be talked to, then click over to another line and relay what they'd heard. No emotion, no news good or bad, just information. There were cans of energy drink lined up amidst the notes and keyboards, the same stuff Gil kept in the refrigerator at the gym. The guy nearest me took a sip from his and picked up a BlackBerry and started texting while on the phone with someone else. He would have given Benjamin a good race. I wondered if attention deficit disorder was one of the job requirements.

A row of six flat-screen TVs hung on the wall above the computer monitors, each one split into four smaller screens showing a different sporting event. In one of the corners I saw a live MMA event going on in New Jersey, a smaller promotion but some good fighters on the card. Somebody I didn't know was going for a kimura from the mount, trying to torque the other guy's arm like breaking off the handle of a little teapot short and stout.

"Here he goes."

I studied the man who'd said it, standing behind the two guys and watching the TVs with a gaze that flitted from screen to screen like a hummingbird. He was tall and lean, late thirties, and looked tan in the glow from the screens. He wore gray slacks and a white dress shirt with no tie, good quality from what I could tell, the sleeves rolled up and the buttons undone enough to show a black T-shirt underneath. He was smiling and working a piece of gum like it held the secret of eternal youth.

"Here he goes, boys!"

I followed where his eyes were spending the most time and saw a horse race.

Something happened that was good for the room, and the man standing clapped once and shook each of the phone guys by the shoulders. There was a set of shelves behind him with more electronic equipment and cords, and he leaned back within an inch of touching the gear and stretched his arms out and over his head. He glanced at us and did a half decent job of looking surprised. "Hey, *there* he is. Lance, buddy, how you doing?"

Lance bobbed his head. "Good, Kendall, good. Thanks. These are my friends, uh, Woody and Marcy."

Kendall made eye contact with me and held it and walked over and shook my hand with both of his and very sincerely said, "I'm Kendall Percy, and it's a pleasure to meet you." He wore a small smile when he talked, something that could easily become a smirk but had no maliciousness to it, and he didn't try to hide the Southern notes that sprawled across his words.

"Same," I said.

He let go with his left hand, produced a business card from somewhere, and held it out between two fingers above our clasped right hands.

I took the card and we let go and I put the card in my pocket without looking at it.

He held my eyes for a moment longer before turning to Marcela. "Marcy, is it?"

"Marcela," she said.

"I wondered, because you don't look like a Marcy. But a Mar*cela*, yes indeed. Can I get you two anything? We got some sweet rolls they finished just before they left, some early catering thing, and doggone if they won't fill you up 'til next Tuesday."

"They said on the way out," Jake said.

"Good enough. But don't let 'em leave without something to drink. We don't want anybody choking to death." Kendall put his hands on his hips and worked his gum. "Now, what can I do for you?"

Lance hesitated, then said, "You know. The money?"

Kendall snapped his fingers. "*That's* right. Aw, man." He waved at the TV screens. "I get caught up. Business. So how we looking?"

Lance crossed his arms, then raised a thumb so he could chew the nail. He was still riding on whatever he'd popped, something with a long plateau and, I assumed, a steep drop-off. He pulled the thumb away and stuffed it under the other arm and said, "Well, I don't have all of it yet. But I have some."

"Some," Kendall said. He winked at me and Marcela. "Well, some is better than none, just about always, right? 'Cept with gunshots and STDs. So how much is *some*?"

"Five thousand."

Kendall whistled. "Five thousand. Okay, so you brought that, but you owe fifteen."

Marcela put her hand over her mouth.

I stared at Lance. Some people thought fifteen thousand was enough to kill three people over. Kendall didn't seem the type, but we'd just met.

Kendall said, "That's about what, 33 percent?"

Lance said, "Yeah, I guess. I don't know."

"It is. A third," said Kendall. "Huh. Okay. Jake, why'nt you go ahead and punch Lance in the guts."

Jake stepped in front of me and sank a fist underneath Lance's crossed arms deep into his belly.

Marcela grabbed my right arm and dug her fingertips in.

Lance dropped to the floor, curling into a ball in the little space he had, and the room turned into a fighting pit.

Jake stood over Lance and put his left foot on Lance's left knee, tucked near his chin. Jake put some weight on it and started to grind the joint against the tiled floor. Lance didn't have the breath to whimper over it, but his face screwed up and his mouth opened to let out a scream that didn't come.

I leaned to my right around Jake to look at Kendall, at the same time trying to slide Marcela behind me.

She shoved my right arm away and started doing something with her hair, getting it all into her fist and tucking it into a loose knot. She kicked her shoes off and started breathing in deeply through her nose.

This was getting out of hand. I said to Kendall, "Call him off."

He gave me that smile and took his time. "That'll do, Jake."

The big man backed toward the door, his eyes on me. He stepped on one of Marcela's shoes and peered down at it, then kicked it out into the bakery.

"Hey," Marcela said.

Kendall said, "Jake here played left tackle at UNLV. He showed up on the first day of practice—from Iowa, of all places—never played a snap before, and started throwing all their scholarship boys around. Played all four years and got his degree in business marketing."

We all looked at Jake.

"Yessir," Kendall said. "We did some business while he was playing, and when he was done and gradu-ated, he comes to me in a suit and tie and markets himself as—what was it? Policy assurance. How do you like that?"

Jake's mouth was open a bit. His pupils were dilated but his gaze was steady, locked in on me. His feet were spread the width of the doorway, and his hands looked like two baseball gloves dangling there.

The two guys at the table had stopped working the phones and keyboards and smartphones and were watching me. They were wiry and pale and caffeinated and seemed upset about the disruption.

Kendall noticed the quiet in the room and said over his shoulder, "You boys keep at it. We can handle playtime over here."

They gave me a hard look for a few beats, then returned to work.

Kendall said, "I can't imagine Lance paid you to come with him; he only has the five grand for me. You don't look like you work for smack or sex—pardon my language, Marcela. So that makes you a friend of his."

"That's right," I said.

"Well, friend, this can go two ways." He held up a finger. "You and the lovely lady can walk out now with cinnamon rolls and enjoy the glamorous night-life and forget all about little old me and Big Jake and Lance here. We'll take care of the business that needs taking care of."

"Or"—the next finger sprang up—"you can situate yourself between Big Jake and his policy assurance duties over a friend who's worth less than a sack of used rubbers. Marcela, again, my apologies." He held the two fingers out. "Okay. Which one?"

I looked at the two fingers. Two was at least as many pieces Banzai Eddie would tear my contract into if he knew I was in this room with these people. All he'd asked was that I stay out of trouble, not sully the good name of cage fighting. And here I was in a closet with bookies and muscle about to get bloody over a deadbeat drug addict who'd taken a bullet for me a long time ago.

I almost wished that guy had been a better shot.

Gil always talked about de-escalation in his self-defense classes, about letting the other person save face so everyone could walk away with some dignity. Kendall had given me options, but they were really the same thing. He was telling me I was going to back down, and I had the thinnest sliver of control over whether I did it with my tail between my legs or shoved up my ass.

Then there was Marcela. Jairo and his brothers liked me, but those Brazilians took family seriously. I'd probably insulted the Arcoverde name just by introducing her to Kendall, and all over Brazil people were getting on planes to challenge me to a fight to the death in the street. They were wasting their time. If something happened to Marcela, Jairo wouldn't even leave my stain for them to spit on.

Still looking at the two fingers, I said, "I'll pay his debt."

Kendall frowned and examined the fingers to make sure they were the same ones he'd always had. "That's not on the table."

"It is now. And that's what's going to happen. I can get five grand right now on top of Lance's. The rest I can get first thing tomorrow morning, and I'll drop it off wherever you want."

"This is tempting, I gotta tell you. As a business owner, money is money, right? I don't care if it comes from hard work or some old lady's purse, as long as it crosses my palm." Kendall wagged a finger at me. "But as a businessman, that's different. I have a brand to consider, a reputation among my peers and clients. Word gets out that someone who owes me can show up with no cash and a tough guy who promises to cover, and I let it happen . . . Guess what? Suddenly everybody's got a tough guy with a fat wallet. Then those tough guys have to find their *own* tough guys, and on and on until I got Bruce Lee, the ultimate badass risen from his grave, in here telling me how it's gonna go down."

He jutted his head toward me, making the cords on his neck stand out. He swallowed and blinked a few times, then laughed and shook himself loose. "So

I'm afraid I have to pass on your generous offer. We're back to the two options I gave you. And, friend—Marcela, I'm going to apologize in advance for this one—let's stop wasting my motherfucking time and get a move on with this horseshit."

I punched Jake in the neck almost as hard as I could.

I didn't want to melt my hand against his jaw, and I didn't want to put one into his belly like he'd done to Lance and have him take it and smile at me.

So I went for his neck.

The neck is a tricky place to hit someone. You put everything into a strike on the trachea with your knuckles, ridge hand, or elbow, the guy chokes to death trying to wheeze through a crushed windpipe. Just give his Adam's apple a good tap, his eyes will bug out and he'll be gulping for days.

Get him on the back of the neck, along or to the side of the spine, and you're into paralysis territory, though it isn't easy. None of that twisting crap. Put him on his knees and grab his forehead from behind and drive your knee against the base of his skull. Or jump on his back and wrap your legs around his waist, get an arm under his chin, and try to turn his vertebrae into a Slinky.

Then there's the vagus nerve, which starts in the brain stem, goes down through the neck near the jugular, and branches out into the chest and abdomen.

One of its jobs is to regulate heart contractions, and if you apply enough pressure to the neck and stimulate the nerve, the guy's heart could shut down.

But I didn't want to do any of that to Big Jake. What I wanted to do was tag him hard enough on the carotid artery to halt blood flow to his brain for a fraction of a second, just enough to hit the reboot button and make him drop.

A short right hook into the side of the neck, and that's what he did.

Jake fell to his knees in the doorway and started to tip forward. He was still technically out, but it wouldn't last long, and I wanted his wind knocked out and his equilibrium shot when he started to come around. I drove my knee into his solar plexus to tip him back up, put another one into his nose and heard a snap, and slapped my palms against both of his ears. I shoved him, and he flopped over his feet into the bakery and landed with his knees bent at bad angles. His hands were still at his sides.

The two guys at the table were frozen in mid-type, their eyebrows almost in their hairlines.

Kendall was staring at Jake, and I could see the gum resting on his back teeth like a little white tumor. He smiled at me. "Jesus Christ in a rickshaw, Lance, where'd you find this guy?"

Lance was still coiled up and indifferent to the world.

Kendall said, "You've been in this kind of room before."

"Plenty," I said. "We're leaving. I'll pay what Lance owes. You forget about him, and if he comes back to do business with you again, you refuse him. Politely."

"You want a job?"

"I have a job. Marcela, can you get Lance up?" I still wanted both arms free.

Marcela slipped behind me and grunted Lance to his feet and got his right arm around her shoulders. He draped off her like his strings had been cut. "He stinks," she said.

"I'll take him when we get outside," I said.

Jake coughed and rolled onto his right side. Even on edge he filled the whole doorway, and I wasn't thrilled about having to step over him.

I asked Marcela, "Can you get through?"

"Yes," she said.

I had to move toward Kendall so she could squeeze Lance behind me.

Kendall didn't give any ground, just stood there with his hands on his hips and that smile. Marcela was almost to the door when he said, "Well, dang it," and turned to the rack of electronics on his left and came back with a flat black automatic pistol that he pointed at my face. "Everybody, sit tight."

Marcela cursed in Portuguese.

"Yeah, I know," Kendall said. "What's your name?"

"Woody."

"Last name Woodpecker? Come on."

I said, "Aaron Wallace."

There was a flurry of clacking from the table. The guy against the far wall read off his screen. "Aaron Woodshed Wallace. Professional mixed martial arts fighter out of Las Vegas, Nevada, USA. Twenty-four and three record." He looked at me and nodded. He was impressed. Hooray.

Kendall took one step back but kept the gun in my face and said, "I knew it sounded familiar, but damn if I could remember where I'd heard that nickname before. You're all over the marquee down there at the—shit, which one?"

"Golden Pantheon."

"That's right. You're fighting *tomorrow*?"

I looked at the clock that was showing Vegas time. It was almost eleven. Tomorrow was getting close to becoming today. "Yeah."

Kendall said, "What are you doing running around with this garbage? You should be resting."

"That's why we're leaving."

"Leaving?" Kendall laughed. "My boy, you just ceased to be a problem and became an opportunity. You ain't going nowhere."

My first thought was that Kendall was going to

keep us here through the fight and put money on me to lose via disqualification. But it was worse than that.

"What are the odds on your fight?"

I shrugged.

"You don't know?"

I shook my head.

"How's that happen?"

"I don't know anything about gambling. I don't care. It doesn't matter anyway. Take your pick."

"Doesn't matter? I can think of a few million people and many millions of dollars who think otherwise."

I shrugged again.

"All right. Steve, get me the odds on this here fight, please."

Steve was the guy who'd looked me up. He was skinny and slouched into his chair and had waxy skin and dark circles under his eyes but couldn't have been older than thirty. His dry, purple lips were too dark for his face and made him look like he was near freezing. Scattered around his workstation were antistress toys—a squeeze ball shaped like a skull, a mini speed bag sticking upright from a weighted base, a tiny putting green he used as a coaster for his energy drink. He did some more pointing and clicking and clacking. "Plus three ten."

Kendall whistled. "Who you fighting, King Kong?"

"Junior Burbank," Steve corrected. "Pretty much

the same thing from the looks of him. Except he's white."

Kendall said, "King Kong wasn't black; he was a gorilla."

"What's the difference?" Steve asked.

"You know better than that. Give me some options."

"Outright winner, plus three ten. Winner by knockout or ref stoppage, Woody is, wow, plus four hundred. Winner by submission, he's plus four thirty." Steve looked me over. "No jiu jitsu, huh?" He looked at the Arcoverde logo on my chest. "What's with the shirt?"

"It's from me," Marcela said. She set Lance against the wall and he stayed there, able to hold himself up but obviously not thrilled about it. "He's good at jiu jitsu." I appreciated her lie.

Steve said, "Yeah? Can I get one?"

Marcela smiled. "Come down to the gym. I'll give you one."

Steve smiled back with those purple lips. His teeth were very white. Overall, it wasn't nice. "I could take yours right now."

The other guy at the table barked a laugh and checked to see how I liked it. He saw I didn't like it at all and returned to his computer screen.

Kendall said, "Behave, Steve." Like he was tired of saying it. To me, he said, "I'm gonna lower this gun because it's getting heavy. Now don't you try anything." He dropped the gun to his side and waited for me to pounce. When I didn't he nodded. "This is what's going to happen. I'm taking Lance here's money and putting it on you to win."

He must have liked the look on my face. "That's right," he said. "You're gonna win, and you're gonna win by knockout. I don't like the odds against you winning by submission, though the money's better, and chances are you'd get floored if you spent the whole fight trying for one; am I right?"

He was, but I let him wonder.

"So I put Lance's money on you to win by KO, and what's the return on that? Anybody? The line is plus four hundred, so that's four hundred dollars for every hundred I put down. That's twenty grand, fella, minus the vig. I know he only owes me fifteen, but hey. For my troubles. And Jake's hospital bill."

Jake sat up in the doorway and let some blood drip onto the floor between his legs. He blew out each nostril and made the drips into a puddle. "I don't need any hospital." His voice was even thicker from the blood and mucus that were plugging his throat.

"We'll see," said Kendall. "I'm gonna put some personal funds down on you too, cuz this is about as close as you can get to a sure thing without buying a dive, but let me worry about that. Now here's the rest, Mr. Woodshed. You lose, and Lance has to go."

"Go?" I said.

Kendall fluttered the gun at his side. "You know what I mean."

Lance sobbed against the wall. He hadn't cried the time he got shot and almost died, but things had been different. We didn't actually think we could die. A lot had happened to both of us since then.

"We'll hang on to him," Kendall said, "keep him nice and cozy. You and Marcela go get a good night's sleep. You win the fight, we can all go out for champagne and nachos. You lose, well, Lance won't bother any of us again. How's that sound?"

It sounded like wet garbage. It made my fists clench and my feet want to slide into their comfortable stance. But it was the best deal we were going to get from the guy with the only gun in the room.

Anything could happen in the fight. With Lance's life on the line, would I find some untapped level, explode with one more burst when I had nothing left, roll Burbank off me when all I wanted to do was lie down for two days?

I would do that anyway. Lance wouldn't make a difference. I glanced at him. He was a sack against the wall, all the spirit gone out of him. He wasn't even watching Kendall and me talk about his survival, just staring off somewhere between the ceiling and the floor, the curved cut on his forehead looking like a wick pushed down into moist wax. He probably wasn't worth helping. He'd end up in another room just like this one—probably not attached to a bakery, but still—in the same bind but without anyone to back him.

And he'd get murdered.

But I owed him. I'd be giving everything I had in the cage no matter what, and if that kept him alive for the time being, so be it.

I'd preserve Lance.

But I knew I couldn't save him.

"Deal," I said.

"Uh-huh." Kendall worked his gum behind tight lips. "Tell you what. Just to make sure you're fully invested in this endeavor, you know—bump the juice for you—how about I hang on to Marcela too?"

The firearm instructors who come through Gil's classes say an assailant twenty feet away can get to you and stab or grab before you can draw your pistol, aim, and fire. Kendall already had his gun out by his hip, but I was only five feet away.

I closed the distance in a lunge and seized his right wrist with my left hand and shoved and braced it against his ass. At the same time I put my right forearm across his throat and gathered a handful of collar and smacked my forehead into his nose. It crunched, and I felt something warm spray my face. Training for the cage made my muscle memory argue with that head butt and my desire to knee him in the groin, but

I prevailed. My left knee lifted him off the floor, and while he was up there, I drove forward and dumped him on top of Steve, who had enough time to wince.

Tipping Kendall back like that had the gun pointing in my general area so I got both hands on it and twisted the barrel and yanked it away. Kendall sprawled over Steve's workstation, desk clutter everywhere, and Steve's head popped up in Kendall's left armpit. I put an elbow across his ear, and his head bobbled around. He sucked air in through his teeth and glared at me sidelong, waiting for the next one.

I turned to Marcela and said, "Run."

She pried Lance off the wall and shoved him through the door, both of them squeezing past Jake, who tried to block them with an arm until Marcela swung her shoe into his busted nose and he needed both hands to scream into. I heard a clatter as they went out in the bakery, then the sound of someone smacking a door open.

Kendall also had both hands cupping his face while he tried to blink the tears away. His knees were drawn up and he could have thrust both feet into me and sent me backward, but his ankles were crossed and all his legs cared about was protecting his balls. Steve was cozy between Kendall and the wall. I pulled the phone handset off its cradle and brought it over the lump of Kendall and wrapped it around Steve's neck. Not to choke, just to tangle.

"Come on!" Steve said.

I looked at the other guy, close on my left. The laugher. His eyes were big enough to have moons. I plucked his headset off and said, "Am I done in here?"

He nodded.

I dropped the headset into his lap, put the gun on the shelf by the door and got two handfuls of Jake's pant legs and heaved him into the room. I grabbed the gun and got through the door without him bothering me. I found a dishrag hanging off a rack in the bakery and used it to wipe Kendall's blood off my face, then my fingerprints off the gun. I ejected the clip and the round in the chamber, all inside the rag, and dropped the whole pile into an industrial mixer filled with soapy water.

I pushed through the swinging doors and saw Marcela and Lance standing at the front door, Marcela on one foot to get her second shoe on. "Go," I said and vaulted the counter and caught up to them before the front door could swing shut.

We ran.

There weren't any cabs drifting along St. Louis so we ran some more. I briefly considered hiding in the construction site until it started to look like a graveyard. Lance possessed the drug user's sprinting ability and

outpaced Marcela and me, his shirttail snapping behind him and exposing the knobs of spine pushing
against his skin. We followed him in the general direction we'd come from but not along the same route.
I hoped he knew where he was going.

We flew into a motel parking lot lit up like a prison
yard, our shadows dropping out in four directions to
mark us as *X*s. I waited for a shout from behind as
Steve or Jake or the other guy spotted us—Kendall
wasn't going to be running anytime soon—but all I
heard was the slapping of our shoes and air driving in
and out through my nose.

Marcela had good form. She didn't waste any
motion and kept her elbows in tight and got her knees
up. I ran like wasps were after me and was glad she
couldn't see it. We dipped into the sharp edge of shadow
cast by a metal carport and almost tripped over Lance.

His burst had fizzled, and he was leaning into the
crook of his arm against the corrugated metal wall of
the carport. The wall was angled out at the bottom so
he could have put his whole body against it, but he
didn't. Instead, he retched and brought up something
that landed with force.

Marcela paced behind him with her hands laced
together on top of her head and avoided looking in
his direction.

"We have to keep going," I said. "Let's get around

more people or find a cab."

"Motel," Lance managed.

"It's too close. We need some distance. Come on. We can walk and talk."

He peeled himself off the steel and shambled along beside Marcela and me. The carport's shadow ended about fifty feet ahead in a dish of gravel, and beyond that was a broad alley that went the length of the block. Where the corners of buildings lined up it spread out into parking lots that would get us to Paradise Road on the left or Las Vegas Boulevard on the right, not technically the Strip this far north but close enough.

When we came to the end of the shadow, it was decision time. Straight down the alley all the way to Sahara and either mix in with whomever else was walking or hail a cab, or cut across the alley and hit the Strip and hope Kendall's guys hadn't fanned out already. We were still close to the bakery, and I wanted more room to move before we got out into the light, but we'd be near the Stratosphere, and enough people would be around to discourage misbehavior.

Hopefully.

"Follow me." I stepped out of the shadow into the alley and started to cross when headlights popped on from the other end of the carport and I heard an engine roar like a blast furnace.

Things slowed down, and I saw the footprints.

It happened like it does in the cage when things are working, when I see the punches starting in the guy's core, flowing up through his shoulder and into his fist. Head kicks take days.

Like that, but I was seeing my own mistakes instead of someone else's. Not as fun.

I stood on the asphalt and watched the headlights sweep closer. The footprints were white and faint but practically glowed against the black parking lot. I had all the time in the world to look back on the gravel and check Marcela and Lance. Their shoes were clean.

I looked down at mine.

Flour.

On my shoes and pant legs, dusted halfway up my calves.

Whatever the clatter was back in the bakery when Marcela hustled Lance out, it must have tipped or busted a bag of flour. And while I was ditching the gun with one hand and patting myself on the back with the other, I'd traipsed through it like Fred Astaire.

No, Gene Kelly.

The van was moving. Not fast but steady, like a crouched leopard bringing one paw forward at a time, trying not to spook the prey until the last second.

From the gravel, Marcela said, "Who is that? Is it them?"

She hadn't seen my feet or the footprints. I could

tell her later. Or not, depending. Without looking at her, I said, "Stay there. I'll lead them off. Find a cab or a cop."

I could squirt between the van and the motel and hoof it back toward the bakery. They'd either follow me or be confused long enough to let Marcela get Lance away. I started walking to the van and it stopped. The headlights dipped a bit toward the asphalt for a moment. I heard a door open but couldn't see which one past the beams.

If it was the passenger, I'd have to deal with him on my way through.

If it was the driver, I might be able to swing around and put him down and throw the van keys over a fence.

If whoever it was had a gun, that would just be unfair and I would submit a protest in triplicate.

I angled to my left and didn't get a chance to find out because behind me Lance got his second wind and bolted down the middle of the alley. I heard the slush of gravel and the van door clap shut. Then the van roared past me, Kendall's bloody face grinning from the passenger window.

Marcela stayed behind the carport. She and I watched as the van caught up to Lance. She said, "No, no, no."

Lance had made it maybe fifty yards, not bad in

that time, and the van shot up behind him and didn't swerve until the very end when it rocked to the left. Kendall opened his door to knock Lance off his feet and send him tumbling against a garbage bin. The hollow boom of it sounded like thunder in the desert.

The van skidded and stopped. Kendall got out and looked at Lance, who was making a sound like a trapped goose. The van's side door opened, and Jake stretched out, grabbed Lance by his hair and belt, and pulled him in. Jake glanced at me and must have asked Kendall something, because Kendall waved a dismissing hand and Jake leaned back in the van and shut the door.

Kendall and I stared at each other for a moment; then he held a thumb and pinky phone up to his ear and pointed at me. "Give me a ring," he said. He had to raise his voice, and I could tell it wasn't comfortable for him with that nose and groin. He got in the van. It took off down the alley and turned right and was gone.

Marcela walked out to me and looked at the flour. She didn't even raise an eyebrow about it. "What do you do now?"

"I guess I give him a call."

"I tried to hold on to Lance, but he's slippery."

"I know. Don't worry about it."

"Are they going to hurt him?"

I said, "He won't be comfortable. But they won't kill him yet. I think."

We watched the end of the alley, waiting for the van to turn around and Lance to pop out laughing and waving at the boys, all a big misunderstanding. They'd toot the horn and be off. Ten seconds of that and it still didn't happen.

She said, "I don't want to see any more tonight. I need a shower."

"I'll get you to your hotel."

Marcela took my left hand in her right and we started walking toward a parking lot that would get us to Las Vegas Boulevard. "I got you," she said, squeezing my hand. "You're not slippery enough to get away."

I tried to smile for her. "I'm not good at getting away." I glanced back and saw that I was still trailing ghost images of my shoes.

They were getting fainter, but they were there.

CHAPTER 10

A cab took us east from the Strip to Boulder Highway. I watched the street behind us and didn't see anyone following.

Marcela thought it was funny I kept checking. "You just want to scare me so I invite you in to protect me."

I hadn't thought of that, but it wasn't a bad plan. She saw me considering her idea and acted shocked by my gall. She pulled the silent treatment the rest of the way, but it was a comfortable quiet, and she wiggled closer to me and got her hip against mine and crossed a foot over my ankle.

We got to the extended stay hotel where Marcela and Jairo and the rest were booked. I expected to see at least one of the Arcoverdes in the lobby with a stack of brochures, glancing through them while he waited for me to bring Marcela back safe and sound.

The place was empty except for a woman behind the counter and a couple in bathing suits peeking around corners until they found the way to the pool and disappeared.

In the cab, Marcela took my face in her hands and turned me so I was looking at her. "Can you sleep?"

"Sure, yeah."

"Okay, go sleep. Tomorrow you'll fight, and all this will be gone." She flipped her hand over her shoulder and kissed the cheek it had been touching. She leaned toward the front seat and told the driver, "Take good care of him."

"What?"

She turned to me. "Okay?"

"Okay."

"I'll see you in the morning. Oh, we can't have those cinnamon rolls now."

"Not likely."

"Lance." She cursed. Then she got out and walked into the hotel.

The cab started forward.

"Wait," I said.

Marcela waved to the woman at the counter and hit the button for an elevator I couldn't see across from the counter. She stood with one foot tucked behind the other, the back foot up on the toes almost like a ballet dancer. She glanced down and brushed something off her shirt, then looked up. The elevator doors must have slid open, but before she stepped in, she saw me and laughed and waved me away, pretending to be surprised that I was still there but knowing I was and posing for me like that.

When she shooed me again, I told the driver it was okay, and we started moving. Marcela rolled her eyes and shook her head at the nonsense, but she was smiling, and I realized I was too.

"She's a cutie," the driver said. "What is she, Italian?"

"Brazilian," I said.

"Oh my."

"Yeah, I know." He got me to the gym, all the overhead lights dark through the windows but the spots above the trophies and medals and certificates shining down in case any midnight strollers wanted to peek in and review Gil's résumé. I went around the side door and punched the code into the security pad and headed for the bathroom.

I got some cold water on my face and double-checked for any damage; no one had hit me, but in situations like that, you can slice your leg on a shelf or bang your elbow into the wall or step in a pile of flour and not notice it for hours. Then you spot it, and it hurts like a bastard.

I was clean.

I checked the mirror again to see how I felt about

Lance. Responsible but not guilty. I could handle that. I would do what I do when they closed the cage door. After that it was up to Kendall, and I figured him for the type who'd keep his word.

Gil had wanted me to get my mind off the fight, forget about Burbank for a while. Done and done. I thought about him for the first time since the weigh-in. He'd probably had a nice dinner, maybe a massage or a soak in the hot tub, gotten laid once or twice. Maybe he was looking in the mirror at the same moment, searching his eyes for any fear or concern and finding none because he was a monster with a game plan and he could tap into his primal being and demolish any man set before him.

I stared into my mirror and almost felt sorry for him.

I used the light from the DVD player and the sound of Roth's snoring to find my cot. I got my head down and was almost asleep when Terence said, "Woody?"

I kept my eyes closed. "Yeah?"

"How was it?"

"Good."

"Gil said you made weight okay."

"Yeah, no problems."

Terence chuckled. "That's not what I heard."

"Well, I guess it wasn't boring."

"Gil said you two acted like a couple of pro wrestlers,

all bug-eyed and red-faced."

"Us *two*? Burbank's the one who came out like fuckin' Elvis."

Terence laughed.

Another voice said, "Is Marcela with you?"

I realized Roth's snoring had stopped. "No."

"Why not?"

"He already got his," Terence said.

I suspected they'd been drinking. Neither had a fight coming up soon, but it was still irritating.

Roth asked, "Can I smell your finger?" and they both lost it.

I said, "Both you two clowns shut up. If Jairo heard you say that, he'd throw you back to Australia."

"Shit," Terence said, "I'd have to swim my ass all the way back."

Roth thought that was hysterical. He was lost to the world.

Terence said, "What'd you two do?"

"Went to Chaos for dinner, saw some sights."

"Mm-hmm."

"Mm-hmm, nothing. Now let me sleep. In case you forgot I have things to do tomorrow."

Roth asked, "Do you dream in Portuguese now?"

I got up and heard him start to scramble, but he wasn't fast enough. I flipped his cot over on top of him.

"Fuck's sake," he said from the pile. He was snoring

again before I returned to my cot.

"I'll be quiet," Terence said.

"Thanks." I closed my eyes and dropped off.

I woke up and had a few precious seconds lying there with my eyes closed before everything came back. I remembered I was going to fight Junior Burbank tonight. A few butterflies showed up with that, but I was looking forward to it.

I remembered Lance and Kendall, and things twisted a bit. Nothing I could do about it except focus on the fight, so I pushed all that away.

I remembered Marcela kissing me on the cheek and the look she gave me just before stepping into the elevator, and my stomach did a little yo-yo thing. I pictured it again and felt good but not the same. I'd have to forget about it and think about something else for a while, then come back to it out of nowhere and see if the same thing happened.

I wanted it to.

I opened my eyes. All the lights were on, and the Arcoverdes were standing by the couch drinking cappuccinos and watching soccer.

Marcela was not there.

I took a shower and had some fruit and oatmeal. I found it best to stick to the usual routine on fight day.

Some guys can ditch the whole program after they make weight, eat lasagna and mashed potatoes and enchiladas and still be ready for five rounds, but not me.

A few years ago there was one guy who got so happy he made weight he celebrated with an all-you-can-eat pancake dinner, complete with a loaded omelet, hash browns, sausage, and a milk shake. And grapefruit juice. It put him way off schedule for quality time, and he was all gloved up, mouthpiece in, posse of yes-men ready to walk him out when he had to take a shit.

It must have been an urgent meeting, because he went in the stall with his gloves on and barely got his jock down in time. The guy he was fighting was out in the cage already, hopping around and staying loose, looking toward the aisle between the folding chairs and wondering what the hell was going on. After ten minutes the bathroom guy's music started back up, and he came out about six pounds lighter and ready for war.

The ref called them forward for the stare down when one of the non-shitter's cornermen ran to the cage and said something to his fighter. The guy got a what-the-hell-are-you-talking-about look on his face, listened again, and by then the ref was yelling at him to step up.

The guy shook his head, and when the ref walked

over to see what the problem was, the fighter told him the other guy just took a dump with his gloves on and left without washing his hands. The ref needed to hear it again. Then—and you could tell he didn't want to—he went over to the other fighter and kept a safe distance and asked him about it. The guy was irate at first, flinging his hands all over the place while everyone ran for cover; then he calmed down and fessed up.

The other guy wouldn't fight him in that state, and the promotion didn't have any extra gloves. The shitter won via Disqualification: Opponent Would Not Fight.

We'd gone over it plenty of times in the gym. Roth was the only guy who would've fought.

So I stuck to my oatmeal and fruit and wondered why Marcela hadn't ridden with her cousins. I hoped she hadn't been grounded. I waited for one of the brothers to say something to me, but Javier and Edson just mumbled to each other and to Jairo, who didn't even glance my way and nodded about whatever they said. The skin on the back of his head looked tight, and his neck was all cables when he turned to listen.

I wanted to get the hell out of the Hole, but Angie was teaching a yoga class, and the kitchen was as far as I could go without looking like a voyeur. I was in there washing my bowl for the third time, almost noon by then, when the three of them came in. I had no idea what Marcela had told them about last night, but it was enough to get them serious and make her stay at the hotel and away from me. She was probably kicking the place apart.

"Woody," Jairo said. He had his arms crossed and must have been making tight fists because his forearms were popping like he had snakes in there.

Javier and Edson stood behind him, looking at me. "Jairo."

"Listen, this is hard because we are friends and we like you. But this thing with Marcela, it is not right."

"I know. I'm sorry. I didn't think it was going to happen like it did, but she shouldn't have been there no matter what. I fucked up."

Jairo's brows came together. His scalp pulled even tighter. "Been where? With you?"

"Last night," I said. "I don't know how much she told you, but I'll go through it again if you want. She was in some danger, but she held her own. It sounded like she's seen much worse. I was impressed."

Javier and Edson fired off into Jairo's ears until he put up a hand and said to me, "Marcela didn't tell us anything. We haven't seen her since she left with you."

"What?"

"She wasn't in her room this morning, either, so I want to ask you where she is."

I felt the blood drop out of my head and crash

into my stomach. I blew between Jairo and the refrigerator, Javier pressing back against the wall to get out
of the way, and found my jeans in a pile near my cot.
I fished Kendall Percy's business card out, opened my
phone, and punched in the number labeled mobile.

Jairo and his brothers were close by, faces somewhere between pissed and worried. I held an open
palm to them and listened to the phone ring.

Kendall clicked on after the fourth ring, and I
could hear him laughing and talking to someone in
the background before he said into the phone, "Kendall
Percy, how can I help you?"

"Where is she?"

"Hey, friend, good to hear from you. Some friend,
though—Lance has been with us all night, and you
can't be bothered. Now that we have your hoochie,
you're on the horn toot sweet."

"Put her on."

"Now, now, you're talking to me for a bit here. Let's
get all this hashed out before things get emotional."

Jairo reached for the phone.

But I turned away and held my hand out again.
"Put her on the phone."

"You're probably wondering how we found her,"
Kendall said. He took a drink of something and spent
some time savoring it. "Lemme ask you this: How
many Arco-vair-days you think there are staying in

Vegas right now?"

I closed my eyes. The shirts.

"Answer is, not many. Only one hotel we could find had any booked. Don't know why she opened the door, but she did. I hope I'm not out of line here, but that girl is a wildcat. If you two've had a tumble, I bet your back looks like a scratching post."

I couldn't bring myself to ask if he'd touched her. If the answer was bad, the worst, I was done. No more fight tonight, no more Banzai Eddie, no more Gil. It would be me dead or in prison for the rest of my life, bits of Kendall and Jake and Steve and whoever else under my fingernails and between my teeth.

Jairo was staring at me with more in his eyes than I'd ever seen from him on the mats or in the cage.

"You still there?" Kendall asked.

"Put her on."

"You're stuck on repeat, brother. Look, calm down. She's fine. We're gentlemen. We've been up all night watching your fights online. Who did the camera work, Stevie Wonder? But hey, you're a pretty good fighter."

"Those are competitions. You've never seen me fight."

"Whoa. Easy. You sound like you're chewing the phone up over there, gonna come through on my end and bite my face off. Hang on." There was a rustling, and I heard Kendall say, "Watch yourself."

Then Marcela said into the phone, "Woody?"

"Are you okay?"

"Yes, but I don't like these guys." And she was gone.

Kendall came back on. "All right?"

I said, "You're coloring way outside the lines on this one. You grab a citizen, a female, from another country? You ever hear of the Trojan War?"

"They beat Notre Dame by three, right? I'm a businessman, son. I thought I told you that already. Now good luck tonight. We're all cheering for you. And like I told you last night, things go bad for you, Lance is adios. Me'n Big Jake will take care of that, and that'll leave Steve here to watch our lady. I'll tell him to be nice, but he's a wily one."

"That would be a mistake," I said. I'd pick Marcela to walk away from it but not unscathed.

"Yeah, yeah. Go get 'em, champ." Kendall clicked off.

I closed my phone and looked at Jairo and the others, waiting, eyes drilling into me, hands opening and closing.

I took all three of them to Gil's office at the other end of the hall from the kitchen. Gil was at his desk surrounded by framed photos and insurance forms and his coffee. His eyebrows raised as he watched me close the door, then go across the room and close the door to the hallway. Angie's voice got cut off midway through a drawn out "And modify . . ."

The Arcoverdes stood against the wall across from Gil and watched me.

Gil looked at me and said, "Morning. What's up?"

I told them everything, but I left out the parts about what I thought of Steve and what he would do to Marcela. A Brazilian rampage through the city wouldn't help anyone. I finished with the part about the phone call to Kendall, Jairo saying I should have let him talk to the son of a bitch, to which I nodded but knew it would have been bad.

When I was done, I stood in the middle of the room, fury boiling from the brothers on my right and Gil's disappointment freezing me on the left. I stood still and let the tornado whip me apart.

Gil picked up the phone.

Jairo said, "Who are you calling?"

"The police." Like that was the only number the phone could dial.

"Woody, did he say anything about that?"

I replayed the conversation with Kendall. "No, he didn't."

Gil started to dial.

"Stop," Jairo said. "What do you think he will do if he sees Marcela's face on the TV?"

I hesitated. "We'd never find her."

Jairo pointed at Gil. "Put that down. We go to

the bakery right now."

Javier and Edson were already through the door to the Hole, heading for the parking lot.

"He wouldn't keep her there," I said.

Jairo snapped his fingers. "Keys."

"We'll have to take two cars." I barely fit in my pickup, let alone me and three furious Brazilians. And I wasn't going to tell two of them they couldn't go.

"I'm driving. And I don't want my truck involved in any felonies." Gil studied me while he lifted the keys out of a drawer. Jairo left, and it was just me and Gil. "I thought we were done with all this."

"Yeah."

"What's yeah? Look at me."

"It's just one of those things. Hindsight, you know?"

"No, because I have foresight."

I nodded.

"Do you want to fail?"

"What? No."

Gil put his fists on top of the desk and leaned over it. "Then why do you keep walking around with a lit fuse, looking for sticks of dynamite to poke it into?"

"It's not like that."

"No? Then what's it like?"

"Hey," Jairo yelled from the back door.

Gil pushed off the desk and walked out. He left his coffee behind.

The chill hung in the room and gave everything sharp corners and edges. It made me tighten up.

I don't like being the one to blame.

I don't like having no control.

When I don't have control, I tend to wrench it back and deal with whatever comes bouncing along at the other end of the chain, sizzling and growling and leaving stains everywhere.

Things were out of control, and I was to blame, and I was starting to lose my temper.

We rode to the bakery in silence except for the directions I gave Gil. I took deep breaths and tried to find options besides what Kendall had laid out. I couldn't find any. Unless something drastic happened to shift the circumstances, Kendall's way was the only way.

Good thing I was in a drastic mood. I even liked the sound of the word, picturing Kendall coming upon the scene with that little smile sliding off his face, saying, "This here . . . this is *drastic*."

We pulled into the strip mall at a little past one in the afternoon and parked far enough away so the people inside the bakery couldn't see The Fight House logo stenciled on the side of the Expedition. We went through the door, the place almost full with people eating slightly late lunches or very late breakfasts. It still smelled good, but there was a mixture of aromas instead of the purity of baked goods.

The girl behind the counter smiled at us before we were halfway to the counter. Her name tag said Hannah. "Hey, guys, welcome to the New Harvest Bakery."

Jairo headed for the hinged gate on the left. "This way?"

I nodded.

"Is Kendall here?" I asked.

"Kendall? Kendall who?" Hannah frowned. Either confused or a great actress.

The customers noticed the change in the room and started to hush up.

"The guy who works in the back room."

Jairo and Javier and Edson went through the gate toward the double doors.

"You can't come back here," Hannah said.

Jairo said, "Bah," and pushed through the doors. I thought about going over the counter to catch up but went for the gate instead.

Hannah looked through the flapping doors. "Alan, I think these guys need to talk to you."

I brushed past her. In the silent dining area behind me, I heard Gil say, "Can I get a large coffee?"

A fortyish guy in dark pants and a white button-up shirt with a gold tie—Alan, I figured, but he was too important for a name tag—was walking toward the doors with a clipboard in one hand, the other waving at Jairo and his brothers. The steel racks were full and pushed against the back wall, and there were a few workers in baker's whites frozen with their hands in dough or sinks of dishes, watching Jairo pound on the door in the corner. The mixer I'd dropped the gun into was churning away at something pale and elastic. I didn't see any flour on the floor with my footprints in it, which helped a little.

Alan made eye contact with me and said, "Listen, Kendall isn't here so just get out and call him. From outside."

I said, "Do you know where he is?"

"No, I don't. I'm sure you have his number, so please—"

Jairo kicked the door in.

Alan flinched and dropped the clipboard. He ducked his head and said, "What? *What?*"

"Kendall will pay for that," I told him.

The Arcoverdes came out. They weren't dragging Steve or the other guy with them, and nothing the size of Jake came tumbling out. Jairo held a computer keyboard, the cord trailing behind him like an empty leash. He looked around the room at the faces. "Any of these?"

I shook my head.

Jairo cursed and snapped the keyboard over his knee. Letters and numbers shot around the room like shrapnel. He threw the keyboard halves into the room and stormed out, Javier and Edson in tow.

Alan put his hands on top of his head. He stared at the ceiling.

"Where is he?" I asked.

Alan didn't look down. "You think he tells me?"

"No cops," I said. Somebody had to.

"Yeah, Kendall would *really* love that."

When I walked past Hannah, she gave me the hands on the hips all the way out the door.

Gil steered with one hand and held his coffee with the other. He said, "Now what? Is there anything we can do? No. Can we go back to the gym and concentrate on the goddamn fight? Yes."

"Call him," Jairo said. "And this time give me the phone."

Kendall answered on the third ring. "Hey, I got you saved in my phone as 'Woodshed.' You know what's funny? I don't have any other people in here under *W*."

"Put Marcela on."

Jairo's hand appeared between the front seats, open for me to put the phone into it.

"You just talked to her, son. She's all worn out from your expansive conversation skills."

"What makes you think I'm not going to try to

win the fight whether you have her or not? Let her go.
You'll still have Lance, you can make your money,
and everyone's happy."

Jairo snapped his fingers.

"Don't you *feel* it, though?" Kendall asked. "The
juice on this is sweet, my man. Money alone can't
match this."

"That's because money isn't personal. This is. And
when things get personal, they tend to get red and sticky."

Jairo tugged on my shoulder. I jerked it away. I
was getting somewhere. Kendall was talking to me,
and I could fix this. Jairo would just yell in Portuguese and put Marcela in more danger.

Kendall said, "You take it personal, that's on you.
I'm on the clock, so it's business. Now Big Jake, degree and all, isn't as professional as me. He's got a big
ole bandage across his nose and two eyes that look
like he's wearing a Lone Ranger mask. He might have
something to say to you no matter what happens."

I leaned forward fast enough to lock my seat belt.
My phone started to crack. "I'll put his fuckin' jaw in
international waters before he gets one word out." It
would have sounded better in Portuguese.

"Woody," Gil said.

Jairo was coming between the seats to get the
phone away from me. Another hand, Javier's or
Edson's, pulled my seat belt backward.

Kendall laughed. "Woo! You're ready for tonight. Don't pop an aneurism or anything. I'll talk to you soon."

"Wait. Wait. Marcela's cousin wants to talk to her."

Silence. I braced myself for the extraction into the backseat.

Kendall said, "Who's that, more of them Arco-vair-days? I think we went past their hotel room when we picked up Marcela." Like it was a date.

"Hold on." I handed the phone to Jairo.

"I am Jairo Arcoverde. Who are you? . . . Okay, Kendall, listen to me now. You know where we come from? . . . That's right, Brazil, my friend. This kind of thing, you do it down there, we take you into the jungle and you never come out."

I winced and looked at Gil.

He kept his eyes on the road and shrugged.

Jairo said, "I know there's no jungle here, but you have desert. I don't know any Jake and don't care about him. Bring Marcela back to me now, and we will talk about how to make this right."

He was talking honor with Kendall. Like discussing gravity with an alien. The concept was familiar, but it just didn't apply.

"No, *you* listen. Hello?" Jairo ranted in Portuguese and crushed the phone shut and threw it into the front seat. It bounced off Gil's coffee and landed between my feet. It looked intact, but it seemed rude to make sure everything still worked right at that moment.

The brothers had what could qualify as a conversation. I didn't catch any of it and regretted not learning at least a few common phrases, like "disembowel" and "leave him in a ditch."

Gil and I sat in the front seat and didn't look at each other, like prisoners in front of the firing squad waiting to see who got the first volley.

My seat moved, and I shifted to see Jairo two inches from my face. He stared into my eyes, nodded, and turned to Gil. "What time until we have to be at the fight?"

"The broadcast goes live at seven, so seven, seven thirty at the latest. I'm sure Eddie wants us there as early as possible."

"Fuck Eddie," Jairo said.

Gil and I nodded automatically.

"What time is it now, one thirty? Yes. Woody, we have six hours. That's a whole night of sleep almost. We will spend it finding Marcela."

Fight days are supposed to be restful. You stay loose, visualize how it will go, and don't do anything that could get you hurt. Burbank was probably playing a video game, watching a movie, taking a nap. I was about to dive headfirst into a scavenger hunt through rusty nails and busted glass.

I rolled my neck and said, "Okay. I know where

we can start. I know a guy." That was the problem and the solution: I always knew a guy.

"All right," Jairo said.

I said, "First we have to go to the gym and drop Gil off. He doesn't need to be in this, and we need to switch trucks."

"Of course," Jairo said. "We have talked about this already. Edson cannot go, either, and Javier will stay with him."

"Why?" I didn't want to push it, but extra bodies meant extra muscle. You have enough of that, and maybe you didn't have to use it.

Jairo said, "Because Edson is mad, and he'll kill the first man we see who might help us find Marcela, and then no one will help us. And Javier will stay with him and hold him down to make sure he doesn't go out on his own to find her."

Gil said, "Can I drop them off at the hotel instead?"

CHAPTER 11

We left them at the gym and switched trucks. My pickup was a ten-year-old Ford F-150, dark gray with black interior. Jairo went inside the gym and came out with bananas and apples and an orange and dumped them on the bench between us. Now that it was just me and him, the mood was calm and focused. We were past the blame and into the resolution, comfortable now that we were doing something.

We had the trust that came from days rolling on the mats and sparring in the cage. You could know someone your entire life, and if you'd never seen them in a fight, you still didn't know who they really were. Watch someone fight the first time you meet them— or even better, be the one fighting them—and you could predict what they would do in just about any other situation.

I got out of the parking lot and started heading north while he peeled a banana and ate it in two bites. He folded the peel over itself and laid it on the floor mat and clapped and rubbed his hands together. "Okay, where are we going?"

"To see a guy Lance and I used to work for. They still run in the same circles, kind of, so maybe he knows something about Kendall or can call someone who does."

"Why don't we just call this guy?"

"Last I knew, he doesn't have a phone. Landline, cell, nothing. Face-to-face is the only way."

"And this guy, he likes you?"

I had to think about that one. "He respects me, but I don't know if he likes me."

"Respect is good."

"I should tell you, though. The last time I saw Chops, he said the next time he saw me he'd kill me. So, you know. Be ready."

I drove north on Nellis Boulevard and watched the graffiti blossom and store windows go from bright and full of merchandise to dark, dusty, and sometimes busted out. The buildings weren't waiting for new tenants; they were waiting to be burned down by thugs or a careless bum or leveled as the Strip continued to feed. The sunlight was flat. There wasn't anything clean or shiny for it to bounce off.

"This isn't the best side of Vegas," I told Jairo. "Sorry."

He shrugged. "This is nothing. I haven't seen anyone shitting in the street yet."

"Be patient."

Jairo perked up at a stoplight when he spotted a skinny guy wearing a Brazilian soccer jersey. He leaned out the window, saw the guy was actually a female with no hair and one boot talking to herself, and made a face like he'd licked a lemon-flavored turd.

I turned east on Owens and ignored the challenging stares and comments from the young hostiles standing on corners—*get a job, at least it's air-conditioned*—and kept going until the houses stopped. One second we were rolling through a neighborhood and the next we were in the desert. The road was still paved, but sand had drifted over the shoulder, and the truck kicked up dust. I could see buildings ahead, some developer's plan to spearhead farther into the frontier and offer a secluded setting along with the big city lifestyle. I hoped it had its own police force. About halfway between the last houses and the outpost, I turned south onto a dirt road stippled with ATV tire tracks.

Not from joyrides. Patrols.

Jairo asked, "This guy lives in the desert?"

"He likes to see people coming. We just ran over a hose that rings a bell in his house, so we're expected."

The track started a gentle incline into low hills, nothing around us but rocks and sand. At the tops of the rises we could see civilization off to the right, like a shoreline from atop the swells. The truck bounced over a final ridge, and the compound was in front of us. I had to stomp on the brakes because Chops had pushed his berm out farther, the wall of earth about eight feet high and covered with scrub. It wouldn't be too hard to climb it, but at the top you'd see that the back side was a straight drop because of the steel retaining wall the earth was pushed against, and while you were standing there thinking about the drop, the crosshairs would find you.

Jairo braced himself against the dashboard, and the truck slid a few feet and stopped a car's length from the gate, a dull barricade of battered sheet metal with rusty barbed wire coiled across the top. "This reminds me of Brazil."

"Smile," I said.

The camera was bolted to an antenna pole about twenty feet inside the berm and pointed right into the cab. It was a newer model than the last one I'd smiled into and was probably equipped with infrared and X-ray and lie detectors and death beams. Someone— maybe Chops, hopefully not—zoomed in on me. The camera panned to the right and gave Jairo some scrutiny. He squinted at it and muttered something.

We sat there for almost a minute; then Jairo said, "What happens here?"

"We wait. The gate opens, or it doesn't."

Another minute. Jairo drummed his fingers on the middle console. "How long?"

I'd sat in this spot for forty-five minutes before with nothing happening, but I didn't want to tell Jairo that. We weren't going to wait that long anyway. It was almost two o'clock, and Marcela was somewhere with Kendall and worm-lip Steve, and Burbank was resting. I was here to get what I needed and move on, and no earth berm or metal wall or amount of violent paranoia was going to stop me. I gave Chops five minutes to open the gate, or I was going over. I kept a smile on my face and hoped the camera couldn't read minds.

The gate shuddered and started to slide open.

The compound looked about the same as I remembered. There were a few more abandoned vehicles spread out across the rocky area leading to the house, but I couldn't tell which ones were new. The first time I'd seen them there was something odd I couldn't place until I realized there was no daylight underneath the frames. The cars were all hollowed out and sat on concrete foundations, filled with dirt up to the windowsills and angled toward the gate in perfect firing positions. I counted ten vehicles, staggered away from the house so a man could work his way from the front door to the gate with minimal exposure.

It was a lot of work, especially since the tunnels probably made the whole configuration moot.

The track led us between the vehicles to the right side of the house and stopped—no fence or barrier, just stopped—at the edge of a gulley that dropped a hundred feet and ended in a washout filled with dry silt and more scrub brush. The ridge on the other side of the gulley was a bit higher and gave a good vantage point over the house, which was why Chops put land mines up there.

The house was a one-story Frank Lloyd Wright built into the ridge. It looked like it had grown out of the rocks after some tectonic shifts. The huge windows that made up most of the structure's exterior had all been replaced with one-way glass, and I watched the truck T-bone its reflection as we drove past the corner and stopped at the edge of the ridge.

Jairo straightened in his seat and tried to peer over the hood to see how much road was left. He eased back down so as not to shift us over the edge.

On our left was the garage door, wooden and a shade darker than the stacked stone pillars that bracketed it. The wood looked a little warped and cracked from the Nevada sun. It was veneer, meant to look like a weak point when behind the thin varnished skin was a steel core that could only be raised with hydraulic pistons sunk into the bedrock.

I shut the truck off and checked the rearview mirror to make sure nothing was rolling toward us to push us into the gulley. Clear so far. Jairo opened his door and I said, "Wait." He cursed and pulled it shut. We sat there for a minute, and I wondered if I should reset my five-minute deadline or continue it from the gate. If the latter, time was up.

I reached for the door handle and had it at the release point when the ground started to hum and the garage door lifted. There were two work boots inside the door, then jeans above them. The boots shifted, and one knee dropped to the cement floor, and I saw the barrel of an AR-15 slide under the door and point at my face.

The door finished its ascent, and everything got quiet. Chops knelt in the middle of the opening and held the gun steady in a compact posture, his elbows tucked in with his fake left hand just in front of the clip. He still had the blond high and tight and thick wire-framed glasses. He was ten years older than me, but his face was smooth and young—paranoia must be good for the skin. I could only see his left eye; the right was dipped down so he could line me up through the optical sight mounted on the rail of the gun. His left eye was open. If it closed I would really start to worry.

Jairo said, "Um."

I put a hand out to soothe him. It probably worked as well as a Band-Aid on a decapitation.

"Show me," Chops said.

I held my hands up where he could see them. Jairo did the same. We waited.

About a decade later, Chops said, "Hey, Aaron."

"Chops."

"What's happening?"

I said, "Oh . . . you know."

"Yeah. You remember the last thing I said to you?"

I put my thinking face on. "I believe you said if you ever saw me again, you'd kill me."

"And here you are." His left eye closed.

I fought the urge to duck under the dashboard until he opened it again, just blinking out some sweat. "I'm here to make it right," I said. Then, quieter, "And to ask a favor."

"Who's that with you?"

I leaned back so Chops could get a better look. "This is Jairo. He's from Brazil."

Chops said, "I don't move people anymore."

"It's not that."

"What then? Wait, no. First I wanna see if you can make it right. This should be good."

"Can you lower the gun?"

He smiled behind the optical sight. "Can. Won't."

Dickhead. "I never told those guys you weren't in the military. They caught me off guard, asking me about your medals, and I didn't know what they were talking about. I guess they figured it out themselves."

"That was my cover with them," Chops said.

"Yes. I realize that now."

"See, I needed them to trust me. They were veterans, and they would respect a fellow veteran."

"Sure."

"So when they came to me after they talked to you and said they wouldn't do business with a dishonorable piece of shit, you can see why I would be upset. I mean, come on."

"I understand."

Chops shifted his stance and reacquired me through the sight. "I had to kill all three of them, man. Three brothers in arms and bury them out in the desert instead of in Arlington with a flag over their coffins like they deserved."

"I'm sorry about that."

"But you know what?"

The punch line was going to be loud. I swallowed. "What?"

"I found out three weeks later one of them was working with the Feds." He lowered the rifle and swung it to port arms. He sniffed. "I would have found out anyway but maybe too late. They did a sweep of the city looking for the guy. Asked me about him, but I didn't even leave a speck of his dust for them to find. But I'll tell you, I wanted so bad to ask the one who'd turned, 'Hey, who's dishonorable now?' You know?"

"Yeah," I said. I didn't really know, but I try not to pick fights with people who recently stopped pointing a gun at me.

Chops spit a white bullet out into the dirt and stood up. He put the rifle on safe, but that didn't mean a whole lot as long as he still held it. "Does your friend there speak English?"

"Yes."

Chops leaned to his left and looked at Jairo. Loudly, he said, "Sorry about that. Just working out an old misunderstanding."

"Okay," Jairo said. "No problem."

"Roger that. So what's this favor? Funny, huh, about that Fed. I go from having to kill you over something to wanting to plant a big wet one on you."

"That is funny." I tried to smile, but it felt more like stemming a gag reflex. "It's about Lance."

Chops frowned. "Lance? What'd he do now? You know I kept asking him about you so I could get in touch and let you know I didn't have to shoot you anymore, but he was never with it enough. He'd fuck up the message."

I said, "Lance is in a bit of trouble, and I'm trying to help him out."

"Money?"

"That's what started the problem, but it's gained momentum since then. He got snatched. He's being held somewhere in the city, and I need to find him in the next few hours." I didn't want to mention Marcela. Chops would understand not leaving a man behind. A woman, he'd try to find a way to exploit the situation because he thought women caused weakness in men.

"Who took him?"

"A guy named Kendall Percy."

Chops took his rifle off safe.

I stopped breathing and sat very still. Jairo followed my lead, but I heard him blink once.

"You know Kendall?" I asked.

"You say my name to him?"

"No."

"Did Lance?"

"Not that I know of."

He looked at me sideways. "Think hard."

I hate dealing with crazy people. They bounce around too much; what's nice one second is blasphemy the next, and if it comes to smacking them around they might like it. "No one said anything."

A breeze came over the edge of the gulley, and Chops turned his face into it and opened his mouth as far as it would go.

I glanced at Jairo. He was watching Chops like he was an ass-shaped bomb—fascinating, but he still wanted to get the hell away.

The breeze died, and Chops stood there with his eyes closed for a few seconds, then said, "I don't know Kendall. I know *of* him and some big hoss he swings around town with when things go bad."

"That would be Jake," I said.

"Maybe. I only heard about them through a guy I work with. From what he's told me, this Kendall is a bit of a cowboy. Likes to make things . . . interesting. When they don't have to be."

"That's my guy."

Chops wiggled his eyebrows. "You going to kill him?"

"Nah. It's not like that." Not yet, anyway.

"Yeah," Chops said. "Why do it for free, right?"

"Who's this guy you work with?"

I thought he was going to pass on that one, but after a few seconds, he said, "He's a shot caller for one of the gangs. Name's Tezo."

"Never heard of him. Is that his first or last name?"

Chops squinted at me. "You tell me."

I frowned. "How would I know?"

"He didn't send you?" The AR was creeping back my way.

"What the fuck? Send me for what? No, I just told you. Kendall? Lance?"

Chops took a deep breath. His cheeks puffed out and turned bright red. He kept his eyes on me, and they started to take on a wet gleam that made me want to blink and rub my own.

"Woody," Jairo said.

I didn't tell him everything was cool, because it wasn't. Backing toward the gate would be a very good way to get shot. Driving over the cliff would be the quickest way out of the line of fire, but if the drop didn't kill us, whatever Chops had wired up probably would.

We both jumped when Chops exhaled and blinked a few times. "Come on inside, and we'll get this op figured out." He turned and walked into the garage.

Jairo grabbed my arm. "This guy . . ."

"I know."

"If he points that gun at me again, I'm not going to like it. I might tell him so."

"I think he's calm now," I said. Jairo kept his grip on my arm until I figured out what he was saying. "Oh. Yeah, I'm with you. If you have to move on him, I got you."

He let go and looked into the garage with a crease between his eyebrows.

I said, "You can wait in the truck if you want."

He scowled at me, said "Psh," and got out.

Chops stood with his back to us, hunkered over a large folding table pushed against the far wall. The sides of the garage were stacked a few columns deep with cardboard boxes that could have held DVD players or frozen organs. Or nothing.

The door into the house was on the back wall to the right of the table. I knew four people who'd been to this place, and none of them had ever been through that door. One of them said if you stood close enough, you could smell something musty and sweet poking around the edges. I kept my distance from the door and breathed through my mouth.

Chops tossed the AR onto some papers on the table like it was a clipboard and shuffled through a stack of manila folders until he found the one he wanted, then turned around. "All right, boys, here's the plan. I'm 99.999 percent sure Tezo can help you out. From what I gather he and Kendall have significant, uh, financial connections, so I imagine Tezo likes to be able to get in touch with him whenever he needs to. But there's no way Tezo will trust you unless you're with me, and I can't leave."

"Why not?" I asked.

Chops pointed the folder at me. "Save all questions until the end. Now, as I see it, the next best thing is for you to take Tezo something from me to prove I vouch for you." He looked at both of us to make sure we were keeping up. I was concerned he might give us his fake hand as the proof, and I would have to ask for door number two, but he held out the folder. "You take him this, and you're golden."

"What is it?"

"Didn't I tell you to save your questions?"

"Aren't you done?"

"Hmm. Go on."

I said, "Can't you just call him?"

"Got no phone."

I pulled mine out. "Here you go."

Chops closed his eyes. "First of all . . . *First* of all, what the fuck are you doing bringing one of those here? Congratulations. You're being tracked right now, and so am I. Jets are scrambling out of Nellis as we speak. Fucking brilliant."

"So let's make the call, and we'll get out of here."

Chops shook his head and grinned. "I don't have a phone. Why would I know any phone numbers?" He bounced the folder off his forehead and kept it held high while he spun around and went through the door into the house. He said, "Back in five," and the door slammed behind him.

Jairo raised his eyebrows at me.

I asked him, "You got any guys like this in Brazil?"

"Crazy, yes. Like this? No. This is pure American crazy."

"We're doing our best to export it."

He started to pace.

I checked the phone display; it was almost a quarter to three. Just over four hours until we had to be at the arena. Some of the undercard fighters might be there already, getting loose and checking out the mat to see where the footing was good and bad.

I joined Jairo, and we paced back and forth and gnawed on the cardboard boxes for a year and a half.

I checked the time again: 2:50.

Jairo walked close to the table. He peered down at the AR with his arms crossed. He glanced at the closed door, then back at the gun.

I cleared my throat, and when he looked at me, I flicked my gaze to the video camera in the corner of the ceiling.

Jairo rolled his eyes and kicked over a stack of boxes. One of them split open and let out a dozen bootleg copies of Neil Diamond's greatest hits. It made as much sense as anything else.

At just past three the door opened and Chops came out with a FedEx shipper wrapped with a few passes of wide brown tape. He started toward me and did a poor job of feigning surprise at the toppled boxes. "Hey."

"Neil didn't mind." I took the package from him. It wasn't heavy. "What's the story here? Am I treating this like the recipe for Coke or nuclear launch codes?"

Chops stood at parade rest and said, "Don't speed."

Meaning don't get pulled over with it. Big help. "We're in a bit of a hurry," I said.

"Well, this'll hurry your ass right to a bunker under Gitmo if you get caught with it."

I handed the package to Jairo and asked Chops, "Where we going?"

"You know Fremont and Bruce?"

"Unfortunately."

"Southeast corner," Chops said. "It's an auto detailing shop."

"And we just go right in?"

He thought about that one. He looked at Jairo. "Hold the package out in front of you." To me: "And keep your hands open where Tezo can see them."

Jairo said, "You'll open the gate."

"As soon as you get to it, brother." Chops didn't move.

They stared at each other for a moment; then Jairo turned and headed for the truck. "Come on, Woody."

I started walking backward. "Thanks, Chops. We're good now?"

"Roger that. But technically you still owe me one."

I slowed down. "I thought the whole Fed thing straightened it out."

Chops smiled. "No, not that. You owe me for the

time I had you in my scope and didn't pull the trigger. Come back with some beers, and I'll tell you about it."

I hurried to the truck and locked the doors, and we got the hell out of there.

CHAPTER 12

Jairo asked, "You know this place?"

"Close enough." We were going west on Owens, back into civilization and traffic. I swept in behind a cab and stuck to his bumper and started making good time. "Does the name Tezo mean anything to you?"

Jairo frowned. "Me? I don't know anyone here. Just you and Gil."

"It sounds kind of Latin, and there are some gangs from El Salvador running around town. So if Tezo means 'God of Death' or something in, what, Aztec, we'd have an idea of who we're dealing with."

"I don't know any Aztec." Jairo pointed at me but didn't look my way. "And something else: I don't care what it means. If he can get us to Marcela, he'll tell us what he knows or take us there, whatever. If I have to pull his arms off, even."

"Let's try giving him the package first."

Jairo picked it up and flipped it over a few times, checking the seams. "What do you think it is?"

I swerved around my taxi escort when he braked for a fare and immediately missed the drafting. "Chops said Tezo and Kendall are connected through money, so maybe account numbers? Probably wouldn't put that in writing, though. Could be shipping routes for something Tezo wants to steal, could be info on a witness for the prosecution. I'm going to assume it's Chops's Christmas list."

"I want to open it," Jairo said.

"For Marcela, don't. People get upset when you peek, and we need Tezo happy. We're going to ask him to give us someone he probably has a profitable relationship with, and I'm still not quite sure how to ask for that."

"We don't ask."

"Jairo, this is tricky."

"No." He dropped the package between his feet like he was done with it. "If this Tezo has any honor at all, we tell him what is happening and he is with us."

"All we know so far is that he deals with Kendall," I said, "so assuming he has honor is out. I'm not saying we go in there on our knees, but we need to be respectful and give him some room before we start knocking things off tables. And Chops said he runs a gang, so chances are good he won't be alone."

"What is this?" Jairo asked. "What is with the bitch talk?"

"Bitch talk?"

"You say *respectful*, he might not be *alone*, and we should be *nice*. No. We smash fucking faces and get Marcela home."

I took a deep breath, and the steering wheel creaked. "I've done that. Sometimes it works; sometimes it doesn't. I'm just saying we should adapt to the situation."

"You've done it before, huh?" Jairo looked out his window. "Maybe you weren't doing it right. Maybe *you* should wait in the truck now."

I almost made the steering wheel into an oval. "I'm trying to keep us from getting killed for no good reason."

"You're trying to save your ass for your big fight." He spit out the window and turned to me. "If it was me, *this* would be the fight. Get Marcela back. Everything else? Gone."

"Man, I have no idea why you think that. Fuck the fight. If I have to choose, it's her. But I'm trying not to have to make that choice."

"You say it, but . . ." Jairo grimaced. "This would never be me. I would not have let them take her."

"I wasn't there," I said.

"I would have been."

"So it would be okay if I'd spent the night in her hotel room?"

The look I got said no.

I didn't mention that he and his brothers were right down the hall when Kendall had come for Marcela. Jairo was looking down on everything from a throne, and anything I tossed out would get swatted away or answered with a lightning bolt.

"I was wrong," Jairo said. I opened my mouth to tell him it was all right; then he said, "I thought you were a man."

I went cross-eyed for two seconds. I had to open my mouth to get enough air. All I wanted was to keep everyone calm and civilized until that wasn't going to work anymore, and this guy had me wanting to pull over and stomp his head through a storm grate.

I was so focused on not jumping across the truck that I almost missed the turn and had to cut across the left lane to the accompaniment of horns and fingers in order to get south on Eastern. We got stuck in a backup for ten very quiet minutes because some fucking moron had T-boned another idiot and blocked two lanes. Once we were clear I pushed the truck up to sixty and risked a ticket until I turned right on Freemont and slowed down so I could look for the place.

"It'll be on the right," I said. "Auto detailing shop."

Jairo was already looking out that window and didn't bother to nod. We were about three-quarters down the block when Jairo pointed and said, "There."

I goosed it into the parking lot of Dan's Auto Detailing and Tire Shop. It was a dirty white cinderblock rectangle with a flat roof and three closed garage doors starting at the left end, each door with two dark oblong windows. Then a door into what had to be the office and from there to the corner a set of large windows showing all kinds of tires and rims. The displays had backdrops, making it impossible to see inside the building.

There was another pickup in the parking lot, but it and mine weren't from the same family. It was lowered with a metallic teal paint job, smoked glass, and chrome rims with some kind of unreadable script across the back window.

I pulled in near the door—glass with a faded poster for Armor All covering the inside—and reached for the FedEx package, but Jairo scooped it up and got out his side. I got out too and waited for him at the bumper. I wanted to revise our strategy of bickering and pouting, but he walked right past and stiff-armed the door on his way inside. It slowed on the way back and thumped shut.

I took a deep breath and listened to the traffic go by and shook my head. Marcela would think this was equal parts hilarious and disgusting. We'd tell her the story, us thumping our chests and butting heads, and she'd roll her eyes and call us idiots.

Or we'd never see her again, and she'd get left somewhere in a pile with the residue of Steve on her. I'd relive the story, trying to convince myself that I'd done everything I could but knowing she was dead and gone because of me.

Or Jairo.

He was probably in there kicking magazines off the waiting room table and jumping on the couch, holding his breath until someone gave him a face to smash. I walked over to the closest bay and cupped my hands around my head and peered through the window. I searched for something shiny catching the light or the back end of a car getting detailed, but there was nothing. Not even an oblong patch of light on the concrete floor.

I looked at the other windows, and it hit me that they weren't dark; they were blacked out. I shoved off the window and bulled through the door and got ready to smash faces.

I almost ran into Jairo. He had his back to me, staring at an old man sitting on a stool behind a counter in the small waiting area. There was a door behind him in the corner that led toward the garage area, but the wire-mesh window was covered on the other side with a piece of stained cardboard. They weren't trying as hard to look normal once you got inside.

Straight ahead was a soda machine with yellowed buttons for RC Cola and Fanta. To the right of that a bowed and dusty couch squatted behind a heavy glass table piled with car magazines and accessory catalogs. The backs of the window tire displays were unpainted particleboard.

"Do you know him or not?" Jairo asked.

The old man slumped on the stool and stared at him with his hands resting on his thighs. He was from somewhere south of the border, probably close to seventy but still with a full head of black hair puffed up into something you could stash an extra pair of saddle shoes in.

I put a hand on Jairo's arm.

He shook it off.

"Jairo," I said.

He dropped the package on the counter and leaned on the chipped Formica with both hands. Something in the counter or the old man creaked. "I want to talk to Tezo. Right now."

The old man opened his mouth. A toothpick popped out from somewhere in there and slid into the corner and danced a bit before coming to a rest.

Jairo reached out to grab a handful of his shirt but stopped just short and made a fist and shook it under his face. "Can you hear me? Do you know what I'm saying?"

The old man flinched but didn't make a sound or fall off the stool. His right hand slid down his thigh toward the counter and disappeared beneath it.

I grabbed Jairo and yanked him back. He tried to get me with an elbow, but I stayed close and bear-hugged him with his feet off the floor.

The old man watched us with his hand under the counter. Jairo saw it and snorted disgust through his nose but stayed with me.

I set him down and got close to his ear. "The windows are painted shut."

"Eh?"

The old man leaned forward and shoved the FedEx package off the counter with his left hand. It slapped onto the floor and kicked up a skirt of dust.

"They're blacked out," I told Jairo.

"So?"

"So whatever they're doing here, they don't want anyone to see it. Take it easy. If we do see it, they might not let us leave."

"I don't give a shit what they let us do." He shook loose and picked up the package.

The old man stared at him. The toothpick went from one corner of his mouth to the other.

Jairo tossed the package onto the counter and

pointed at it. "This is from Chops. Woody, tell him."

"That's from Chops," I told him. We could have said it was from Martians and gotten the same response.

He blinked and kept his hand under the counter, and that was it. The door in the corner opened, and a stocky Latin kid with a bandana around his face and a sawed-off shotgun walked across the room to the door and turned the dead bolt. He put his back against the door and looked at the package like it wanted to date his mother. The shotgun was pointed at us by default.

I glanced through the open doorway into the garage area and saw a taller guy standing about ten feet inside under an overhead fluorescent light fixture with his hands in his pockets, relaxed. He looked damn near bored. His black hair was slicked back and he was clean shaven, but there was something all over his face. After a few seconds he said, "Chops sent you?"

"Yes," I said.

He nodded at the package. "And that?"

"Yes."

"What is it?"

"I don't know."

He took his time, moved his hands to the back pockets. "Is it a bomb?"

"I hope not. Are you Tezo?"

He tilted his head up to the light with his eyes closed. "Yeah, I'm Tezo." His head came down. He sized us up and didn't seem impressed. "Come on back. And tell Pelé there to chill out. He almost got shot by *mi papi.*"

Jairo stomped through the doorway, and I followed him into one of the five worst rooms I've ever been in.

No, scratch that.

One of the three worst.

The smell hit me first. Like someone tried to clean a hot butcher shop with bleach and dope smoke. My eyes started to water, and through the blinks I could see Tezo smiling about it. Jairo pulled his shirt up over his mouth and nose and held the package out to him. Tezo looked at it and pursed his lips but kept his hands in his back pockets.

The door closed behind us. The kid stuck the shotgun into Jairo's back and kept it there while he used the other hand to check for weapons, wires, whatever.

Tezo watched but didn't seem interested. He was about as tall as me and maybe forty years old. The something all over his face was tattoos. He had more ink per square inch than a hundred dollar bill. His forehead, ears, cheeks, and neck were covered in black lettering and icons; I could pick out a tombstone on his neck, a pair of dice near his right eye, three dots in a triangle between his eyebrows, and *SUR* in gothic letters across his Adam's apple. Everything else would have required closer inspection, and I was fine where I was.

The kid moved to me and gave me the shotgun/frisk combo. I didn't have anything except the truck key and fob; the cell was in the center console, and I rarely had a good reason to carry a wallet.

Tezo caught me looking at his ink and gazed back at me with eyes that did not reflect any light.

I was suddenly fascinated by the ceiling.

We were in the garage bay closest to the entrance, the one I'd tried to peek into from outside. Black garbage bags were taped over the bay door windows. A dividing wall of more bags, broken skids, and stained tarps had been set up on the other side of the bay, putting us in a narrow space that ran from the front of the building to the back. The place looked like it hadn't been used for detailing since the Model T chugged around.

To my right, past Jairo, there was a card table with a guy sitting at it and an expensive-looking leather couch with two more guys, all of them in their late teens, shaved bald, and staring at me and Jairo. The two on the couch were playing a football game on a huge plasma TV but had it paused so they could look tough without distraction. They had some tattoos on them but nothing like the wallpaper job on Tezo.

I didn't see anything that looked like it smelled

horrible, so it was either one of the guys or something on the other side of the tarps. The kid finished the frisk, stepped to the door, and got both hands on the shotgun again.

Jairo waved the package at Tezo. "So you want this or not?"

"Who are you two?"

"Just the messengers," I said. I'd let him see what Chops sent before we got into any personal favors.

"Why'd he send two? The package ain't that big."

The kid at the card table snorted.

"We can get into that," I said, "but we'd like to establish some trust first."

Tezo's eyebrows pushed two black devil horns up toward his hairline. "Oh, you would? Well, I'll tell you, I only trust my dog and my boys who I've seen kill someone with my own two eyes. Not my old lady. Not *mi madre*. And you're both too fucking ugly to be my dog, and I ain't seen you kill anyone yet."

I liked him better when he was thinking. "Not trust, then. Let's go for professionalism. You want us to open it?"

Tezo moved toward the dividing wall. "Slow."

Jairo ripped the tape apart and got a corner of the package in his mitt and held it against his leg with one hand so he could pull with the other.

Tezo shook his head. "I say slow, this fool gets a

live wire up his ass."

"We're on a tight schedule," I said.

"Who gives a shit?"

Jairo sweated and cursed and got the corner to break and pulled a two-inch strip off the end of the package. He dropped it and stuffed his hand in and came out with a mess of shredded newspaper. All three of us stared at it. Jairo let it fall and went in, came out with more shreds.

"What the fuck?" he said and pressed the edges of the envelope together so he could see inside. He stabbed a hand in and pulled out a single sheet of paper folded in half. Looked into the envelope once more. He held the paper up and frowned at me.

I wasn't happy. "What's it say?"

Tezo plucked the sheet away from Jairo and unfolded it. He blinked a few times and smiled. Looked at me, then Jairo, the smile getting bigger. Without looking away, he told the kid at the card table, "Make some calls. Get everyone here. We're gonna have a show tonight."

To us, he said, "Get on your knees."

We didn't move.

Tezo looked amused; then that was gone. "Get down."

"Wait a minute," I said.

The kid behind us jammed the shotgun into my right shoulder blade. It hurt.

"Get the fuck down," Tezo said.

"What is this?" Jairo asked.

"Down!"

The kid was looking at Jairo when I turned and grabbed the sawed-off barrel and pointed it at the ceiling and push-kicked him in the bladder. His legs went out from under him, but he held on to the gun, and I had to bend over to keep him from pulling the trigger. I was ready to stomp on the back of his head when I heard people shouting at me. I stared at the black automatics aimed at me from the couch and card table.

Jairo had his hands near his ears and was in a half crouch.

Tezo had a gun out, a short and blocky chrome revolver, but it was pointed at the floor. He said, "Let go of him and turn to me."

I did. The kid scrambled up behind me, and I braced for it. But Tezo shook his head, and the kid settled for breathing on the back of my neck. He had to get on his tiptoes to do it, so good for him.

Tezo said, "So stay on your feet. Whatever. You're gonna be walking soon, anyway."

"What's on the sheet?" I asked.

Tezo turned the paper around so we could read it:

2 4 Pit
Truce?

I tried glaring at it until it made sense. Sometimes it works. "Meaning?"

Tezo tucked the pistol into the back of his pants and took his time folding the paper until it would fit in his jeans pocket. "Chops and me, we had a misunderstanding a while ago. Lately we've been, uh, actively unfriendly toward each other, you know? But now it looks like he sent you two as a makeup gift. I guess you had a misunderstanding with him too, huh?"

"No, look—"

"You look," Tezo said. He pulled an oily yellow tarp aside and let one of the video gamers slip through into darkness. The other gamer got off the couch and walked over and put his pistol in Jairo's ear. The shotgun settled against the vertebrae at the base of my skull. A string of caged work lights came on in the area behind the tarps, and through the opening I could see where the smell was coming from.

They took us through the triangular opening, and we had to stop three steps in at the edge of the concrete. The two overhead doors on our left were completely boarded over, and the combined garage bays made a large space. The six-foot-wide walkway we were on went around the area on three sides like a capital *C*. The fourth side, on our right along the rear of the building, was wider and had a square room sticking out of the far corner. It also had a four-tiered set of bleachers that faced the middle of the room, where the pit was.

"Down," Tezo said. "All the way."

The kid behind me kicked me in the small of my back, and I went in. It was an eight-foot drop onto the moist dirt, and I landed off balance and had to roll to absorb the impact and immediately wished I'd stayed on my feet. The dirt was spongy with a stagnant liquid that had probably started out as water, but after mixing with blood and piss and shit, it had become something entirely new. I stood with my arms out from my sides and let the stuff slough off me in chunks.

The pit walls were vertical panels of particleboard nailed together with scraps of wood and sheet metal, three panels at each end and five along each side. That made the pit twelve by twenty. The panels were swollen and rotten at the bottom from the fluids, and the rest of the surface was covered with random stains and matted blood, hair, fur, and feathers.

I felt the juices seeping into my shoes. It burned. I searched for higher ground, but there wasn't any.

We were in a swamp.

Jairo had landed on his feet and was facing Tezo and the others.

Tezo tapped a heavy boot on the pit's edge. "Come on, big boy. Put your fingers under here just for a second."

Jairo scowled at me. "What is this?"

"This is . . . not good." I didn't mention how it had been his idea to come in like we had. Maybe it was moot, but I didn't feel responsible for us being in the pit. You know, small victories.

He turned back to Tezo. "We didn't come for this."

"Nobody does."

"We came for my cousin."

Tezo said, "Your cousin ain't here, *esse.*"

"You might know where she is. That's why we came." Eight feet down in a pit, standing in a CDC Petri dish, Jairo still managed to exude authority.

Tezo squatted down at the edge. "Tell you what. You the one comes out of there, we'll all go find her and bring her back here, yeah? For another kind of show."

That got Jairo's fingers up there. He moved faster than Tezo anticipated and got his right hand on the lip and pulled so he could reach for Tezo with his left. He touched his shirt, but Tezo tipped backward out of range and got to his feet with a little more urgency than he probably wanted to show in front of his crew. He spit on Jairo.

Jairo bellowed and punched a dent in the particleboard and screamed at them in Portuguese.

"Kendall Percy," I said.

Tezo looked at me and things got quiet. "What?"

"Kendall Percy. We're here for him."

Tezo nodded at Jairo. "I thought you were here for his cousin."

"Long story," I said. "Bottom line, we're here for Kendall."

He nudged the kid with the shotgun. "Anybody here look like a Kendall to you?"

I said, "Chops says you know him, work with him."

"Chops is the piece of shit that put you down there; you think he's the rope gonna pull you out?"

"Do you work with Kendall or not? He has a lot riding on us being somewhere tonight."

"Besides here?"

"I don't think he'd appreciate you sticking your dick in his soup," I said.

Tezo stared at me.

Something warm from my tumble into the pit slid off my forehead into the corner of my eye and started to wiggle. I fought the urge to dig it out.

Tezo kept staring and pulled a cell phone out of his pocket. No hurry. I pictured him engulfed in flames, strolling toward a fire extinguisher. Added it to my bucket list. He flipped the phone open and thumbed to the number he wanted and put the phone to his ear. "Hey, it's me. You know some big boys trying to be hard, looking for some cousin?"

I held my breath.

"They in the pit right now," Tezo said. "Both, yeah. The white one says you guys got something going."

I tried to read his face while he listened, but it looked the same as it always did.

"Yeah? Okay." Tezo flipped the phone shut and sniffed and took a year putting it in his pocket.

"What did he say?" Jairo asked.

Tezo leaned forward so he could look past the edge of the pit at him. "Who?"

Jairo spat some Portuguese.

"Oh, that wasn't Kendall," Tezo said. "That was Big Jake. You know him?"

I let my breath out.

Tezo said, "Yeah, Big Jake says, 'Let the best man win.'"

CHAPTER 13

Tezo nudged the kid with the shotgun and nodded toward the bleachers.

The kid walked around the pit and sat on the top tier and lit up.

Tezo said, "We got some people coming for this, so relax. Stretch out. Only one of you is getting out of there, so you might want to start hating each other now."

He marched through the tarp with the others and left us with the kid on the bleachers, who watched us with a flat face and dead eyes.

I'd been in fighting pits before, and I knew how to get out of them. Nothing like Tezo's sewer, but the concept was the same. Thunderdome bullshit. Fighting to the death is rare and a stupid business plan; there's no profit in fighters getting killed. But the smell in this place was unmistakable, and Tezo wasn't interested in careers.

Muscle memory from all the way back to the empty swimming pool kicked in. I started to pace and survey the floor, if you could call it that. There was standing water in the corners, enough to drown a man in if I could get on his back and push his face down.

The footing's terrible, so nothing fancy. Short, hard punches. I shook out my arms.

Forehead into nose, temple. Again and again. I rolled my neck.

Elbows into throat, knees into groin. I pulled my left knee up toward my chest, then my right.

Don't let him grab hold, because he won't let go. He's bigger and stronger and a black belt in jiu jitsu.

He was watching me, staring me down.

Don't put your eyes on me. I'll close them for good.

I would make it out.

No, he wasn't staring. Just watching. I stopped pacing.

He was Jairo.

I came back. Marcela. Burbank. Lance. I bent over and put my hands on my knees.

Jairo squished over and squatted next to me.

"I'm sorry about this."

"We need to get out of here."

The insight made me smile. "That's true."

"Isn't Jake Kendall's man?"

"Yeah."

"Why would he let you fight in here?"

"I have no idea," I said. "I busted his nose, so we aren't exactly best friends. But still, Kendall wants me in the Burbank fight."

A thought hit me then, and Jairo saw it on my face. His eyebrows went up, then came together. His jaw muscles knotted around each other. "If Marcela is dead already, they won't want you in the fight tonight. If she's dead, they want us to die here. This is a blessing to them."

"I know." There had to be another explanation why Jake would leave us in the pit. If it was because Marcela was dead—and probably Lance too—there wasn't any reason to get out. "Maybe he's working against Kendall behind his back. Wants him to fail."

"We have to get out. At least one of us. Marcela is waiting, either for us to get her or get them." He nodded. "Okay, so which one of us?"

"They're not gonna let one of us leave the building. Whoever doesn't die in here is going to either keep fighting until he does or get shot. Or stabbed. Or strung up for dogs to work on."

Jairo stared at the wall. "If we get out of this hole, we can fight our way to the outside."

Outside. We were one wall and ten seconds away from it, but it may as well have been a date with Marilyn Monroe. "Do you have a chain gun I don't know about?"

"There's only one guy in here." He scooped up a handful of the muck. "We can throw this shit at him until he moves, and you boost me out so I can take him." He waited for a response, then followed my gaze to his hand. In the muck were two human teeth and a tan, mushy dog's paw. Jairo tilted his hand and let it all slide off.

It hit him where we really were.

A grave.

We waited. We asked the kid what was happening, got the blank look in return, and waited some more.

Things were picking up on the other side of the dividing wall. We listened to raucous welcomes and laughter as people arrived for the show. Three times the tarp opened, and I looked up for Tezo, but it was just people peeking through the opening for a preview. They made excited sounds and talked in Spanish.

I asked Jairo, "Do you know what they're saying?"

"Some. It's not good for us."

It got loud as more people arrived. Someone turned on music. The soundtrack for getting ready to watch two men fight to the death? Reggae.

I don't know how long we waited in the pit. It felt like five and a half days. When the tarp opened and Tezo came through, my guts tried to wrap around my spine. Tezo held the tarp aside for a string of men and women who filed around the corner by Jairo and found spots on the bleachers, maybe fifty people altogether. Most of them were young, late teens or early twenties, but a few were older with faces like old potatoes. Nobody seemed to mind the smell coming from the pit.

The thugs from the couch helped the elders to the lowest tier and made sure they were comfortable. They smiled with no teeth and murmured to each other and passed a pouch of chewing tobacco around. One of the women saw me watching and waved. I gave her the finger and she hooted.

When everyone had a seat, they started pointing at me and Jairo and jabbering and laughing; then the cash came out. A fat guy in a white tank top and janitor's pants collected the money and took notes on who bet on who, what, when, how. Nobody cared about why.

In MMA, you train with guys in your weight class knowing you might have to fight them in the cage someday. The only way to keep the other guy's respect and look yourself in the mirror is to give it everything and see who gets his hand raised. Some guys from the Japanese and Brazilian clubs flip it around and refuse to fight their training brothers out of respect. If one of their guys has the belt, the second-best fighter waits until his champ loses; then he's first in line to avenge the loss. On the other hand, American fighters will generally fight their mom as long as it's the main event.

If you do have to fight a friend, the best part is knowing you're going to crack beers afterward and tell the story over and over. It's a warm fuzzy when your friend says, "No one ever hit me as hard as you did."

I glanced at Jairo, breathing fast in and out through his nose despite the stench, his face tight and his eyes closed. His mouth was moving in a pattern, and I realized two things:

One, that he was praying.

Two, I didn't want to hit him.

For the first time in my adult life, I was scared to fight.

When the audience got their bets down, they threw whatever was left in their pockets at me and Jairo. Loose change, wadded-up Kleenex, crumpled cigarette packs. Someone sailed an unused condom like a Frisbee at Jairo, and it bounced off his forehead and landed in the muck between his feet.

He opened his eyes, picked it up, and brushed it off. He looked into the crowd and said, "This is five years old. Why don't you go get laid instead of watching this?"

The crowd turned on a skinny guy in his twenties sitting on the top tier with a bandana wrapped around his eyebrows and shoved him and laughed

and called him names. A few of them changed their
bets after that, using wit as a gauge for fighting ability.
I was a massive underdog.

Tezo walked around to the edge of the pit on my
right so he could look down at us and across to the
bleachers. "You speak Spanish?"

I shook my head.

"Too late to learn. I'll keep it in English for you."
Super guy. He surveyed the bleachers, which quieted
down for him. "Business first. These two are a gift
from Chops, so unless I say otherwise, he's off-limits."

Some of the males seemed disappointed; there
went a chance to kill someone for Tezo.

"Hey, you know Chops. He'll fuck up again and
get back on the shit list. That happens, don't wait so
fucking long to make a move, huh? All right. Business
is done. Now for pleasure." Tezo stared at me, then
Jairo. "Ready?"

I looked across the pit at Jairo. Neither of us was
ready for this.

"Go," Tezo said.

I stood still.

Jairo took one step forward, then brought his
foot back.

The crowd despised him. Fifty people in that
small space sounded like a train derailing. They stood
and hacked their hands at us and couldn't believe we

weren't eager to kill each other.

"What the fuck is this?" Tezo said. "Go. *Go*."

Ignorance is a good way to buy time, and I'm a natural at playing dumb. I shouted to Tezo over the crowd, "What's the goal?"

"The what?"

"Knockout? Submission?"

"Please. All that scar tissue on your head and you don't know where you are?" He kept his gaze on me and pointed at Jairo. "You, kill him." Reversed his gaze and finger: "You, kill him."

"What are the rules?"

Tezo pulled the chrome revolver out of his pants and said, "I'll let you know if you do something wrong. But don't hold your breath, huh? Now let's see something, or one of you is fighting on one leg."

Jairo took another step forward. Didn't step back. Kept coming. By the time I realized he wasn't going to stop, I was almost cornered in my end. He had a wide stance to keep from slipping in the muck, and my left leg wanted to zip into his groin, but I kept it planted and pushed off to my right. His hands reached out, looking like they did part-time work dropping cars into crushing machines, and I slapped them away as I slid around his left side and ended up at his end of the pit.

Jairo stood at my end and shook his arms loose and rolled his neck and came at me again. He spread his arms out, and it looked like he could have tickled both walls. He closed in like a trash compactor, like a hawk zeroing in for the bash and snag.

The crowd started making screeching sounds with their arms out.

Jairo crossed the middle ground into my space, watching me to see where I was going. I looked left and he leaned that way; then I darted right but he was already there. He got his left hand on my shirt and pulled me in. We were close to the bleacher wall, and the light changed as people crowded the edge to look down on us.

Jairo grabbed the back of my belt with his right hand and snaked his left hand over my right shoulder and got another handful of shirt and hugged me close. I dropped my weight down to avoid getting hip-tossed into the sludge.

But Jairo didn't try to throw me. He pushed and held me away from him at bent-arm length and ducked and put his face directly above my right knee. Muscle memory put my hands on the back of his head and brought my knee up. A half inch before it connected I shoved his head away, and my knee went past his ear.

The gang whined about how close they'd come to seeing blood.

Jairo let go and skidded away. Squared up, he raised his hands and slopped toward me. I got ready to sprawl to defend his takedown shot, but he surprised me again by throwing a straight left that missed by two feet, then standing in the pocket with his fists next to his cheeks.

I had no idea what he was doing. First he put his face in front of a cannon; then he wanted to stand and bang. His striking had gotten better since he'd come to Gil's, but that was like a shark's walking improving when it washed ashore. We were fighting in a grappler's dream—bad footing, confined space, no time limit—and one of the best grapplers in the world wasn't trying to take it to the ground. So I asked him, "What the fuck are you doing?"

"Saving Marcela," he said and threw a right jab I could see coming since last Christmas.

I moved my head and waited for him to reel his arm back in. When he did he kept that hand low and his chin out. His gaze flicked to my left hand, like he was waiting for it. A hook would put him down. I couldn't throw it. I glanced at Tezo up on my left. The revolver was still out, and he was tapping it against his leg. If we didn't knuckle up quickly, someone was going to get shot.

Jairo hadn't given up; he just thought it was inevitable only one of us was going to get out of the pit alive. He'd thought it through and decided Marcela had a better chance if I was the guy who got out.

Flatterer.

Bottom line, though, we were just in advanced negotiations with Tezo. When he put us in the pit, he gained more from one of us dying than keeping us both alive. We had to change that. We had to become more valuable or useful alive than dead. Standing in that cesspit, there was only one route: put on a fucking spectacular show.

Step one was getting both fighters to actually fight.

Jairo dropped his hands even lower and looked at my left again.

I slapped him with it. Hard. It sounded like two planks of wood clapping together.

The crowd in the bleachers inhaled as one.

Jairo's eyes popped wide. His mouth opened and pulled toward the cheek I'd stung.

I had a few reasons for slapping. It's humiliating, it sounds great, and if we made it out of the pit and I got the reward of fighting Burbank, I didn't want to do it with broken hands.

Jairo's hands stayed down so I cracked him again, open-handed on the other cheek. While he tasted that I kicked him in the shin.

"Ay."

I said, "That's right," and shoved him.

He jutted his chin at me and said, "Come on. Just do it."

I stuck my finger up his nose and kicked him in the other shin.

"What the fuck?" He shook his head and snorted and rubbed his shin. "Woody—"

I slapped him in the ear once, twice, dug my foot into the mud, and launched a grapefruit-sized chunk that hit him in the throat. It splattered around his neck and dribbled down his shirt and must have smelled like he was wearing a diaper necklace.

And that did it.

Jairo charged and the bleachers cheered. He came with his shoulders square and his head low. I tried to smack him again, but he ducked and got his head outside my left shoulder and bear-hugged me off my feet. He crushed me against the plywood at the tarp end of the pit. The wood flexed enough to cushion the blow some, but I wouldn't take it over a massage. Jairo yanked me off the wall and spun to his left and pulled so he was almost behind me, hooked his left leg in front of mine, and shoved me forward.

I went face-first into the muck. I tried to brace the fall by putting my arms out—a good way to get a broken elbow in the cage—but my hands sank six inches into the dark brown sludge and plowed forward. Jairo dropped his weight over my shoulders and drove my face down. I shut my eyes but couldn't do anything about my nose and ears; the mud slid in, and I could feel things squirming in my nostrils. Something in my left ear spoke high-pitched German. I thought Jairo was punching me in the back, but I couldn't be sure.

I pulled my arms in and did a push-up with him straddling my kidneys. He tried to shove me down, but my head was slick with filth. His left hand and arm slipped into view, and I hooked it with my left arm and rolled that way. He tried to wrap his legs around to take me with him, but I powered out and stood over him. He lay on his back and invited me into his guard.

I dug everything out of my ears and looked at it. What I saw made me want to stomp somebody in the groin. That would pretty much end the show, so I blew my nose at Jairo and told him to get up.

The bleachers were coming apart from the jumping and stomping. The people were screaming at us in Spanish and making some tongue sound that must have been a battle cry of their ancestors. Or hip-hop lyrics.

Jairo stood. He shook his arms to get the muck off and gave up after three tries. Came forward again.

I put a teep kick into his belly and left it there long enough so he could grab it. When he did I bent my leg and leaned forward and slapped a Thai clinch behind his head, pulled his ear close to my face. "Don't you cut me, you crazy fucker."

He jerked his head back and frowned at me, but I was already falling. I let my right leg shoot out from under me like Jairo's pulling had thrown me off balance, then flopped in the sewage. Jairo dropped down in half mount and drew back to hammer me in the face.

I hoped he'd figured it out.

His fist slammed into the muck a quarter inch from my ear and made a geyser four feet high. I crossed my forearms in front of my face, and he flailed away at them, half the time skipping off into the muck and letting me take a breath while he reset his base. Every fourth or fifth punch he'd slam one into my ribs for realism. I believed him.

The bleachers liked watching me get pummeled but wanted variety. Or at least some blood. They booed and threw things again.

I started returning punches between every second or third from Jairo, tagging him in the ribs and shoulders like I was going for his face but he was too fast for me, and that made them happy for a few seconds. When they began to boo again, I flicked my gaze over to the right, letting Jairo know I was going to sweep him that way; maybe me in top position for a while would cheer them up. He winked at me and I tried not to grin.

I planted my feet and was starting to buck when Tezo shot Jairo.

The sound of the gun in that confined space made me flinch and cover my head for real. I tried to get my shoulders into my ears. The bleachers cut to silence. I felt Jairo topple off to my right and heard him hit the muck. I checked to see if Tezo was going to keep shooting; the gun was up but not pointed at anyone, and it was hard to tell with all the ink but Tezo looked slightly disappointed.

"I was aiming for your knee," he said.

I knelt between him and Jairo, who was lying on his left side and not moving. His right arm was bent and tucked next to his head like he was doing old-school crunches. I tugged on the arm, but it wouldn't budge. Sometimes when a person got shot in the head everything seized up, like instant rigor mortis.

I tried again with more force behind it, and his whole body started to roll so I let go. The pinnacle of the Arcoverde bloodline, dead in a filthy Las Vegas garage fighting pit. Marcela was as good as gone. Because of me. I wanted to be furious but couldn't find the traction for it. Just kept slipping into misery.

The arm rose and Jairo looked furious enough for both of us. "I've been shot."

I cleared my throat. "Where?"

He peeled his hand away, and fresh blood coursed from a deep groove in his right trapezius muscle. It looked like a baby crocodile had taken a bite out of him and gotten all muscle, no bone or connective tissue.

I reached out to help him keep pressure on it, saw the slime on my hands, and pulled back. The wound wasn't bad, but if he stayed in the pit longer than two minutes, he'd die from rampant infection in four. I found the cleanest part of the bottom of my shirt and tore it off, slipped it between the groove and Jairo's hand, and pressed it all down. "Hold that there as tight as you can." I faced Tezo. "You like money?" I had no idea what I was saying.

"You like dick?"

The bleachers laughed, their first sound since the gunshot.

"Get us out of here. Now. Get him cleaned up. Then you and I can talk about how you can get some nice new money."

"How much money?" Tezo asked.

I pointed at Jairo. "It goes down every second he bleeds."

"Where's this money coming from?"

"I got a sure thing on a fight tonight. Ticktock."

Tezo sucked a tooth. Shrugged. "Okay. But he stays in the pit while we talk. I like what I hear, maybe he gets a Band-Aid. I don't, you go back in, and we'll see how both of you fight with holes in you."

CHAPTER 14

Tezo said something in Spanish and the bleachers emptied, the gang members and elders shuffling and grumbling single file through the tarp. The music started again on the other side.

One of the couch guys and the shotgun kid stayed and rummaged behind the bleachers and came out with a twelve-foot aluminum ladder spattered with paint and drywall mud. The feet were caked with dry sludge from the bottom of the pit, and they sank six inches when they dropped it in near me. The kid put the shotgun on Jairo, who was a serious threat sitting against the wall and wincing. The other one had his black automatic on me.

"Out," Tezo said.

"I'll be fast," I told Jairo. I climbed the ladder and looked down. He was staring at the rotten plywood, hugging himself to keep the blood from flowing. For the first time since I'd met him, he looked small.

Tezo walked around the corner near the garage doors and headed for the room in the corner. I followed, passing the guy with the automatic. He had *Parasite* tattooed like a necklace beneath his throat.

"What time is it?" I asked him. It felt like we'd been in the pit for days, but it couldn't have been more than two hours, tops.

"Fuck you thirty." He fell in behind me, and I heard the shotgun kid pull the ladder out of the pit.

Tezo went through the door and waited in the center of the room. It was a small space, maybe twelve by twelve, and looked like it used to be an employee bathroom. The walls were bile-yellow and dirty. An old metal bench was pushed against the left wall with a row of coat hooks over it. Three gray sinks hung off the wall across from the door under a cracked and crusty mirror. In the corner there was a window made up of square glass blocks that let in light but blurred everything, and on the right wall I could see two slightly cleaner silhouettes where the urinals used to wait. The pipes were still there, but they'd been capped with spigots. The stall in the near corner on my right was miraculously intact, but the door was closed, and I wanted to believe all it hid was a toilet so I didn't peek.

A stained claw-foot bathtub full of trash and a few inches of water squatted under the urinal shadows. There was a framed rectangle of tight wire mesh leaning against it, big enough to cover the top with some overlap. It looked like something out of an exhibit from a serial killer's experimental period. Parasite closed the door behind me.

"So?" Tezo asked.

I opened my mouth, and Parasite kicked me in the lower back. The air went out of me like an untied balloon. I collapsed.

Tezo kicked me in the belly. More air went out, stuff that had been hanging out in the bottom of my lungs so long it smelled like middle school. The two of them each grabbed an arm and hauled me to the tub and dumped me in.

My head cleared the end near the stall, but my feet stuck over the other end so my shins cracked against the lip. Tezo bent my legs and smashed the mesh lid over the top and sat on it. Parasite joined him, his ass directly above my face. I was wedged in with my head squished between my left shoulder and the mesh, which dug into my forehead and would turn into a cheese grater if I moved too much. The water and trash combined to make a cold and jagged nest.

Tezo reached behind him and turned on one of the urinal spigots. More cold water fell on my side and back. "Comfy?" he asked.

I tried to talk and got out something in baby goat language. I shifted as much as I could to take the bend out of my neck and said, "This isn't going to get you any money."

"You got time," he said. He had to raise his voice over the hiss of the pipes. "This is my negotiating table. You like it?"

Parasite laughed.

I pushed with everything against the mesh. It could have been welded on. Wrappers, butts, and Lotto tickets sloshed around my face, and the water was over my hips. I could feel broken glass scraping against the bottom of the tub when I moved. I wanted to kick against the lid but couldn't get my legs straight, and it was too cramped to roll onto my back to get my knees pressed against the mesh. I tried to use my hands and forehead to push, but Parasite bounced a few times and put an end to that.

I fumbled around behind my head and found the drain, but it was a hard pile of caulk or putty stuck in the outlet pipe. It was there forever.

I started to panic. I'd never been drowned before, so my body didn't know what to do. My breathing had no rhythm, just ragged gasps and spurts as I jerked and squirmed between the water and the wire grid. The water slapped at my chin. Everything else was underwater. Objects floating in the tub bumped against me and rode currents into my jeans and neckline.

"I'm fighting tonight," I said, "on the Warrior card. Main event. Put money on me to win, and you'll walk away happy."

"Is there a fix?"

The water was at my chin. I yelled about Marcela and Kendall as fast as I could and told Tezo there was no way I was going to lose the fight. The last few words were gurgled out. The water was up to my nose when somebody turned it off.

Parasite shifted to the end of the mesh so Tezo could look down at me from over my legs. "What's your name?"

I had to tilt my head back and get my eyes under the water to get my mouth above it. "Wallace."

Tezo got his phone out again and did the staring routine while he made a call.

I kept busy by shooing trash out of my nose so I could breathe and rolling side to side as much as I could to get the water moving. After a few rolls it started to slop over the edge of the tub onto the tile floor, giving me more room to breathe.

"Hey, it's me. Hold on." Tezo leaned over and looked at his feet and the water spreading across the floor. "Knock that shit off," he said to me.

I rolled faster. I could tell by his face he wasn't a

fan of insubordination, but he let it slide. What was he going to do, take the lid off and make me stop?

He brought the phone back up and said, "Is there a guy fighting tonight named Wallace? . . . Yeah . . . No shit? I'm gonna put some money on him."

I shifted, slightly more comfortable knowing I was getting out soon.

Tezo listened for a few beats and said, "Can I bet on a fighter to lose for not showing up? . . . Fuck. Okay, let's go fifty—no, a hundred grand, Wallace to lose." He closed the phone and opened the faucet.

Tezo stared down at me thrashing and dying. "Go easy, son. It's a bad way to go, but it don't have to be as bad as you're making it."

I pressed my lips against the mesh and sucked air and pushed with everything I had. Nothing moved.

Tezo said, "I'd put you back in the pit, but now that you're a pro fighter I can't afford the licensing."

Parasite thought that was hilarious.

The cold water poked into the outside corners of my eyes, and I had to shut them. I grunted air in and out and tried to mash my nose against the wires to keep water from flowing into my sinuses.

Then I couldn't breathe at all.

I tried again and couldn't bring any air in. Not even a wet gurgle. I had to push against the wire mesh to make my face drop into the water. I opened my eyes, and everything was pale and hazy.

The edges were closing in.

Then the paleness moved, and I saw Tezo's face again, grinning at me like it was the happiest day of his life. Parasite's bare ass hovered over my mouth.

"Kiss it," Tezo said into the water.

I shot back up and pressed against the wires and tried to get air, and Parasite dropped his ass again. No more air. I could hear them laughing.

My eyes started to bulge. The water was churned and foamy from the faucet flow, and everything I did sent the surface bobbing up and down through the mesh, creating a whirl of ripples and waves. Garbage swirled like a filthy cosmos. I pushed up for one last shot at air, ass flavor and all, but some trash wedged between my forehead and the mesh. I pulled back and the water moved the stuff—a bloated French fry, a condom, and a long, used hypodermic needle with brown crust on the inside of the cylinder—in front of my face.

I carefully pinched the extended plunger between my thumb and forefinger. I closed my fist around the plunger and the barrel and shoved the needle into Parasite's right ass cheek three times like I was sending Morse code.

Parasite screamed. But he didn't move.

I jabbed him five more times, moving left to right,

hoping to find a nerve that wouldn't let him overcome the pain. Red clouds fanned into the water. Parasite loosed a steady screech but kept his weight on the lid. It looked like Tezo was holding him there.

I pushed the needle in as hard as I could and swirled it around. I felt the vibration through the barrel as the end of the needle scraped against bone. After the third revolution Parasite sprang off the lid and slipped on the wet tiles and went down.

Vesuvius had nothing on my eruption from the tub.

Tezo dumped off the end of the tub and skidded against the wall under the window with the wire lid on top of him. I stood up, hardly noticing the weight of my wet clothes or the loud music coming from the other side of the door. My teeth were bared.

Parasite was in front of the tub with his pants down, leaning on his right hand and knee. He planted his left foot and tried to put weight on it, but the tile was too slick and his foot shot straight out.

I didn't give him a second chance to get up.

I grabbed the top of the stall with my left hand and the rim of the tub with my right and vaulted out. Parasite looked over his shoulder in time for my foot to smash into his ear and send his face toward the floor. I let go with both hands and was careful but fast while I closed the distance and dropped my left knee onto his spine. His head snapped up from the impact, and I smacked it down with a palm strike that started at my shoulder. His nose splattered against the tile, and he screamed into the puddle.

He turned his head and cocked his arms like he was going to do a push-up, but I rose on my knee long enough to bring my right foot around so I could stomp my heel on the back of his hand twice—once to break the bones and once to move the pieces around. With my foot still moving back, I pivoted on my knee and let all my weight flow into the tip of my right elbow. I crushed that into his ear. It sounded good.

The tension went out of his body. Maybe three seconds had passed since I got out of the tub. I roared something non-English into his pulpy ear. This was not MMA or anything I'd learned on Gil's mats; that muscle memory had been overruled by something that waited in the mud of my primordial soup until the dark waters got churned up enough. Now it was frolicking in the lather, and somebody was going to die.

I left him there and turned on Tezo.

He'd shoved the lid off and was trying to get his hand behind him to pull the revolver out of his belt, but he was on his side and slipped on the wet floor, pinning his arm beneath him. I closed in as fast as I could, and Tezo rolled onto his back to free his arm. He grabbed the gun, and my feet went out from under me. I tipped forward and landed with both my forearms across his right one, crushing it against the tiles.

Tezo hissed with pain and tried to punch me with his left. I ducked and let him crack his hand against the top of my head. Brought my right knee up to pin the gun hand and put all my weight on it, posturing over him with my left foot planted next to his face. He was jammed in the corner so there wasn't much room to work. He tried to push me off with his left so I pulled his arm straight and dislocated his elbow over my knee. It sounded like snapping a fistful of dry spaghetti.

When Tezo opened his mouth to scream, I hit him with a short left hook that bounced his head off the wall. Again. Again. His legs went stiff. He was looking at me but not on purpose. I bounced his head again, smiling at him until a voice of reason finally spoke up in my head and said I was going to break my hand, so I switched to elbows.

I slapped the gun across the floor and yanked Tezo out of the corner so I could get my knees into his armpits. I drove elbows into his temples and bounced them off his eye sockets until my shoulders began to burn.

I stood and tried to pick up the tub to drop on his face. When I couldn't lift it, I blamed my shirt. Halfway through getting the thing off, the heavy, wet material sticking to my back and bound up around my shoulders, I realized I was exhausted.

I let my shirt fall back down and sat on the edge of the tub. I wheezed air in and out through clenched teeth. I was spattered with blood, and spittle trailed down my chin. Compared to Tezo and Parasite, I looked like a Calvin Klein ad.

Tezo's face was gone. The parts were still there, but they were on the wrong side or upside down or only attached by blood and hair. The tattoos made less sense than before. He was breathing, but I think he regretted it. Parasite was still facedown, huffing into a pink puddle with his ass in the air. The needle punctures looked angry.

I checked my hands. They were scraped and bloody but intact. They were not shaking. I rinsed them off as much as possible in the tub. Most of the pit muck was gone from my thrashing in the water, but the stench was still on me. I'd need bleach or fire to get it off.

I felt my elbows; they'd be swollen from the collisions with Tezo's facial bones but no chips or nerve damage. I got to my feet and nothing gave out or protested. My breathing was close to normal. I tilted my head and tapped it with the heel of my hand to get some water out of my ear, and that was when I heard the music.

Jairo.

I cracked the bathroom door and put my eye to the opening. I could just see the top of Jairo's head in the pit, facing toward the bleachers. Good. At least he was on his feet again.

The shotgun kid was showing me his right profile, standing over Jairo with a sloppy grin on his face. Everyone else was still on the other side of the tarp. The kid loosed a stream of brown juice through his teeth that arced above the pit and dropped like a mortar shell behind Jairo. I didn't see him move or duck to avoid it. The kid laughed and took a step backward and started working his cheeks, constructing the next salvo.

The shotgun was on the lowest bleacher seat behind him. He'd see me before I could get to him or it. I thought about Tezo's gun and Parasite's black automatic. If the kid made me shoot, the whole gang would swarm in. Worse, the old women.

The kid threw both fists over his head and puffed his chest out—he must have hit the target—then grabbed his crotch and laughed and had to bend over to keep the vine of spit that fell out of his mouth from landing on his shirt.

I opened the door and started moving, my gaze on Jairo so I could give him the hush hush when he saw me.

Instead, he saw me, threw the bloody scrap of shirt

at the kid, swore, and ran to the side of the pit near the tarps. I almost called him a stupid motherfucker but realized he was getting the kid to turn his back on me completely. Jairo jumped and got his hands on the lip of the pit and pulled and kicked against the rotten wood for momentum.

The kid gaped at him for a beat and finally turned around for the shotgun.

Which I had in my hands.

He pulled a fish face and shiny brown spit welled from his mouth. He was just a kid, couldn't have been over seventeen.

I hit him in the throat with the bottom corner of the gun butt and let him deflate over the edge and down into the pit.

Jairo smiled over his shoulder at me and let himself fall back in. He winced and tried to see the hole near his neck, fresh blood oozing out.

I watched the tarp and said, "Get out of there before your back gets infected and falls off."

He slopped over to the kid.

I held the shotgun level on the tarp flap until the sounds of wet violence stopped in the pit; then I set the gun down and put the ladder in.

Jairo climbed up, and I pulled his good arm to help him with the last few steps. He was covered in blood and shit and mud and tobacco spit. For the first time, his bald head wasn't shining. He looked me up and down and asked, "How did you get so clean?"

We got into the bathroom and closed the door and put the bench against it for show. Jairo peered at Parasite and Tezo like they were part of a spoiled food exhibit and grimaced, but he seemed impressed.

I told him, "We have to clean that hole out."

He nodded and leaned over the tub while I ran cold water from the pipe over the bullet wound. The water had a rusty smell I hadn't noticed before and was much quieter outside the tub, but it was loud enough for me to watch the door in case I didn't hear the rabid mob burst in. I squeezed the flesh near Jairo's trapezius to flush the wound, and the water running off him turned from pink to red. He hissed and swore.

"That's going to hurt," I said. Blood kept slipping out of the raw groove in ribbons and the water didn't have any morphine in it, so I tore another scrap off my shirt, wrung it out under the water, and twisted the faucet shut.

Jairo pressed the new scrap over the wound, his eyes shut and his teeth showing.

"Good for now?"

"It's nothing."

Brazilians. I went around him and dragged Tezo farther out of the corner so I could get a good look at the glass cubes in the window frame; they were mortared together and caulked around the outer edge, but it was all old and cracked and crumbly.

I rammed a corner of the wire mesh lid into the glass. It chipped a cube and made a horrible sound, but it didn't have enough weight to do any real damage. I glanced around the room. The sinks were bolted to the wall. Tezo was too floppy to put through a window.

The tub.

"Help me tip this over."

"What about this?" He held Tezo's cell phone up.

"Too small."

"No, we call Kendall. Or Jake. We find out about Marcela first."

"The crowd could come in any second. We have to get out of here."

"No," Jairo said. "If they hurt her, we find out now. That way I can kill people here and not have to come back."

I started rocking the tub side to side. "Window first, then call."

"I'm calling," Jairo said.

I got the tub past its midpoint and dumped it over. Red water and trash and silt rushed around Tezo's body and Jairo's feet. He shuffled through it in an attempt to wash his shoes.

I reached for the phone and was more than mildly

surprised when he handed it to me. I put it to my ear and didn't hear anything. Checked the phone and saw no call had been made. "Liar," I said.

Jairo shrugged, then winced and swore at his shoulder.

I hit the down arrow to get to the call history and saw the letter *J* for the second most recent call: Jake. I scrolled past the most recent call and was about to dial out when I looked at the most recent call again.

The person Tezo had called to see if I was fighting and to bet on me to lose. The contact was saved as *BE*.

Banzai Eddie.

"Motherfucker," I said.

Marcela first. But I had to be sure. I called the BE contact.

Three rings. "This is Eddie." Lots of noise in the background, people talking and music blasting.

I went for deadpan psycho: "It's me."

"What's up, killer? Hey, I'm getting pulled five hundred ways right now. Can you talk to Benjamin?"

Benjamin, head of marketing for Warrior.

"I'll call you back," I said. Cut him off.

"Who you calling?" Jairo asked. "What about Marcela?"

"Right now," I said and called Jake.

He answered after the second ring. "Hey, how'd they do?"

"Better than expected," I said.

"Who's this?"

"Woody. Put Marcela on."

"Where's Tezo?"

"Lying at my feet with blood in his lungs. His face looks like a butcher's garbage can. Put her on." If Jake had a number for anyone else in the gang, he could hang up and call them. We'd be fucked. I heard talk and rustling on the other end.

Kendall said, "How you doing?"

"Is she okay?"

Jairo held still and dripped and listened.

"Who, Marcela? She's fine. Why?"

"Let me talk to her."

"What for? Hey, you ready for tonight?"

"Kendall."

He sighed. "Hold on." More rustling. I heard him ask someone, "Why's he so grumpy all the time?"

I recognized Marcela's breathing before she spoke. "Woody?"

Somebody took the bulldozer off my shoulders and cut the noose around my neck. I gave Jairo a thumbs-up. He crossed himself. "Are you okay?"

Marcela said, "Yes, we're at the place, the one—"

I heard a yell and the phone thumping around. I closed my eyes and held my breath.

I heard Kendall say, "What'd I tell you about

that? Now you don't get to watch this no more. Steve, change it back to ESPN." He returned to the phone, a little out of breath. "Goddamn. She's a sly one, huh?"

"Did you hurt her?"

"She's *fine*," Kendall said. "For now, anyways. You even gonna ask about Lance?"

"Fifteen minutes, wherever you say. We trade Marcela and Lance for Tezo."

"Tezo? Who gives a shit about him?"

"Why is Banzai Eddie in Tezo's phone?"

Silence. Then a clicking sound, like Kendall was doing something with his gum while he did some hard thinking. Then, "All right, son, listen. Up 'til now you've been in a game of checkers. You're about to fall onto a chessboard; you get what I'm saying?"

"No."

"See, that's why I think it's best you sit tight and let this play out the way it's supposed to."

"Which is?"

"Now that you're all *informed*, I guess that's for you and Eddie to discuss," Kendall said.

"So he and I will discuss it. Let Marcela and Lance go."

"Sorry. They're my queen and king on the board. Well, queen and pawn maybe."

"Our deal is still on. I knock Burbank out, and they come back safe."

He chuckled. "You just go out there and do your best."

"What the hell does that mean?"

"No time, boy. Your first Pay-Per-View broadcast just started. Damn, there's your face! You look sweaty. Okay, gotta go. See you on live TV in, what, maybe an hour or two?" He hung up.

I looked at the time display on the phone: 7:05. "*Motherfucker.*"

The tub went through the glass cubes on the first try with me on one side and Jairo on the other. The back feet got hung up on the sill so I tipped it out upside down. We both scrambled out onto the cracked asphalt. I filled my lungs with street exhaust and stale grease from a nearby restaurant and almost cried from the euphoria.

I hurried to the front corner of the building and looked around. The parking lot was full of chrome and tinted windows, probably ten cars and trucks in all. Someone had ridden a chopped Schwinn and left it leaning against the front of my truck. There was a narrow path from us to the truck, bordered on the left by the garage doors that would never open again and three of the parked cars on the right. It looked wide enough to get the truck through, but I was in a glass-half-full kind of mood.

I didn't see anyone milling around the parking lot while they waited for me to return to the pit, but the tinted windows on the cars could have hidden an army. I thought about the guns lying inside on the tile floor. The drivers zipping past would keep going if they saw a group of guys yelling at each other in the parking lot; they'd drive into poles and buildings and call the cops if they saw guns. I said to Jairo, "Get ready."

We started moving. I dug into my wet pocket and pulled out my key fob and punched the unlock button. The truck's hazard lights blinked once and the horn bleated. Nobody opened a car door or came out of the building.

Jairo grabbed the Schwinn and sent it rolling into the passenger door of a lowered Impala.

I winced and waited for the alarm to start wailing. Nothing.

We got in the truck and squeezed through the narrow gap between the cars and building and shot past the corner. I dropped off the curb into the street and floored it and checked the rearview mirror. The smashed window gaped like a ragged wound, and I waited for Tezo's mangled face to pop up in it, but it never did.

CHAPTER 15

I turned left on Maryland Parkway, a block before the
Strip. This time of night on a Saturday, Strip traffic would
be slower than amputee bingo. I popped the console
open and got my phone out—seventeen missed calls,
all from Gil.

Jairo peered into the console and took out a fistful of drive-through napkins, dropped the shirt scrap
onto the floor mat with a splash, and pressed the
whole stack against the bullet wound.

I scrolled to Gil and made the call.

"Jesus, Woody, where the hell are you?"

"We're on the way, ten minutes, maybe fifteen."
I could hear noise around him, people talking and
laughing and some smacking that was probably someone hitting focus mitts to warm up.

He must have moved or turned because the sound

faded. He said, "Did you find her?"

"No."

"Shit, okay. Well, you gotta get here as soon as you can. The doctor needs to check you out before the fight or else you forfeit, and Eddie's hollering about how you won't get a job fighting colds in this town if you don't walk through the door five minutes ago. It's fucked up, but he seems pretty anxious to pull the plug on the main event."

He was talking fast and I was driving fast; I wanted to tell him to grab Eddie and choke him until I got there. It took me a few seconds to catch up to what he'd said. "Forfeit?"

"Disqualified for a failed physical."

"Christ, can't they stall?"

"What's happening?" Jairo asked.

Gil said, "Why would he do us any favors? You know he wants Burbank to win anyway."

"Yeah, about that . . ." I came up on a yellow light on Sahara and watched it change to red and saw the rims of the crossing cars start to spin and blew through the intersection. Horns protested into my exhaust. "Eddie's into something with Kendall."

"What?"

"I don't know any details, but he's got something to do with Kendall grabbing Marcela."

Jairo crushed my right forearm, letting me know

I hadn't mentioned that to him yet.

Gil said, "Are you sure?"

"Long story, but yeah. If he comes close, stuff his ass in a closet until we get there. I got some blanks he needs to fill in."

"Where are you?"

"Passing the country club near Desert Inn."

"Fuck, hurry."

"I know." I had to brake for a car turning right and almost clipped the rear bumper cranking around and pushing my speed up.

"Is Jairo with you?"

"Yeah, right here."

"Is everyone okay?"

"More or less." Probably better to let Gil see Jairo's wound than mention he'd been slightly shot.

Gil said, "I got Javier and Edson here with me; they're about ready to chew through the walls. Where have you guys been?"

"Man, I don't even know where to start. I thought we were close to her, but things got out of hand."

"Jesus. What is this? How did this happen?"

"I know. It's bad. I gotta go. I'm at Flamingo and it's snarled up." I shut the phone, dropped it in the cup holder and turned right on red, despite the traffic turning left from the northbound lanes.

Jairo held tight and said, "What's going on?"

I bobbed and weaved through traffic and told him what I knew. That took seven seconds. Then I told him what I was pretty damn sure about. Ten minutes into it we skidded to a stop in the service area behind the Golden Pantheon Casino.

A guy in a black security coat tried to intercept us halfway to the door. "Slow down. You got a pass to park there?"

We swept past him on either side, and he went for Jairo's sleeve before seeing what was smeared on it. "All right, hey—"

"Take it up with Eddie," I said.

He started talking into a radio as Jairo and I went through a big metal door into the service corridor that ran beneath the arena. I looked left and saw signs for the casino and hotel so I turned right and went blind.

A cameraman stuck a white light into my face and started walking backward as I stumbled toward him.

Jairo put one hand up to shield his eyes and tried to grab the camera with the other.

"Don't do that," the cameraman said. It wasn't the same guy who'd interviewed me and Gil at the gym.

"Which way to the prep rooms?" I asked. I still couldn't see anything, but I wanted to at least be fumbling in the right direction.

The cameraman said, "Goddamn, what've you

two been doing? Wrestling pigs?"

"Which way?"

"Behind me. Can you walk slower?"

I shielded my eyes and looked around him and noticed a group of suits farther down the corridor. "Eddie."

The cameraman scurried backward and pivoted to his right to capture everyone in the shot.

My eyes worked again, and I saw Banzai Eddie staring at me. If Kendall had called and warned him that I knew he was involved with Marcela somehow, he'd run. Maybe trip Benjamin and leave him behind to get more time. Instead, he dismissed the suits except for Benjamin and the two of them walked toward us.

I said to Jairo, "Don't do anything yet."

When Eddie was close he glanced at the cameraman. "There's no sound on that, right?"

"Just pictures."

Eddie turned on me, all smiles and shoulder claps, but his voice came through his teeth in a hiss. "Brah, what the fuck? You think I need this? You think I need *you*?" He used a handshake to pull me next to him and spun his body so we were side by side walking down the corridor, the cameraman in front of us with the spotlight in my eyes.

Behind us, I heard Benjamin ask Jairo, "What's that smell? Is that you? Is that *blood*?"

I looked at Eddie like I was going to eat his face.

He pointed at the camera and said, "Don't give me that look. This is piped onto the big screens, so fucking behave yourself. Listen."

The sound of the crowd welled and rolled down the corridor from somewhere ahead. The ceiling shook with stomping feet and heavy bass.

"Every time we show you or Burbank the place goes ape shit. You know how hard it was to put this together? Any idea? And you come strolling in here at seven goddamn forty-five? All dirty and *moist*? I got a long memory, and I hold grudges like they're fucking stock in Google."

"That's true," Benjamin said from behind me. "You better listen."

"You remember where you were two days ago?" Eddie said. "I can make that seem like a vacation."

Eddie jabbered away. I blocked him out to keep from committing murder on live TV. I tried to look past the camera's spotlight. The corridor made a circle around the perimeter of the arena, and I could see only forty yards ahead before the curve cut my line of sight. I scanned the sparse security guys and entourages but didn't see Gil.

Eddie was saying something about validating his concerns. We passed two closed doors; there were pieces of paper taped up with names of fighters written in black marker. I heard mitt work and music coming through the doors. The next door was open and the prep room was quiet; it belonged to one of the guys out in the cage.

The camera light went off. "Thanks, Mr. Takanori. Got it." The cameraman spun and hustled away.

Eddie jabbed a finger at the floor. "You want to disrespect me? Here's what happens—"

Enough of that shit. I grabbed him by the back of his belt and his blue silk tie and carried him through the door. Straight across from the doorway was a low leather couch. I turned Eddie horizontal and heaved him into the cushions. He bounced off and landed on the floor and rolled. I stopped him faceup by putting my foot on his throat.

The door closed. I looked back. Jairo had Benjamin in a one-armed rear naked choke; the other arm was holding the napkins, which sagged with blood. Benjamin kicked and pulled on Jairo's arm with everything he had.

Jairo locked the door with his free hand and nodded at me. "Take your time."

I looked down. "Where's Marcela?"

"Get the fuck off me!" Eddie thrashed and tried to kick me.

I caught his foot near my waist and levered it toward his head. His leg was short and inflexible. "Where is she?"

"I can't *breathe*."

"I'm not even putting weight on you."

Eddie started to gurgle.

"Jesus." I took my foot off his throat. He gasped like a man saved from drowning. I dropped down and put a knee in his belly. He grunted and tried to sit up. I got a handful of his faux hawk and kept him down. Put my face a few inches from his.

Eddie licked his lips. "I'm in pain," he said. Like he was surprised at how it felt.

"Where is she?"

He brought his hands up to hit or push me, then folded them on his chest and was ready to have a conversation. "I don't know who you're talking about."

"Kendall took her last night. Where?"

Eddie's eyes popped. "How do you know Kendall?"

"You first."

"Shit. Ah, can you get off me? Can I just sit down on the couch?"

"I'm comfortable like this."

He took a breath. "I owed some people money. A lot of money. I knew Kendall from other transactions, and he offered to buy the debt. Pay it off for me. In return, he wanted a sure thing on a big fight, something he could cash in on through his sports book."

Eddie licked his lips again. "That sure thing is you."

I heard a thump behind me. Turned and saw Benjamin in a heap on the floor, snoring softly.

Jairo shrugged. "He wouldn't stay still."

I turned back to Eddie. "How am I a sure thing to win?"

Eddie frowned. "Win?"

"Kendall bet on me to knock Burbank out."

"No, he didn't."

"He took Marcela and Lance hostage last night and said if I didn't win by knockout they were both dead."

Eddie gaped. "He did *what*? First of all, I don't know any Marcela. Second—"

"But you know Lance?"

"Skinny guy, kind of greasy?"

"That's him."

"He works for Kendall."

I said, "As in, places bets through him?"

"As in, is on his payroll."

I had let Lance fool me. I wanted to kick myself in the face. If I thought about it too long I'd actually try. "Go on."

Eddie said, "I have no idea why Kendall would seek you out, let alone say he bet on you to win." He blinked a few times. "Actually, I do know. He's a crazy fucking cowboy lunatic. And he's going to get us all killed. Dammit. Why did I let him in on this?"

It was rhetorical, but I wanted the answer. "Why did you?"

"I told you, he offered to buy my debt."

"How'd you fuck up so bad a guy like Kendall was your bailout?"

"Hey, man," Eddie said, "everybody owes somebody."

"So you'd rather owe him than . . . who?"

"Some bad folks. You don't know them."

"Tezo?" I asked.

Eddie looked at me like I was levitating. "Tezo? How the fuck—no, not him, but how do you know Tezo?"

"Can you smell me?"

"Uh, yeah."

"If that doesn't explain it, you're lucky," I said. Eddie didn't mention Tezo had also bet on me to lose. One thing at a time. "Who did you owe?"

Eddie closed his eyes. "The Yakuza."

Jairo gave a low whistle at the door. He was impressed, which impressed me. Japan and Brazil are closely connected in the fighting world, and that means money. And money means organized crime. The Arcoverdes had dealt with the Yakuza before, and every time Edson started talking about it, Javier and Jairo shut him down.

I said, "All right, I can see why you'd rather owe Kendall than the Yakuza. But there had to be other options."

"I can't believe I'm getting lectured by the fucking Swamp Thing."

I thumped his head against the floor. Lightly. Sort

of. "I'm not lecturing you; I'm trying to figure out how this fits together so I can take it apart. Why Kendall?"

Eddie let out a breath. "Because guys like him, they don't last. He doesn't have any discipline. He does shit for the thrill, not the profit. He's lasted longer than anyone thought, but he's going to end up in a hole in the desert or thrown off the Hoover Dam eventually."

"Hopefully before you have to pay him back."

Eddie shrugged.

I didn't know what to say or do. I took some weight off Eddie, but he didn't try to squirm away.

He said, "Listen, man, whatever Kendall's been up to, it's all him. Yeah, I put you in this fight hoping—shit, *knowing*—you'll lose, but kidnapping? Murder? That's not my style. I'm all business."

"Funny, that's what Kendall said."

"Yeah, well, his business is being crazy. Mine isn't."

"Call him."

Eddie fished his phone out. "Can I sit up?"

"No."

He held the phone in front of his face and found Kendall's number. Cleared his throat and sniffed a few times while it rang. And rang. "No answer."

I took the phone and waited for it to go to voice mail. It didn't. Just kept ringing. I closed the phone and gave it back to Eddie. Overall, I believed him. He screamed a little when I hauled him upright and sat him on the couch, but he recovered quickly to smooth his tie and hair and watch me pace.

"So he bet on me to lose?"

"Just like everybody else," Eddie said. "But a lot more than most."

"But why all this? Why the ruse with Lance, why Marcela, and why tell me to win by KO or they're dead?"

Eddie crossed his legs. "My guess? Knowing Kendall, he just wants to watch you freak out. He wants to put as much pressure on you as possible, and when you fail, he wants to see you crack."

I couldn't get my head around it. "How is this a sure thing? I'm not taking a dive. This isn't a fixed fight."

"As close as I can get. This isn't Japan. If I tried to fix a fight at this level here, too many people would sniff it out."

"What if I win?"

Eddie looked sad for me. "Brah, come on. You're going to get manhandled out there. We did our best to hype it up as a grudge match, but everyone knows you don't stand a chance."

I stopped pacing. Eddie tried to hide beneath the couch cushions, but I wasn't focused on him. "Will he really kill her?"

Jairo stepped away from the door to listen.

"No doubt," Eddie said.

We put Benjamin on the couch and smacked him around until he woke.

"He'll have a headache," Jairo told Eddie. "Give him ice water and some aspirin."

Eddie looked skeptical of Benjamin in general. "Yeah."

The door opened, and one of the undercard fighters, a lightweight kid named Piper, jumped into the room with soggy tape trailing from his hands. He and his cornermen were hopping up and down and whooping and beating their chests. Piper saw Eddie and froze. "Oh, shit. Hey, Mr. Takanori."

"Eddie, please. And congrats. Great fight."

"Thanks, thanks." Piper looked at our faces and landed back on Eddie's. "Dude, have you been crying?"

"No. Hey, we have to run, but Benjamin here needs your couch for a few. Just ignore him."

"No problem," Piper said. To me: "Good luck out there."

"Thanks. And congratulations."

"Hell yeah."

Jairo and I followed Eddie out the door.

Behind me Piper asked, "Who shit their pants in here?"

Eddie pulled us farther down the hall toward what I hoped was our prep room. People wanted to stop Eddie but resisted the urge when they saw and smelled Jairo. I still stank, but he had wavy lines coming off him. We came to a closed door with my name taped to it.

Eddie faced me and said, "Look, just give a good show. There's no reason to embarrass yourself."

"You never answered my question. What happens to Marcela if I win?"

"Man, with Kendall, I have no idea."

"He told me, win or she's dead. You say if I win, his bet goes to shit and she's dead. Which one of us is right?"

"Which one involves more money?"

"So she's gone either way."

"I didn't want to say it."

Jairo kicked a rack of folding chairs. Parts tinkled onto the concrete floor.

I tried to think it through, find a gap I could get my fingers into and pry.

"I gotta go," Eddie said.

"Just hold on."

"Dude, there *is* a live show going on right now."

"Be quiet and hold still, or I'll make you eat your hair."

"Okay. Jesus."

There had to be a gap. The mess with Chops and Tezo was connected to Kendall, but it was a dead end. Eddie owed Kendall, so he didn't have any leverage.

But like Eddie said, everybody owes somebody. "Did Kendall pay off all your debt?"

Eddie shrugged. "I didn't ask. All I know is, I don't have to wince when I start my car anymore."

"Call somebody in the Yakuza. Somebody who'll talk."

"About what?"

"Kendall and whatever deal he worked out with them."

"Why?"

I put my nose in his eye. "Just get your goddamn phone out. And first thing, ask if Kendall's there watching the fights. Maybe these guys are all pals now."

Eddie looked like he regretted life. He got his phone going and walked a few yards away and stuck a finger in his ear.

I asked Jairo, "You want to go in the room and get everyone caught up?"

"I want to choke this little shit and make him cry some more." Jairo grabbed the knob.

"Two knocks if that needs to happen. Keep Gil in there, will you? If it's not too late, I don't want Eddie holding any grudges against him."

Jairo nodded and went in. I heard rapid-fire Portuguese before the door closed.

Eddie put his phone in his pocket and walked over. "My guy is pretty low on the org chart—nobody higher up bothers to talk to me anymore—but he said Kendall didn't offer cash. He offered a payoff, something big. And everyone is *very* interested in your fight."

"Was Kendall there?"

"He said no. Why?"

"Because if he was I'd say fuck all you and your bets and go get Marcela."

"Mm-hmm. That seems unlikely."

"Maybe to you. So, what, Kendall rolled your deal over to them? Told them to bet big on me to lose?"

"Good a guess as any," Eddie said. "Or put his own money down, with some of the winnings going to them."

"Why didn't you make them the same offer?"

"Man, I do that, they'll want a say in everything. Pretty soon we'd have a straight-up judo guy who doesn't speak a lick of English wearing the heavyweight belt." He shook his head. "No, I gotta have a buffer between them and the sport. Even if it's an asshole like Kendall."

I chewed on it all until Eddie said, "Seriously, dude, I have to go. Are we good?"

I gave him a look that made his eyelashes curl.

"Okay, no, then. I'll come see you after the fight. We'll get this figured out, yeah?" He was twenty feet away with his back to me by the time he was done talking. Suits and production staff swarmed him, and he was gone.

I was alone.

I took a breath. When you game-plan for a fight, there are two ways to go. One way is to play into your opponent's style and try to beat him at his own game. If he's a puncher, punch harder and faster. Grappler, take him down and tear him apart. It works sometimes. Other times, people wonder what the hell you were thinking on the way to getting knocked or choked out.

The other way is to know his plan and do everything you can to turn it upside down and inside out from the beginning. Get him off balance, lost. Throw his shit out the window. Make him think about what to do next while you split his face open and crack his ribs.

Now I knew Kendall's plan: he needed me to lose.

Was counting on it.

I opened the door and Gil was right there. "Woody, Jesus, we—what're you smiling about?"

"I want to get in a fight."

CHAPTER 16

Gil closed the door behind me. A shirtless Jairo was speaking in Portuguese, his left hand flying all over the place miming assault rifles and bad driving while Javier and Edson tried to hold him still so they could poke at his wound.

There was a TV on a rolling cart showing the live broadcast. The camera zoomed in on Eddie glad-handing on the way to his seat. Somewhere between the hallway and there he'd changed suit coats.

Gil said, "You two smell like shit farmers. Did he get shot?"

"Yeah, listen. I just talked to Eddie. He and Kendall—"

"Does it change the game plan?"

"No. Wait, kind of. I don't have to win by knock-out anymore."

"No shit? So now you can use your stellar jiu jit-su to win. Tell me the rest later. Get your ass in the shower; I'll go find the doctor to clear you. Hey." Gil pulled me around to face him. "Where you at?"

"I'm here."

"Shaky?"

"No."

"You can't take her in there with you. Remember what we drilled, what we worked on. You stop to think about it, it's already over."

I nodded.

"Showers are through there."

I took as much time as I could in the hottest water I could stand. The blood came off easy, but I had to spend some time on my feet getting rid of the grime from the pit. I felt pretty good. Great, in fact. With no one pointing a gun at me or trying to drown me, I had time to think about what I had to do: destroy Burbank.

After the weigh-ins, the Burbank fight had become personal. All the smack talk and will-imposing aside, he and I truly did not like each other. But with everything that had happened since then, the grudge with Burbank seemed about as personal as automated phone sex.

Fine by me. It's hard to fight professionally and personally at the same time. It clouds things, makes you slow. Now there was no more confusion about who bet on what and why. Everything was condensed to what happened in the cage, where I lived. It was time to punch the clock and do my job.

That simple.

Right. Like touching the back of my head with my foot.

I toweled off and got into my cup and shorts, which still smelled like fabric softener, so I spent a few precious moments with them pressed against my face to combat the stench Tezo's pit had lodged in my palette.

Edson poked his head around the corner and caught me inhaling. He looked concerned. I nodded at him and he vanished.

Jairo walked in a few seconds later for his turn in the shower carrying rolls of gauze and tape and a tube of antiseptic ointment. "If Eddie is right, if it doesn't matter what you do in the fight—"

"It matters."

"How?"

"Kendall said something to me about chess. This whole thing with Eddie and the Yakuza—the bets and debts, his entire strategy to come out on top—depends on me losing. If I lose the fight, he's free to do whatever he wants. And you and I know that means she's gone. If I win, the only piece he has left is Marcela, and he can't throw that away. She'll be his insurance."

Jairo didn't like it. "I don't like it."

"It's the best we got."

"What if you're wrong?"

"I'm not."

"How do you know?" he asked.

"Because I can't be."

The doctor was waiting for me in the prep room. He was a young, skinny guy, looked like he did a lot of running. He listened to my heart and lungs and went through the usual stuff, making sure I could see and hear and didn't have any preexisting cuts or broken bones. He took a long look at my lumpy eyebrows and leaned in close to frown at some scrapes on my knuckles. I held my breath.

"These look like they're on their way to infection. Hit them with some alcohol and ointment after the fight." He told me good luck and had me sign something and took off.

Gil rooted around in his giant bag and came out with my gloves and some focus mitts. "Glove up. Let's get you loose."

I shook my arms and rolled my head. "I'm already loose."

"Shut up and get over here."

I strapped the gloves on and followed him over to the mats.

He clapped the mitts together and said, "One-two, easy to start."

I relaxed into my stance and let the right jab out and the left cross follow.

"Nice, sharp," Gil said. "Javier, get warm. We're gonna do some sprawls after this. Woody, keep your chin down." He swatted at my head with the left mitt to prove his point. "Get behind that shoulder."

I knew what he was doing and it worked. He wanted to keep me focused on the technique and let muscle memory run the show, get me out of my head and live in my hands for a while. My body was one piece, the punches flowing all the way up from my toes. Good rhythm, power and snap.

We added a knee at the end of the one-two— jab-cross and grab the crown of his head in the Thai clinch and drive the knee into his belly. Keep him in the clinch and sneak some elbows across his face. Between combos Gil looped some half-speed strikes at me with the pads. I covered up and countered three times faster.

"Good," Gil said. "Let's work some ground. Bait the powerbomb, just like we worked on. If they come back here with a camera, you get up quick and just shadowbox. No reason to show Burbank anything. Javier, you ready?"

"Yes," Javier said. He had his shirt and shoes off

and walked over to the mats stretching his wrists and fingers. Edson guided Jairo into the room with a towel around his waist and a fresh white rectangular bandage taped from his collarbone to the top of his shoulder blade.

"How is it?" I asked.

"Not bad. It has a pain rhythm to my heartbeat."

Gil pointed at the giant bag. "I got Advil and some of your T-shirts and some warm-up pants that might fit. You're gonna have to free ball it."

"Lucky pants." Jairo got dressed while he and Edson talked in low voices near the TV. It showed an empty cage and a rowdy crowd under spinning colored lights.

"All right," Gil said, "Woody, you just got taken down and Burbank here has side mount, so let's work on what we drilled yesterday."

I laid down on my back with my knees up, and Javier dropped next to me and put his chest across mine with his head over my left arm.

Gil said, "Slow now, slow. Nobody's getting hurt on fight day. Woody, get that knee through."

We worked it until someone rapped on the door. It opened and a guy wearing a headset ducked in. "Twenty minutes. You ready?"

"Good to go," Gil said.

The headset vanished and Hollywood Andersen, one of the top two cutmen in combat sports, floated in. He was near sixty and had worked on the prettiest faces in boxing and MMA and kept them that way. He smiled and pointed to the couch.

The brothers cleared out and I sat down.

Hollywood spun a metal folding chair backward in front of the couch and sat down with his tackle box between his feet. He peered at my lumpy eyebrows while he unwrapped a new roll of gauze. "No offense, but I don't want to spend all night trying to keep your face from falling apart."

"How is that offensive?"

A state inspector came in and closed the door behind him. He nodded to everyone and stood behind Hollywood to make sure he didn't include any engine blocks or kryptonite in my wraps.

Hollywood said, "Just try to keep that meat loaf you call a forehead out of the way of his fists, all right?"

"There goes the game plan."

He laughed and pulled a strip of tape off the roll. "All right, all right, what's it gonna be? The knockout wrap or the tapout wrap?"

I stuck out my left hand. "Knockout."

Hollywood wove a tapestry of tape and gauze over and through my knuckles, across the back of my hands, around my wrists. Grapplers and jiu jitsu guys usually like a looser, lighter wrap so they can grip and hold and squeeze; strikers like it tight and hard. When he was done, it felt like I had wrecking balls hanging off my arms.

The state inspector approved and signed Hollywood's work. Hollywood should have autographed them too; Michelangelo would have admired the sculptures.

Gil got my fighting gloves on, and we taped them down, and the inspector liked that too. I stepped into my sandals and pulled my Arcoverde T-shirt with all the sponsors on it over my head, and things started happening fast.

The guy with the headset jumped through the doorway and said, "Ready? Ready? Come on."

Gil and the Arcoverdes and I followed him into the hallway where a camera crew waited. Six burly security guards in slacks and maroon blazers filled in around us.

"Right here," the headset said, then, "No, come with me."

He led us toward a black curtain and a wave of sound that would make a riot cop ditch the Taser and call in the tanks.

The headset stopped us about thirty yards from the curtain and said, "Wait for my signal; we want to get you walking to the music."

I asked Gil, "What'd you pick?"

The speakers answered: "Superbeast" by Rob

Zombie. I could barely hear it over the crowd. Colored lights and strobes sliced through a gap in the curtain. Gil stayed close and talked to me. I didn't really listen, but it was familiar and solid. Jairo offered me water. I shook my head. He worked his fingers into my neck and shoulders.

The headset said, "Yeah? . . . Okay, let's go!"

Someone pulled the curtain aside, and the cameraman backed through the opening with his lens pointed at me. I walked through and looked up. At first all I could see was a huge, boiling mass of arms in the air, waving, shaking fists, throwing middle fingers and devil horns, but mostly clutching cups of beer.

The arms gave way to faces pulled into all sorts of arrangements, none of them pleasant. Anyone rooting for me was vastly outnumbered, and I hoped they had the good sense to either keep quiet or fake it. Burbank's fans had been lathering up since the weigh-ins and wanted blood, and if I didn't give them some, they'd settle for anything red and warm.

"Let's move!" the headset said.

The place got louder. Canada braced for an earthquake. The lights popped and blazed. Gil yelled something in my ear, but I couldn't hear him. He pointed straight ahead. Past the camera, past the faces leering into the corridor to taunt me or cheer me, past it all, I saw the cage.

My oasis.

I took a step toward it. Another. The crowd screamed toward liftoff.

By the third step I was running. I blew past the cameraman and left the security guards behind. Gil and Jairo and the others almost kept up, but I was going home and couldn't get there fast enough.

I made it through the gauntlet of hands and ran into Hollywood again at the bottom of the steps to the cage door. I pulled my shirt off and kicked my sandals somewhere.

Hollywood grabbed my shoulders and held me still. "Easy, son, it'll still be there in a minute." He had a gob of Vaseline waiting on the back of his latex glove and pulled half of it off, looked at the flesh and scar tissue around my eyes, and went back for the rest. He smeared it across my forehead and around my orbital bones and down my cheeks, a thin barrier that would hopefully reduce the friction between my face and Burbank's gloves and keep me from getting cut right away.

As for the elbows and knees, well, I'd just have to block those with the back of my head instead of the front.

"Go get 'em," Hollywood said.

I turned and Gil and Jairo were there.

Gil hugged me and said, "You know what to do."

He stuck my mouthguard in and gave me a sip of water.

I clamped down and liked the pressure in my jaw.

Jairo kissed me on the cheek and hugged me. "Marcela, she's smarter than all of us, and she's not worried. Okay?"

I nodded.

"So don't worry. Just kill him."

I turned toward the steps. I showed one of the Warrior referees my mouthguard and rapped my cup, and he checked my hair and skin for grease.

"Clear for takeoff," he said.

I ran up the steps.

CHAPTER 17

I stood in my corner and faced the fence during Burbank's entrance, focused in on Gil and Jairo and whatever they had to say that I could hear over the crowd and music. The music cut off and I could hear Gil better. Then Jim Lincoln, the Warrior announcer, took the center of the cage and started his roll on the microphone and everybody shut up.

"Ladies and gentlemen," Lincoln said, sounding like a movie preview, "this is the co-main event of the evening, pitting two honorable warriors against one another in a battle of heavyweights."

I turned around and saw Burbank for the first time since the weigh-in. He only took up half the cage and looked twice as big as when we'd fought three years earlier. He smiled at me. His mouthpiece had something printed on it, but I couldn't tell what. That was odd, because his mouth looked big enough to hide a van.

I checked out the arena. The only people sitting down were the cage-side officials and commentators. Davie Benton was there in a headset, grinning and talking and moving his hands like he was bending something in half while the play-by-play guy, Ken Vincent, nodded.

The biggest house I'd fought in before tonight held five thousand people. The Golden Pantheon could hold five times that, and people were standing in the aisles and blocking fire escapes. I couldn't even see the upper tier of seats.

"Knock that off," Gil said behind me.

I came back down to the cage and the man across from me.

Lincoln had been working up to a crescendo, and I didn't know he was talking about me until he pointed his note card my way and said, "The only fighter to defeat Junior Burbank: Aaron . . . Woodshed . . . Wallace!"

The crowd treated me like I'd canceled weekends. I nodded at them.

Lincoln must have decided I wasn't going to be carried outside and thrown off a bridge. "And in the red corner, standing at a massive six feet six inches, bringing a ten and one record into the rematch. Warrior fans, here is Junior . . . Burbank!"

Jesus might have gotten more noise, but only if he came out dancing. Burbank held his arms out and turned in a slow circle, his head back and eyes closed to take it all in. He stopped while he was facing me and opened his eyes and smiled again.

The crowd ate it up like free steak.

Lincoln said, "The referee for this matchup is Mel Wilkins."

Wilkins walked to the center of the cage, and Lincoln ducked behind him so he could get the microphone under his chin. Wilkins waved me and Burbank toward the center.

I walked to him and tried not to let Burbank's stomp across the canvas affect my balance.

Burbank came more than halfway across and pushed against Wilkins's outstretched arm. Wilkins tried to move him and should have practiced by knocking mountains over with a straw. He said something about a clean fight and obeying his commands at all times.

I worked my mouthpiece and nodded and didn't blink.

Burbank tipped his head toward mine until our foreheads touched. He pushed. I pushed back. Wilkins tried to pry us apart. I smiled at Burbank. I was going to eat his head.

He smiled, and I could read his mouthpiece:

Marcela.

Everything stopped—heart, lungs, brain. Drops of sweat halted halfway down my face and waited.

Burbank laughed at the look on my face.

Wilkins said, "Now touch gloves, and let's have a good fight."

I couldn't raise my gloves, but it didn't matter.

Burbank strolled to his corner while the crowd screamed its throat raw.

I backed into my corner and heard Gil over my shoulder: "He's gonna come out fast. Weather the storm and wear him out. Lateral movement. He'll make a mistake before you do. Make him pay for it."

I tried to tell him about the mouthpiece but couldn't find the air.

Wilkins pointed at me. "Fighter, are you ready?"

For the first time in my professional career, I wasn't sure. But I nodded.

He pointed at Burbank. "Are you ready?"

Burbank roared.

"Fight!" Wilkins moved out of the way, and someone shot a torpedo at me from the other side of the cage.

Burbank ran across the canvas and got to me before I could take three steps. He faked an overhand right and shot in for an immediate double-leg takedown. I sprawled and pushed him toward the canvas, but he drove forward and backed me into the cage and tried to get his long arms behind my thighs. I kept my legs straight and punched him in the back a few times. It would have been a good way to crack open some oysters or walnuts.

My breathing was all over the place. My heart rate couldn't decide on a tempo so it cycled from jackrabbit to hummingbird.

Burbank tried to pull my legs in again, but I fought it so he settled for picking me up. The world tilted and spun, and I clamped my hands around his head to keep him from whipping me onto the canvas. I still landed on the back of my head and shoulder blades. I went loose and let the impact flow through me. My left knee made a cameo near my face and went back where it belonged.

Burbank knelt in my open guard and tried to smash my face with a hammerfist. I got my hips up and extended away so his hand only caved my chest in. I put my right foot on his shoulder but couldn't move him. He was bolted to the floor. He brushed my foot to his right and scrambled into side mount, but I rolled to my left away from him and squirted out of his paws and got back to my feet. He stayed on one knee for a moment and smiled, showing a glimpse of her name, before he rushed me again.

The crowd sounded like it was pressed against the

cage. I could feel its breath on my back. I moved to my right and sent a jab out that hit nothing.

Burbank squared up with me and stalked forward, following me around the perimeter of the cage. He planted his left foot, and I flashed a low kick into the inside of his knee. It cracked home and felt good, but he didn't seem to notice.

I moved back, and he faked another overhand right and darted in with a takedown attempt. I jumped away and stiff-armed his head and hit him in the ear with a glancing shot. He got up and plowed forward again.

I retreated.

I was thinking way too much. About Kendall, Big Jake, Tezo, and how they were connected to Burbank— the monster I was locked in a cage with and the only person I should have been thinking about.

No, fuck that. I shouldn't have been thinking at all.

Acting and reacting.

Fighting.

Despite Gil's best efforts, my main strategy is I can take more punishment than the other guy. I'll stand in the pocket and throw punches and knees and elbows and come out on top because I hit harder and can take a harder punch.

Burbank was different. I couldn't plant my feet to throw any power punches, or he'd take me down. I couldn't kick above the legs, or he'd take me down. I had the powerbomb bait if it did go to the ground, but our brief meeting down there had me concerned. Burbank was immovable, and the one punch he'd hit me with so far felt like a traffic accident. If he got me down and kept me there, I was done.

He tried a left-right combo and shot for the double. I slipped the left, blocked the right and got knocked sideways, and danced away from the takedown.

The crowd despised me. I was denying their gladiator his right to competition. They wanted us to stand and bang until he caught me and I went down so he could pounce and tenderize my head until the ref jumped in.

I didn't like it, either. I wasn't used to moving backward. But standing in the pocket with his power was too risky, too easy for a flash knockout from something I didn't see coming. He followed me and tried the one-two combo again. He grimaced, and I saw Marcela's name. He drove forward after the combo, and I sprawled for the ensuing takedown, but it didn't come.

A left hook came instead.

A fist big enough to plug a pool drain caught me on the side of the head, and everything went black.

The sounds returned first.

A fuzzy roar that started to pull apart into distinct voices and impacts. I heard Gil screaming and Wilkins, the ref, telling someone he should defend himself. I tried to find who he was talking to, but my head wouldn't stay where I wanted it to; it kept bouncing up and down and side to side.

I looked straight up and saw Burbank above me, smashing his fists into my face. I had my hands behind his head and was trying to bring him closer to keep him from getting full power behind the punches. He was in my closed guard, between my legs with my ankles crossed behind his back.

I had no idea how long this had been going on or how we'd arrived here.

Burbank hit me again, and Wilkins said, "Cover up, fighter. Do something or it's over."

I couldn't see out of my right eye. I tried to open it and everything was red and it wouldn't stay open. I was cut. Burbank hammered at that eye and pushed my head to the left to get the blood to flow into it. I patted him on the head and face with my fist to show Wilkins I was still in it.

I had to get on my feet. I pulled my legs up into a high guard to coax Burbank into the powerbomb. He pushed them back down and dropped an anvil onto my stomach and smacked me in the face with a house.

Wilkins leaned over me and asked, "Can you see?"

I didn't answer him. I was busy.

"Can you see? I'll stop the fight if you can't see."

"I can see. I'm fine," I said.

Burbank laughed and punched my rib cage sideways. I pulled high guard again, and Burbank leaned back and got one foot underneath him. He was going to try to pick me up and drop me on my head, and I'd let my legs fall and be on my feet.

No.

He scooped his left arm under my right leg and pried it off and spun me on my back and dived into side mount. Where he could do some real damage. He put his left elbow over my eye and ground it in to make sure the gash didn't close. He kneed me in the ribs and punched me in the guts. I laid there and listened to the crowd howl and the sound of my body getting beaten and took it.

I was still waiting for everything to slow down like it always did when I fought. When I could see things coming and predict and react and counter without thinking. I was still waiting when the bell rang to end the first round and Burbank pushed off my face to get up and left me in a spreading pool of blood.

The crowd chanted Burbank's name.

Hollywood went to work on the cut over my eye with Vaseline and diluted adrenaline to close the cap-

illaries. Jairo rubbed my shoulders and put an ice pack
on the back of my neck to shrink the blood vessels
that led to my face.

Gil squatted between my feet and poured water
into me and offered encouragement: "That was fucking disgusting. Where did you learn any of that? I've
never seen it before, and I sure as hell didn't teach it."

I worked on breathing. "He's got her name on his
mouthpiece."

He either didn't hear me or didn't care. "What
the hell were you doing flopping around on your back
like that?"

"I went for the powerbomb. He didn't bite."

"Well, then you were right to lie there and get the
shit kicked out of you. Jesus, find another way to get
up. Better yet, don't get taken down in the first place."

"How'd he get me down?" I asked.

"Huh?"

"What did he do?"

Gil took a closer look at me. "Shit, were you out?"

"I don't know. Maybe."

"If you don't know, that's a yes. Forget it. Lateral
movement. The first chance you get to throw power,
do it. He hasn't tasted any yet, and he won't like it.
And he's going to try to take you down right away and
get more blood in your eye, so don't let that happen."

"Okay," I said. "Am I still bleeding?"

Hollywood looked hurt. "Come on. You're good for now, but it ain't built to last."

Wilkins told everyone to clear the cage. Hollywood gathered his things and patted my knee and hustled out the door.

Jairo leaned in. "She's watching. You're a fighter. Don't try to win for her; just fight for her." He checked my eyes and nodded, took the stool out of the cage.

Wilkins walked to the center and the bell rang.

Forget Kendall. Eddie. Tezo.

Marcela was watching.

Everything slowed down.

Burbank did his starting block sprint again and shot toward me. I could see his calves stretch and bunch up to push him forward. He leaned over his toes and put his center of gravity too far ahead. He crossed the midpoint of the cage and pawed a jab out and judged me to be at the right distance and shot in for the takedown.

I launched into a flying knee that crunched into his neck and jaw with his full weight behind them. He went limp. I toppled over his back and landed on his legs. I spun around and took his back with my knees at his sides and pounded my fists into the sides of his head. He was rocked but had the presence to cover his head with his forearms. I battered them and tried to sneak into gaps and switched up with some punches to the ribs to bring his hands down.

The crowd may have gone quiet or kept hollering; I don't remember hearing them after that point. I listened to Burbank grunting and breathing and punched him again and again. I must have hit my forehead on him or the canvas during the tumble because my blood was raining onto his back. A few drips at first, then a steady stream as I shook the cut open with my efforts.

Wilkins stepped toward Burbank's head and said, "Do something, Junior. Do something."

Burbank snugged his arms tighter and covered his head so all I could see was the back of his skull and his spine, both illegal targets. A rear naked choke was out of the question; his arms and shoulders and neck were too massive to snake anything through.

I did the only thing I could do. I stood and backed away and waved him to his feet.

Wilkins said, "Up, Junior, up."

Burbank peeked out from his arms and saw me standing. He pulled his knees in and tried his feet. He was still wobbly from the flying knee.

"Turn around. Face each other," Wilkins said. When Burbank finally got around, Wilkins said, "Fight!"

I moved forward. I wanted to be in the pocket, trading blows. I just had to hit harder.

Burbank retreated. His legs were unsteady and

his eyes were glassy. I followed and tried to tag him, but he kept his head moving and his hands up. The punches that did land couldn't get through to anything important. I cut him off with an angle, and he shot in for a takedown so I had to sprawl and give him room again. He backed up and I followed.

We did that three times, and I was ready to fire another flying knee when Burbank shook his head, stood his ground, and threw a slow right jab. I stepped in and hit him with a straight right and a left hook to the liver that felt like it touched his spine. He bent around the punch and heaved a left hook at me that I stepped inside of and snuck a right uppercut that grazed his chin but didn't do any damage.

Burbank wrapped his arms around the small of my back and pulled me into a Greco-Roman clinch and spun to walk me over and crush me against the cage near his corner. He drove the top of his head into the cut over my eye and pushed, not technically an illegal head butt but not very classy, either. He dropped down and tried to secure a double-leg, but I had my hips against his shoulder and my legs spread. Blood poured down my face and into my eye.

Burbank's cornermen yelled at the ref to check my eye and stop the fight.

Wilkins watched me closely. I blinked the blood out and made sure he could see my open eye. Then

Burbank drove into me, and a fresh flow welled out and filled my eye socket. I shook my head but couldn't get the eye back open.

"Stop! Stop!" Wilkins said.

Burbank let go and stepped back, and I got ready to die.

"Doctor time-out. We gotta look at that cut. Go to neutral corners. No, that one, Junior, over there. Woody, come with me." Wilkins guided me over to a neutral corner.

The physician, a blonde woman about forty years old, came in the cage with a commission representative and looked at my cut. Towels came over the cage, and I used them to soak up as much blood as possible. "Can you see okay?" she asked me.

"Yes, fine. Please don't stop the fight. Please."

"I know. I know." She examined the cut again and looked into my eye. She seemed concerned.

It couldn't end like this. I'd fight until my blood ran out if they let me.

But they wouldn't.

The doctor shook her head. "I don't know."

"I can see fine. Hold up some fingers."

"That's for brain damage." She watched the blood course down the outside of my eye and down my cheek. It wasn't going directly into the socket, which was all I could hope for. "If you can keep it from pooling, I'll let it go on. But if you end up on your back or side and that eye closes again, I'm calling it."

"Okay, yes," I said.

"For your own safety."

"I know. Thank you." I bowed to her and tried to hug her. She cringed.

They all cleared out of the cage, and I heard Gil yelling at me. I looked over and he was pointing at his liver saying, "Attack it! Attack it!"

I checked Burbank. He was leaning to his right, grimacing and protecting that side. That hook must have done some good work. I could see Marcela's name on his mouthpiece. I wanted to hit him hard enough to put it in the fifteenth row.

Wilkins warned me, "I'm watching that cut now. You ready? Ready? Fight!"

Burbank and I both moved forward with our hands up. From way out of range, practically California, I threw a left push kick that extended enough to compress Burbank's abdomen over his liver. He grimaced and went to one knee. I had the left hook loaded and my eyes popped wide, and everything started to tense when the bell rang.

Wilkins jumped between us and sent us to our corners. Burbank's guys had to help him to his.

Hollywood went to work on me again. His hands

moved like he was playing a tiny piano on my eyebrow. Gil gave me water while Jairo wiped me down and put the ice pack on the back of my neck.

Gil said, "Man, that liver is ripe for picking. He can barely stand."

"I was close," I said, "this close."

Hollywood shook his head. "Hold still, guy."

"That liver is gold," Gil said. "It'll open something for sure. Just don't let him catch a kick and take you down. I guarantee he won't let you up. Watch for the takedown again right after the bell. He's desperate."

"Got it."

"What are you going to do?"

I smiled at him. "I already told you. I told everybody. I'm going to knock him the fuck out."

Burbank didn't rush out for the takedown. He extended his arm and walked toward me. The third and final round, and *now* he wanted to touch gloves, a show of respect for a tough fight. I had a feeling he also wanted the extra couple seconds of recovery it would give him.

I gave his hand the finger, and he lowered it. He kept his right elbow tucked into his ribs over the liver. That brought his hand away from his face. He tried a left jab, and I moved to my left and countered with a straight that snapped his head back.

His right hand came up and exposed the liver. I cracked a left kick into it, and his eyes bugged out, squeezed shut, and he nearly crumpled. I swarmed him with punches, but he ducked and covered and survived it and shot in for a takedown. I stuffed it and had to back off to keep him from wrapping me up.

Blood landed on the canvas in front of me. I was leaking again.

Burbank tucked his elbow back into his ribs. When he stepped forward, I whipped a left kick into the nerve above his right knee. He halted and I tried a one-two-knee combo but didn't get through to the liver; that elbow was in there too tight. I pushed off and hit him with another leg kick. He leaned to his right to protect his liver even more. His liver had full control of the rest of his body: protect me at all costs.

I threw a jab-jab-leg kick. He barely noticed the jabs and spent the whole time bracing for the kick in case it rose to his abdomen. I gave him one just to break the anticipation. It bounced off his elbow, but he winced and tried another takedown with one arm. I sprawled and shoved him to the mat and stepped back so he could stand.

He did, and then he pounced. Burbank closed in fast with his elbow tucked. He was going to get me down and smother and pound on me until the end of the round and win by decision or doctor stoppage from the blood.

He cut the cage off and backed me up. My heel hit the fence, and I came forward with the one-two combo and threw the left kick again. Burbank braced his elbow and leg to check it, but it wasn't going to either of those places. My shin smashed into his face between his eyebrows and his nose. He turned into a rag doll. His mouthpiece spun out, and he dropped to the canvas and stared up at the lights.

I drove toward him to finish it, but Wilkins got there first and protected Burbank with his body and waved his hand in the air yelling, "That's it! That's it!"

I turned in a circle and put my hands over my face. When I took them down, Gil and Jairo and Javier and Edson were there, and we all fell into a mess on the canvas that made everyone in the crowd sick.

They got Burbank on a stool and gave him some water. The doctor returned and watched Hollywood close the cut over my eye with some tricks he'd learned in Haiti. I tried to see Burbank, but there were too many people milling around the cage. If he was in real bad shape, they'd take him to the hospital before I could talk to him about the mouthpiece.

Hollywood cleaned me out and put a few butterfly bandages over my eye, told me to get stitches.

Jairo yelled into the camera in Portuguese, and it sounded like he was talking to Marcela.

Wilkins tugged me to the center of the cage and raised my hand while Lincoln announced me as the winner by knockout. Some of the fans cheered me, and some cheered a great fight. Most booed.

Some tan guy in Ralph Lauren congratulated me and posed for a photo while I got sweat on his suit and frowned in Burbank's direction. Through gaps I could see him nodding and shrugging to his cornermen. So he was talking. I pushed my way toward him and got to the layer of cornermen when a hand caught my arm.

Banzai Eddie.

Benjamin was with him, looking like a soft, saggy version of himself. Eddie shook my hand and clapped me on the shoulder and smiled. He had the executive talent of appearing and speaking in polar opposites: "You really fucked me here, you know?"

I grinned back. "Yeah." I do not have that talent; I was genuinely happy about it.

Whether he was curious or concerned, what Eddie said next may have saved his life. "So what happens to your girl now? Can I help?"

"In the prep room. We'll call Kendall."

"Sounds good. Hey, you're one of my superstars now. I gotta take care of you, right?"

"Don't ruin it."

"Fantastic." He shook my hand again for the

cameras and pushed his way through Burbank's crew. He rubbed his vanquished poster boy's head and talked into his ear. Burbank nodded and apologized, which made Eddie shake his head and talk some more. Probably telling him, "Great fight. Don't worry; you'll be back." Leaving out, "As long as the crowd pays to see you."

Eddie finished and backed out, and I slid in before the cornermen could close him off again. They congratulated me and I thanked them.

When the love fest was over, I said, "Give us a minute."

They moved a few feet away, and I knelt in front of Burbank.

He smiled. "You got me again, you asshole."

My smile was tight. "Yeah, neither one was easy. You got plenty of time. You'll be on top eventually."

"When are you going to retire?"

I had to laugh at that. Then: "So, about the mouthpiece."

He waited.

"Anything you want to tell me?"

"About what?" he asked.

"Marcela."

"Oh, you know her? I hope she said yes."

"What? Why was her name on your mouthpiece?"

One of his cornermen reached over my shoulder and handed him an ice pack. Burbank folded it in half and pressed it between his eyes, which were already showing the raccoon bruises he'd sport for a few weeks. "Some dude gave me ten grand to write her name on it with a Sharpie. Said he was going to propose to her during the fight."

"Was his name Kendall?"

Burbank squinted to think about it and winced. "Ah, I don't know. I didn't get his name."

"So you don't know Kendall? Big Jake? Tezo?"

"No, man. Those all sound like cartoon characters." He laughed. "Shit, maybe I do know them and you hit me so hard I forgot."

I let out a lot of air. I respected Burbank and wanted to like him now that the fight was over. He was just a piece on the chessboard like me. "Great fight, man. The toughest one I've ever had."

"Yeah. Let's do it again in about twenty years."

Some of the crowd wanted high fives or fist bumps on my way backstage. I let Edson take care of it. Eddie was waiting outside the door of the prep room talking with a group of young guys in suits. None of them had adopted the dyed faux hawk yet, but it was the last stage until full assimilation. I wondered which one of them called in the bet Tezo made against me.

Eddie saw us coming. "It's the . . . eye of the tiger. It's the thrill of the fight, ri—"

"Get your phone out," I said. To the suits: "Beat feet."

They looked at their chunky watches and decided it was time to be somewhere else.

Eddie watched them go with envy, then fished a sheet of paper out of his inside pocket. "I got a list here of guys you can fight next."

"Are you on it?"

"Come on, man."

Gil reached past me and plucked the list. "You and I will talk, Eddie."

Eddie made a show of leaning around me to say, "Thank you. It's nice to have some professionalism." He looked at me to let the point linger. Two seconds later he had his phone out. Smart guy.

"Start dialing," I said.

We piled into the prep room and watched Eddie work his phone. Gil yanked my gloves off and started working on the right hand tape and gauze. Eddie handed me his phone.

Kendall answered on the third ring. "Well, well. Congrats, champ." The gum was getting worked like a balloon in a car wash.

"Are they knocking on your door yet?"

"Who's that?"

"The Yakuza."

Eddie winced.

Silence on the other end.

I said, "Let me talk to her."

"Still don't care about Lance, do you?"

"Now that I know he works for you? Not really."

"Damn, you have been a busy boy today, huh?"

"You have no idea. Put her on."

"That's a tough one right now, sport."

I stopped breathing.

The gum clicked and snapped. Kendall said, "We're what you might call *in transit* at the moment, and there was some concern sweet Marcela would jump out of a moving vehicle—mostly because she said she would—so she's in the trunk."

"But she's okay."

"For now," Kendall said. "But I gotta tell you, you put me in a tight spot here. My day is pretty much shot to shit at this point."

"Boo hoo."

"Fair enough. Point is, it's no longer entirely up to me whether she stays in one piece or not. So here's the updated agenda: There's some boys with fast little cars and loud guns who're looking for me. They're gonna want a shit ton of money or someone to cut up, preferably me. I could try to give them your girlie, but I figure, why not give 'em the guy who owed in the first place?"

I did not glance at Banzai Eddie. "Okay."

"So let's trade. Marcela for Eddie. I don't care how you get him to me or what state he's in, as long as he's got enough air left in him to scream for the Japs. And just you and him; I got a call from Tezo about an hour ago, sounded like he was talking through a mouthful of marbles. I don't need any more crazy fucking Brazilians around me."

"Where and when?"

"Start your engines. We're headed to a place Lance says is safe as it gets in this town. Says you know it—some kook named Chops?"

I handed the phone back to Eddie. When he reached for it, I shoved his arm across his throat and stepped in. I got my shoulder against his triceps and my arms around him in an over-the-shoulder hug and lifted him off the floor. I squeezed his arm into his neck to cut off the blood to his brain. He made a sound with no vowels and started to kick at my legs.

The rest of the room was silent until Gil yanked on my arm. "Hey, hey."

I turned to him. "If you want to leave the room, I understand. This has to happen."

Gil sized it up, looking for a way to get Eddie free of the arm triangle. Eddie's kicks were getting weaker. Gil was watching me choke out my one chance at a successful career, watching me retreat from the next step in my life and piss on it. He could have taken my legs out, attacked my groin, gouged my eyes. Instead, he ran his hands over the stubble on his head. "Jesus, Woody. Tell me you know what you're doing."

"I do." Eddie stopped moving. I could hear him breathing deeply next to my ear.

"Tell me I won't need to mortgage the gym for legal fees."

"You won't." I set Eddie down on the couch and put his phone in my pocket.

"Whatever you're doing, it *has* to happen?"

"Yes."

Gil closed his eyes. "What do you need?"

"I need your bag."

I carried the bag through the corridor and tried to make it look lighter than it was. Gil made us do farmer's carries with heavier weight, but at the gym I didn't have to smile and thank other fighters and trainers when they congratulated me on the win.

I could see the exit fifty feet ahead on the left when Benjamin shuffled out of a doorway directly across from it, working his phone. He raised it to his ear, and my pocket started to ring. Benjamin heard the chime in stereo and frowned. He took the phone away from his ear and listened, looked toward me.

Then he noticed Jairo walking next to me, and he physically shrank. Benjamin brought his phone back up and said, "Hey, no, what?" and spun and disappeared through the doorway while Eddie's phone continued to ring in my pocket.

We went through the exit. My truck was still there; the security guard wasn't. Jairo helped me shove the bag into the passenger seat. Eddie groaned inside.

Jairo said, "Woody, let me help. Javier, Edson, all of us."

"Can't do it."

"Because Kendall said so? Fuck that guy."

"I agree. But this is going to be fast and loud. If I get you killed saving Marcela, I'm not going to feel great."

Jairo scoffed and gestured at the bullet groove in his shoulder. "Who can kill me?"

"Go with Gil. I'll take her to the gym."

"If you don't?"

I thought about it. "Join the Air Force. Get assigned to Nellis. Drop a bomb on Chops's compound."

He frowned.

"See you soon," I said. I left him standing in the parking lot and headed northeast toward the desert.

But first, one quick stop.

CHAPTER 18

I backtracked through the streets and turns Jairo and I had flashed through on the way to the arena. This time I obeyed the speed limit and traffic lights. No reason to hurry just yet, and my right eye was swelling shut, throwing my depth perception off. I squinted into the oncoming headlights and did a pretty good job of not running anyone over.

Eddie stirred in the duffel bag. He asked someone a question and screamed quietly.

I smacked the bag. "Hey. I'll let you out of there if you stay quiet and hold still."

"Whozzat?"

"Woody."

"Where . . . It smells in here."

I reached over and tugged the zipper open a few inches. Fingers poked through and peeled it open the rest of the way. Eddie sat up out of the bag and blinked. He looked around. "Brah, what the fuck? My head . . ."

"It doesn't last. This is what you need to know: We're going to get Marcela. If things go right, you'll be fine. If they don't, you're on your own."

"No. Let me out."

"I've knocked out three people in the past few hours, all of them bigger and tougher than you, and I'm still ready to go. Sit still and shut up or I'll put you in the glove compartment."

"What do you need me for?"

"Moral support."

"Fuckin' liar. Where are we going?"

"North. Then east."

"Nice. Thanks. Can I at least get out of this bag?"

"As long as you run when I tell you to. Otherwise, stay in so I'll have some handles."

Eddie muttered and fought his way out of the bag. It was a close contest. "Dude, why does everything around you stink?"

I felt a little sorry for him. Coming out of Gil's sweat bag into the truck, with the dried sludge from Tezo's pit caked on the seats, probably had him wishing I'd dot him once on the nose.

I turned right on Fremont, drifted into the left lane and let the truck roll at idle speed. No one was behind me to complain.

Eddie said, "What the hell is that smell, anyway? I'm cracking a window."

"Stick your head out far enough, you might smell the source."

"Huh?"

"But I recommend you duck." I came to a full stop outside Tezo's garage and held the horn down.

After ten seconds the old man poked his head out of the office and saw me. I gave him the finger and he disappeared. Five seconds after that the place turned into a hornet's nest. The door flew open, and half the guys from the bleachers stormed out waving guns and automotive tools. The other half and the old people had either left or learned their lesson. I hit the gas and watched all the headlights pop on in the rearview mirror.

I wouldn't call what happened next a car chase. I drove; they followed, but no one bumped onto the sidewalk or T-boned another car at an intersection. They were smart enough to hang back and wait for me to get cornered or make a wrong turn. I got north to Owens and turned right and watched a few of the cars peel off left and right at side streets. I spotted them paralleling me, trying to anticipate a turn and be there to cut me off. They got snarled up in the residential traffic and eventually fell back in behind me.

A low-slung pickup came within kissing distance of my rear bumper for a block. I looked in the mirror and saw Tezo's swollen head in the passenger seat. He should have been in a hospital, maybe the coma ward. The tattoos were temporarily hidden in the cuts and bruises. He was talking into a cell phone, his puffy mouth barely moving.

Eddie cranked his head around. "Who's that?"

"You don't recognize your buddy Tezo?"

He stared. "*That's* Tezo? I pictured him being less . . ."

"Mauled? You've never met?"

"No, just over the phone."

"To place bets against your fighters, that kind of thing, right?"

"Gambling is legal," Eddie said.

"Yeah, you should know. He was halfway to drowning me when he called you to place that bet."

"No shit." Eddie was still mesmerized by Tezo's piñata head.

We crossed North Hollywood and the houses petered out. Tezo must have figured out where we were heading; the string of tinted windows and chrome rims got aggressive. They looked for clear spots to pull ahead of me, but their clearance and tires weren't designed for the dirt road, let alone the ditches and humps alongside. I sped up and they fell back.

Eddie faced forward again and said, "So, what, we're having a meet out here? You need me to negotiate with Tezo?"

"No, he'll be busy."

"So what the fuck am I here for?"

I got the truck to fifty on the washboard road. "Mostly, to be scared."

"I ain't scared."

I got Eddie's phone out and called Kendall.

He picked up right away. "Hey, I can see you on the security camera. How are just you and Eddie driving all them cars?"

"Tezo found me," I said. "Get that gate open."

Kendall said something away from the phone, came back. "Your boy Chops is *not* a fan of yours right now."

"Likewise. But if he doesn't open the gate, Eddie's gonna get chewed up out here and you'll have to deal with the Yakuza yourself."

Eddie said, "Who is that? Is that my phone?"

I dropped it and got both hands on the wheel and floored it toward the crest that flattened outside the compound.

Eddie fumbled his phone off the floor and hit a button. "*Kendall?* You're taking me to that cowboy? In the fucking *desert?*"

"You can jump out and talk to Tezo, tell him why he shouldn't have bet a hundred grand on me to lose. Or run like hell and wait for the Yakuza to find you. Or we top this crest and if the gate's not open, we smash into it and won't care what happens next."

I glanced over at him.

He was scared.

The truck roared briefly when the wheels left the ground at the top of the crest. The dull metal wall was still rattling open. We landed and slewed before straightening out, and I had to twist the wheel to the left. Chops probably had a database of vehicle widths, and the opening froze at what looked like two inches wider than my side mirrors. The right mirror hit the gate and flapped on its hinge against Eddie's window when we squeezed through. The gate was already closing.

I crushed the brakes.

Eddie rolled onto the dashboard and bounced back onto the seat.

The truck slid. I'd waited too long.

Then the gate clamped against the passenger side, and the sound of metal grating on metal made me wince. The gate pinned the truck against the wall. I hauled Eddie out my door and pulled him into a run up the driveway. The entire compound was blacked out; I could see the outline of the house and a car parked outside the garage against the night sky. Everything else was a shade of black.

Eddie's shoes were offended by the gravel and tried to take him down. He caught himself on my arm, got upright, and said, "Don't leave me here with Kendall, man. You do that, I'm gone. And that means Warrior is gone, and you're back fighting for gas money."

"I know. Now shut up and keep moving."

I looked back. Headlight beams searched the sky from the other side of the crest, then dropped and silhouetted my truck wedged in the gate opening. The first car, maybe still Tezo's, braked and started to slide sideways. The second car came over the ridge and had to crank right to avoid hitting it. Guys were already spilling out of the first car and running toward the gate.

I almost carried Eddie the last fifty feet of the driveway. The car outside the closed garage door was a late model Cadillac. Eddie ran around and crouched behind it. I thumped on the trunk lid. "Marcela?"

A gunshot came from behind me, a loud crack that bounced off the far wall and rolled back before it was interrupted by another shot, then another.

"She's inside," a voice said.

I took my lips off the Cadillac's rear bumper and my shoulders out of my ears and turned around.

Chops was standing in his trench twenty feet away, the AR leveled across the hood of one of his dirt-filled vehicles toward the gate. I flinched when he squeezed off another round. Shapes were scrambling over the side of my truck, tumbling over each other to lie flat in the bed or get to the other side of the wall. When there were no more targets, I waited for the gun to turn toward me. Chops had sent me into a pit to die; shooting me would be self-defense.

He had his eye pressed to the scope, a dim ring of green light oozing out around his glasses. He kept the gun trained on the gate. "What'd you stop for? It was open far enough."

"I got a little sideways coming through."

He grunted. "Well, I told you all this was gonna happen someday."

I looked closer. It was hard to tell with my right eye swollen shut, but I think he was smiling.

"How many out there?"

"At least five or six cars' worth."

"So anywhere between six and sixty."

A shot came from the gate; compared to Chops's rifle it sounded like a cap gun but I ducked anyway.

"Don't bother," he said, "these guys can't shoot for shit. The ones who come up from Central America—Tezo's one of 'em—are hard-core. Military training and cold as ice. But most of these idiots are Vegas born and raised or transplanted from LA." He fired three shots. "I just hit your truck. Sorry. Look at them

out there, holding their firearms sideways like they're
in a rap video. Is Tezo down there?"

"Yeah. Look for a swollen head."

"Roger that. Hey, about the Tezo thing. I'm glad
you made it out. How about your friend?"

Goddamn crazy people. "He's okay."

"Nice." Chops fired again. "Oh, that was tight. So
how about I shoot these guys for you and we call it even?"

"I think you'd shoot them anyway."

"Technicalities. Oh yes, please try to come over the
top of the wall. Please. Who you got there with you?"

"Banzai Eddie." I looked behind the Cadillac,
but he was gone. Shit. If he tried to make it down the
canyon wall, he'd fall, trip a claymore mine, and/or
start a nuclear countdown. "Eddie?"

"Seriously, dude, who *are* these people?" The
voice came from under the car.

I reached under and felt cloth and pulled it.
Eddie came out and I stood him up. I asked Chops,
"Where's Marcela?"

"Garage." He kept his wooden hand under the
AR's foregrip and used his right to pluck a remote
hanging off his tactical vest. He tossed it my way, got
his finger back on the trigger.

I picked up the remote and hit the only button.
The garage door raised two feet and stopped; the open
space at the bottom was a black maw. I hauled Eddie

toward it and rolled him through and followed.

I could have had both eyes swollen shut; it wouldn't have been any darker inside. Tiny comets trailed across my vision. I tried to pick shapes out in my peripheral vision, but having one eye didn't help.

Eddie bumped into me and grabbed my shirt. "Who's that?"

"Stand still."

Somewhere ahead, Kendall snapped his gum and said, "You gotta shut the door for the light to come on."

I hit the remote. The door eased down and thumped on the concrete. Overhead fluorescents burbled into life and I squinted my left eye.

Eddie let go of my shirt and shielded his eyes against the brightness.

Kendall said, "You look like you been in a fight."

He didn't look much better. The tussle in the bakery had left him with a swollen nose and bruises around his eyes. He was sitting on the concrete steps below the door to the house. Big Jake towered next to him, his eyes on fire behind his mask of bruises and swelling. He looked much worse than Kendall; his nose was taped in place and had cotton plugs to keep the blood from falling out.

Lance was in the far right corner, where piles of

shit belonged, with his arms tucked against his ribs. He gnawed on his right thumbnail like it was heroin flavored, looking at everything but me. I had nothing to say to him.

Steve was in the other corner. He was paler than I remembered. His purple lips were compressed and pulled toward his chin. The bottom lip was split and puffy. His left arm was in a sling, and two of the fingers on that hand were splinted and taped together. He glanced at me with concern; then his gaze flicked to a low stack of cardboard boxes, and his face registered real fear.

Marcela was sitting on the boxes smiling at me. "Hello, Woody." She got a good look at my face and sucked in a sharp breath, jumped off the boxes, and walked toward me.

"Sit still," Kendall told her.

She ignored him.

"You see?" Kendall asked the room.

Marcela held my head and frowned at the right half of my face. "Your eye."

I touched her waist and her stomach and back. "I'm fine. Are you okay?"

She hitched a thumb at Steve. "Better than him."

"Did he . . . ?"

"He asked for a shoulder rub." She shrugged. "So I rubbed his shoulders against each other."

Steve looked like he was going to cry.

Eddie nudged me. "Is this Marcela?"

"Be quiet." The garage muffled the sound of Chops squeezing off four rounds. Smaller calibers responded like lame applause.

Kendall stood. "Sounds like the O.K. Corral out there. Are they inside the wall?"

"If they are, they're facedown in the dirt."

"Mm-hmm." He cracked his gum and patted a flat black automatic pistol against his leg. "Hey, Eddie, you want to come with me to see some fellas?"

"No," Eddie said.

"They wear nice suits too."

"No."

"Well, good thing it ain't up to you." Kendall glanced at me. "That Chops guy gave you the door opener?"

I nodded.

"Lemme have it."

"Not a chance." I had my thumb on the button. I could hit it and shove Eddie and Marcela through, but with the fluorescents off we'd all be silhouetted against the dim light from the driveway. Easy targets.

"Jake, go get it."

Big Jake came forward, grinning despite the pain it must have caused.

When he was halfway between me and Kendall, I put the remote on the floor and raised my heel over it. "One more step."

He stopped. Looked back at Kendall, who peered around Jake's shoulder and said, "What, you're going to trap us in here? The door into the house is locked."

"I've been fighting in cages all day. This is just another shift." I put my focus on Big Jake. "You get someone to set that nose or do it yourself?"

He blinked. "Myself. I've done it before."

"If it doesn't set right, I know a guy. Had me breathing through both nostrils after five years of the left side only. And your boss is dead in the water."

"Hey," Kendall said.

I told Jake, "The rest of us can walk out of here and go our separate ways. He's chum."

"Watch your mouth," Kendall said.

Jake nodded toward the front of the garage. Sporadic gunshots and Chops's replies still cracked. "Isn't that Tezo out there? Looking for you?"

I shrugged. "I've seen Chops shoot before. I'm not worried about Tezo anymore."

Kendall stomped his foot. "Jake, get your big ass over here out of the way."

Jake stared at me. If he stayed where he was or came forward, I could step on the button and barrel the three of us out before Kendall got a clear shot. I let my foot sink down. Jake stepped back so he was next to Kendall again.

The gun was already up. Kendall smiled and didn't blink. "Now how about I shoot you and take that thing at my leisure?"

"That's not the deal. Businessman, remember?"

"Yeah, that was when I *had* a business. All I am now is a man on the run, thank you very much. And if me and Eddie are the only guys who walk out of this garage, who's gonna tell the story about me being unprofessional?"

"I won't," Eddie said.

Kendall pointed at him. "No shit, you won't. The only boys you'll be talking to don't speak good English anyway."

Steve shifted in the corner. "What do you mean, 'only guys'? What about the rest of us?"

"Sorry, Stevie. We part ways starting now. Everybody's fired."

I said, "Did anyone else in here bring a gun?"

Kendall frowned. "What kinda question is that?"

"He has one." Marcela pointed at Steve.

Steve glared at her. "Fuck you."

I said, "Steve, will you please shoot Kendall so we can all go home?"

Kendall turned and shot Steve in the chest. The sound of it shattered through the enclosed space and made everyone jump. Eddie hid behind his hands. The bullet punched a hole through the sling fabric and knocked Steve into the corner, where he sank to the floor and gaped at Kendall.

"Don't look at me like that, Steven. I can't take it. Were you really gonna shoot me?"

Steve looked at the blood spreading across his chest and said, "No. Here." He reached his lower back with surprising grace and pulled another black automatic out. Held it toward Kendall butt first. "Here. See? Take it." His strength gave out, and the gun fell into his lap.

Everyone stared at it.

I stomped the button and the lights went out.

The door shook the ground as it raised. The weak light that cut in underneath died out a few feet inside the garage; the rest of the place was ink. Someone stumbled over a stack of cardboard boxes and went down hard. I pulled Eddie and Marcela away from Steve and the gun.

Kendall squeezed off four shots, working his way from where we had been to Steve's corner. His face popped into view with each strobe of flame from the barrel—eyes shut, mouth open, gum hanging out. He may have been laughing.

I hit the boxes stacked along the right wall and started throwing them down between us and Kendall, anything to absorb bullets and keep us from being outlined on our way out the door. I pushed Eddie and Marcela that way, tried to whisper at them to get their asses outside but yelled it instead.

Someone ran into me and grunted. Someone who stank.

Lance.

I put a right hook into his guts, about the same spot Jake hit him the night before. He crumpled, and I tossed him onto the barrier between me and Kendall.

Kendall fired again and something buzzed past my face to smack against the wall. A voice that could only belong to Jake bellowed, and someone else yelped.

Two more shots, the concussion waves rocking through the space, and Jake yelled again.

Time to get out.

I dropped to the floor and rolled and cracked my shoulder against the door. I looked under, saw Marcela and Eddie crouched behind the Cadillac's engine block. Marcela had Eddie by the tie. I had to flatten out facedown to squeeze through into the driveway.

Marcela slapped the car. "It's locked."

"Okay, okay." I looked for Chops. He'd moved while we were inside, and no one was shooting anymore. My night vision was jacked from the fluorescents and muzzle flashes, but I could see my truck still wedged in the gate. Four other cars were scattered behind it, two with the lights still on. I didn't see or hear anyone moving. "Let's go. Down the driveway."

Maybe it was the swollen eye. Maybe it was because I was so focused on getting everyone out. Either way, I should have gone to them, worked around the back of the Cadillac. But they came to me, and when Kendall scuttled out from under the garage door on my right side, I didn't see him.

I heard the gun scrape on the concrete as he pushed himself to his feet. My brain and body were screaming at me to duck, roll, drop, but all I could do was turn my head.

Too late.

Kendall stood with the gun and that sideways grin, that *gotcha* face, and I got to watch it change to shock when Marcela flowed behind me and drove her fist into his throat. She got both hands on his gun wrist and pushed it up, then piled him backward into the garage door and slammed her forehead into his battered nose. Kendall screamed but didn't let go of the gun.

Marcela pulled Kendall's right arm out straight and hooked her leg over it. She made a small adjustment and dropped her weight on the back of his elbow while she yanked his wrist up. The joint sounded like twenty knuckles cracking when it gave out. Kendall made a screaming face, but no sound came out. The gun came loose. Marcela threw it over the edge of the driveway into the canyon.

Kendall melted onto the concrete and tried to wipe the blood and tears out of his eyes with his working arm. "Jesus. Ah, what the fuck did you do to me, you crazy bitch?"

Marcela responded in Portuguese and kicked him in the knee.

"All right, knock it off. Shit." He managed to get his feet under him and work his shoulder blades up the garage door. He looked around and laughed. "What a cluster fuck, huh?"

I stepped toward him.

Marcela yanked me back. "I gave him enough."

"He—"

"It's up to me," she said. And she was right.

Kendall looked around again. "Hey, where's Big Jake?"

"I think you shot him," I said.

"Oh yeah. Bastard tried to get my gun. You believe that?" He peeled himself off the door and wavered, staring down the driveway. The gridlock made him swear. He let his right arm hang and fumbled across his body with his left to get the keys out of his pocket. He shuffled past us and said, "All right, Eddie. Those Yakuza, they ain't gonna like what I tell them. I'm sending them all your way. You're on your own now."

Eddie looked at me. "You're letting him leave?"

I didn't answer.

Kendall got in his car and struggled to work the keys in, eventually got it started. It was a quiet car. He had to lean over and shift into Drive with his left hand.

Marcela pulled me toward the garage door out of the way. I brought Eddie with me.

He said, "Don't be stupid, man. Don't believe for a second he's done with you guys."

Marcela nodded. "He'll get lost in the desert. We'll call the police on him."

"Maybe," I said.

"Maybe?"

Kendall took his foot off the brake and let the car roll toward the ravine. He hit the lip at an angle and skidded sideways out of view. It was a good way to get down the slope at a controlled speed.

I turned Marcela around and got her facing me. Put my hands over her ears. She frowned for a second, saw the look on my face, and brought her little hands up to cover my ears.

"What are you two doing?" Eddie asked.

Whatever Kendall ran over on his way down the slope, it made a fireball big enough to lift his car into view for a moment; then it was gone.

We took our time down the driveway.

Chops was waiting for us at the truck, surveying

the lumps of clothes scattered around the gate. None of us looked too closely. He rubbed his hands together. "Busy day tomorrow."

"Tezo?"

Chops motioned toward the wall. "Tried to come over the berm. I checked the tattoos. The neck ones, anyway. No hard feelings?"

"I'm too tired for those. Can you let my truck out?"

"Sure, yeah. Hey, these two, do they need to be debriefed about all of this?"

"I'll handle it."

Close to one in the morning in Vegas, so traffic was as bad as ever. The holes and cracks in the windshield didn't help. I drove west on roads that would not take me past Tezo's garage.

I dropped Eddie behind the Golden Pantheon. Before he got out, I asked him, "What are you going to do about the Yakuza?"

"I have no idea." He looked like someone had cut his puppet strings. He spoke to the dashboard. "So, what? I guess I owe you one now?"

"Everybody owes somebody."

"Shit." He got out and I drove away.

I found my phone. Twenty missed calls, all from the gym. I brought up the number, but before I could start the call, Marcela took the phone out of my hand and put it in the glove compartment.

"Hey."

"Pull over."

"Where?"

"This place, the restaurant."

"You're hungry?"

"Woody, shut up and do it."

I pulled into the lot.

"In the back under that palm tree."

No one else was parked nearby. I rolled into a spot and looked at her.

"Shut it all off."

I turned the key.

She grabbed it out of the ignition and put it in the glove compartment with the phone.

"Jairo—"

"They will all wait." Marcela pulled her shirt over her head and started on mine.

"Easy," I said. "I'm sore."

She laughed. "Just wait."

MEDALLION

P R E S S

Be in the know on the latest
Medallion Press news by becoming a
Medallion Press Insider!